ELIZABETH AMBER LOVE

This is a work of fiction loosely based on the life of Pedals the bipedal bear. Names, characters, businesses, places, events and incidents are either the products of the author's imagination or used in a fictitious manner. Any resemblance to actual persons, living or dead, is purely coincidental.

*Dedicated
to
Pedals,
New Jersey's Beloved
Bipedal Bear*

CHAPTER ONE

The church basement meeting room smelled of rancid wood polish from the 1970s. The linoleum tile on the floor and the wall paneling hadn't been updated since then. The Skylands Organization for Animal Rights was allowed to use the space for only a few dollars to contribute to the electric and heating bills. Members brought their own coffee and refreshments. They were expected to anyway, but some routinely mooched off others.

"This meeting of SOAR will come to order." Mick Hoffman didn't have a gavel, but his tenor voice boomed loud enough for everyone to hear. He stood behind a long table in the middle of the five board members.

"We'll get right to it this evening without wasting any time. Does the board approve the minutes of the last meeting?"

In unison, the four seated members said, "Aye."

"Old Business." Mick remained standing. "Our most important campaign of this year is again about the bear hunt. We've been doing great work in reaching the community better. I'll turn it over to Ursula Applegate, who has been handling our internet communications."

The metal folding chair screeched as Ursula backed it up because of the one leg missing a rubber tip at the bottom. She stood from the front row and walked over the corner of the acting dais table.

"Thank you, Mick and board members." Ursula clutched her phone in her brown hand despite not needing it while she spoke. "The social media engagement has gone up on the two biggest platforms. It would be better if we could afford promotional posts. You may have heard that LifeLook only shows about five percent of your followers your actual content unless you pay them."

In the second row on the aisle seat, Miriam Vanderwal pursed her lips enhancing the wrinkles she already had. Her white hair was in an immaculate twist and shellacked with hair spray making it damn near bulletproof. Miriam was not interested in anything that would cost more money. They were a grassroots organization with hardly any donations. Members mostly foot any bill that came up. Though when it mattered most, money poured into the account.

Ursula noticed Miriam wasn't the only one not happy to hear about a possible expense. She honestly didn't like the idea of a non-profit group having to pay essentially extortion money for people who want their announcements to actually see them. That was out of her control. Her role was to present their options and run their social media. Jon McHugh was the board member in charge of all communications, but he stuck to the old school direct mail campaigns, an email newsletter, posters, and billboards. In the back of her mind though, Ursula couldn't help but wonder if Miriam was simply a racist who didn't want to hear what she had to say about anything.

"Look, I don't think it's fair that users have to pay for people to see their posts. We're not *The New York Times* or anything and we certainly don't have the bank accounts of celebrity members like PETA. So I have a proposal."

She went back to her chair and retrieved a notepad and pen. Tucking her phone into the front pocket of her tight jeans, Ursula freed up her hands to make a small chart in the steno pad. She flipped the cover over and found a blank page. She drew a couple lines and then listed the names of everyone present down the rows. Across the top, she wrote the names of the social media sites that needed the most attention: LifeLook, Boffo, and InstaSnap.

She looked around the room to see if anyone's body language could ease her alienation. Her eyes made contact with the dark-haired, ruggedly attractive man in the seat at the far end of Miriam's row. Peter Medvedovich never spoke much in the meetings unless someone asked him a question. She didn't know anything about him except he was a photographer and liked herbal tea instead of coffee when he came into Applegate's Country Store. He wasn't exactly smiling, but under his neatly maintained scruff, he wasn't scowling either. That was better than looking at Miriam's lemon-soured expression.

"If I can have volunteers who already have accounts on these sites or people who would be willing to make new accounts, I'm more than happy to give you all tutorials whenever you have time. The more accounts that make posts and share posts, the better it looks and the more engagement we'll generate. Otherwise, it's just the official account and my shares of the posts. Fortunately, my friends online share a lot of my stuff."

Mick stood up again and looked like he was ready to argue. As luck would have it, it wasn't that he didn't support Ursula's proposal to increase the online presence. It was the content that was controversial.

"Ursula, last year you admitted that we got the most engagement from the graphically violent photos at the check-in stations. I think we need to get back to doing that. Show the public that the state of New Jersey allows hunters to murder mothers and cubs. It's vile, but in this day and age, people react to the gore."

It definitely was not what Ursula wanted to hear. She knew it was true. Her head lowered and her eyes dropped down to look at her scuffed up hiking boots.

"Look, I'm sorry, but you know I'm right."

"I know, Mick. It's very true. The bloody baby cub photos get people talking. I hate looking at them just like everyone else, but if that's what you want me to post, I will."

Peter Medvedovich's head turned away and his gaze shifted to nothing in particular on the wall. The gruesome photos discussed were his photos. Other people did have their own from cell phones, but Peter was the official photographer for SOAR. He traveled around the state to the various stations where the harvested bears were brought for weighing and permit checks. He had thousands of photos of gorgeous living bears of all varieties too, but those didn't get people to open their wallets or write to their state representatives.

"Pete, make sure everyone can access the cloud folder of last year's slaughter. And make sure all the pictures have our watermark, okay?"

Peter nodded and muttered a quiet, "Okay."

Ursula resumed her quest for people to sign up as the SOAR social media army with their current user names or a note to let her know that they wanted help setting up accounts. She passed the notepad around and the last one to sign it was Rona Medvedovich. Ursula assumed she was married to Peter.

"Hey, Pete, any chance you can project some of the photos up on the screen so our new members can see what we're talking about?"

"Sure, Mick. Give me two minutes." Peter was less than excited to see his photos of bleeding bear cubs and adults displayed on a sixty-inch backdrop. Seeing them in person and again on his computer were enough to make his stomach turn.

Rona got up and helped. She pulled the white screen down from the ceiling using the dangling string on the end of the chain's loop. Peter wheeled a serving cart to the middle aisle. He unzipped his personal projector and connected it to the wireless signal of his phone. Everyone noticed how Peter favored his mostly-functioning right hand and arm because of the more extensive trauma to his left.

"Thanks, Pete." Mick and the board members shuffled to either side of the screen behind their table. A portion of the photo was cast over Mick and for a split second, the blood of the bear corpse looked like it was coming out of Mick's mouth. He explained each slide for the group.

"Let's see. This shot was taken at the Whittingham Wildlife Management Area over in Newton." Mick let everyone digest the horror scene before calling for the next slide. "This one is from Pequest in Warren County. As you know, Sussex and Warren are the counties with the biggest kill numbers."

"We get the idea, Mick. Do we really need to go through these?"

It wasn't that Dolph Glazier had a weak stomach. His gut was spent. He'd seen enough of horror in Vietnam and again when he spent his life trying to help people. He managed to go through college when he got back and eventually became a social worker specifically trying to save kids who needed loving adoptive families. He hated abuse and torture whether it was an animal or a person.

"You don't have to look, Dolph, but we have some new folks who might need to see this."

Ursula was among the new roster of members. She joined SOAR after hearing about them in the newspaper articles showing their protests of the bear hunt. She didn't have a lot of time to volunteer for things like protests while she managed the country store and greasy spoon her family left to her. She offered to run the SOAR social media since it was something she could do throughout the day and evening when she had moments to spare.

"One more thing," Mick said, "Walker has been spotted in the Rockaway area again."

Rona looked at Peter. Her eyebrows furrowed down and she gently shook her head. For a second, the sides of her black bobbed hair hid her face. Before Mick could continue, she spoke out.

"Can you clarify who Walker is since, like you said, there are new folks here?"

"Sure." Mick asked Peter to find a video. "Seen here in this clip — there are tons like this — Walker is a black bear that usually walks upright on his hind legs. It made national news. People weren't sure if he was a person in a bear suit. Some still don't believe he's real."

"Has anyone been able to examine him to see what's wrong with his front paws?" Ursula had seen the videos many times. She was initially among the skeptics until so many news articles and amateur videos were posted.

"As far as I know, he's never been treated or examined by a vet. We keep tabs on him as much as possible through the media and personal accounts." Mick hated to admit when he didn't have all the answers.

Dolph asked Peter to pause the video. He walked over to the screen and pointed to the deformed front arms of the bear.

"You can sort of see it here: Walker's left arm doesn't have too much use. He can't use the paw at all, but he seems to be able to bear weight on it once in a while. I've studied a lot of the videos and he has more normal use from his right front paw, but even that isn't one hundred percent."

"What happened? Was he born that way?" Miriam's look changed from sourpuss to genuine concern.

Dolph continued. "People mostly speculate that he was hit by a vehicle and the untended injuries didn't have a chance to heal the way they would have if they were pinned properly. It also could have been a snare trap. We're not sure."

"Why are those legal in New Jersey?" Rona was angry. She slapped her hand on her thigh.

"They're used for fur animals like beaver. They require a special training course and a permit." Dolph believed it was best to your know your enemy and in this case, the hunting association was specifically the enemy. They had the state Environmental Protection Agency wrapped around their proverbial finger.

Rona stood and gripped the back of the chair in the row in front of her. "Look, I'm not against hunting completely, but some of these practices are inhumane. Bottom line. Snare traps for fur? Why are people still using real fur? Animals hunted for food is as far as I can personally justify. Over population needs to be addressed a different way."

"I think most of us would agree with you, Rona. I've been vegan since the 80's, but I understand letting the animals starve to death is not in their best interest as a species. I don't want to talk about fur right now." Dolph gave a head nod to Mick signaling for him to take over.

"Thanks for all the info, Dolph. Back to the matter of Walker, I'd like to see that he's protected from the bear hunt. If we can save even one, that's going to help. We'll simultaneously keeping pushing for the hunt to be called off, but it's only a month away and they begin selling permits soon."

"I think as part of our social media push, we should share as much about Walker as we can. Tag our local politicians in the posts. Beg them to stop the massacre and to protect Walker who has become beloved by the neighborhoods." Ursula saw some of the news coverage of Walker. People who spotted the bipedal bear walking through their yards and rummaging for food. They didn't have any complaints about him. He had never been aggressive to anyone or to any pets.

Mick wasn't ready to stop at a social media blitz. He wanted to take stronger action. He crossed his arms while standing next to the screen. His voice was firm like he was issuing orders rather than leading a democratic group.

"I propose we request that the Division of Fish and Wildlife safely capture Walker and relocate him to a preserve. Until we can find one appropriate, maybe he can wait out some time temporarily at Musky Park."

The crowd was not in unanimous agreement the way Mick expected them to be.

"We can't capture him!" If anyone looked closely enough at Rona's eyes they might have seen the tears forming. "He's a wild animal. He's supposed to be free to roam where he wants. To migrate. To have a family. Just like any other bear!"

Miriam agreed with Mick and eventually Dolph did too. Ursula watched Rona's reddened face glow with perspiration.

"I agree with Rona. I think we should request that Walker becomes a tagged and tracked bear by the state, but that he's free to roam. It's a reasonable compromise. They do it with only a certain number of bears anyway and I've seen it work with shark activists."

"What do you mean, you've seen it work? You can stop people from fishing a specific individual shark?" Mick didn't buy Ursula's idea and thought she was too much of a "Millennial activist" to be taken seriously. Let her do the internet posts; her generation is good for slacktivism.

Ursula swiveled in her metal chair. She didn't have the same bravado to stand up and bark orders to make her case.

"No. You can't stop anything from happening to a tagged animal. But, you can use it to generate a ton of community support. The tagged sharks all have Boffo feeds where people who are the administrators for their research write posts in the voice of the animals. The tracker maps are published so anyone can see what migration route they take. It's a wonderful approach."

"I don't agree with that at all either." Rona wasn't backing down. "He's a free animal. A tracker means that hunters who are after a unique trophy, the dead disabled bear, would be able to find him with even less sportsmanship than they show now. No! No way would I support that!"

"Valid point. I hadn't thought about that."

Ursula swiveled back and tried to make herself invisible in her seat. She felt foolish and ignorant. She should have thought of the way hunters would use the information before opening her mouth. Her ex-boyfriend was one of them. She knew a good portion only wanted the trophies and weren't after food sources.

"All right then. We have a couple options to consider. I say we table it for now and have a special vote in two or three days depending on where we can get space to meet up."

"If we do it after hours, we can always meet at my store." Ursula felt like it was one way to participate without throwing another monkey wrench into the volatile pool of emotions.

The meeting wrapped up. Ursula went to the front table to retrieve her steno pad to see who signed up. She managed to recruit Rona, Peter, Mick, and five others to her social media army. She slid her notebook and pen into her bag when she sense someone close enough to be encroaching her personal space.

"Hi, Ursula. I'm Rona Medvedovich. We haven't formally met."

"Hi. Thanks for signing up to help me out. I've seen you in my store, haven't I?"

"Applegate's? Yeah. It's a charming place you have. I'll try to come in more often. I'll be able to drag Peter along if you can start carrying herbal tea blends that aren't in little bags."

Ursula smiled. Not often she came across tea infusion snobs. Her customers were satisfied with Lipton or the occasional orange spice.

"People have been hounding me to get espresso, lattes, and chai flavors. If I had the money, I would do it. I have a plan. It'll get there. But for a while we're still no-frills."

"Not to worry. I like it just fine." Rona turned her head away. "Peter! Come over here."

Peter finished packing up his projector and joined them at the front of the room.

"Hi." He reached out his right hand to shake which made him self conscious around strangers. Ursula's mother had a friend with hands like that from rheumatoid arthritis; able to use them and get through daily life, but had to make some adaptations.

"Hi. I'm Ursula, but you probably figured that out."

"My brother is a man of few words. You'll get used to it. He's more of visual communicator."

"Shut up. I can speak for myself."

"Oh, you're brother and sister? I wasn't sure. Not that it matters." Ursula blushed with embarrassment. "I just mean it's so great that you have someone close to you who supports your cause. My girlfriend wasn't too happy about my joining SOAR. She already thinks we don't have enough time together."

"We better get going. It was nice to meet you — officially, that is." Rona touched Peter's elbow as a gesture to move along.

Mick and Dolph were the last ones to leave, entrusted with locking up. Ursula exited through the door that led directly to the lower parking lot around back. She had a half an hour drive to get home to her apartment above Applegate's.

CHAPTER TWO

Ursula entered Applegate's Country Store from the rear entrance. Adriana was inside locking the front door and switching off the lighted Open sign in the front window above the "Devora Zhukov for State Senate" campaign poster. The chairs were already upside-down on top of the tables. The floor was swept and everything looked pristine. Adriana was a better substitute than Ursula's current afternoon part-timer, Tayleigh. Ursula still desperately need reliable help as good as Adriana. It wasn't fair to keep expecting her girlfriend to do the work for free.

"Thanks for closing up for me." Ursula dropped her bag on the counter next to the cash register and slumped over onto her arm.

"You're welcome. Rough meeting?" Adriana tossed a tea towel over the front counter and it landed on the stainless sink. She rubbed Ursula's back and kissed the side of her head.

Ursula moaned. "That feels so good. I feel like I was beat up. I guess my muscles hate when people yell at me."

"Someone yelled at you? What the hell?"

"Well, no... sort of in a way, I guess. We were just talking about this bear all of us want to save and no one can agree on how to do it. Apparently my suggestion was abysmally stupid."

"Let's go upstairs and relax. Can you manage that or do you still have things to do?"

"Nothing other than a blazing hot shower and checking social media," she saw the look on Adriana's face which said that will take forever, "and I promise that will only take thirty minutes max."

"I'll believe it when I see it."

The upstairs residential space was two floors. When Ursula's parents died, she divided it up and rented out the second floor for office space and she lived alone in the two-bedroom apartment on the third floor. After a long day, she felt like her ascension up all the flights of stairs was a crawl. Her days began at five. Staying out until ten might seem like a normal schedule, but not when running the store alone was so demanding. Her other part-timer Kylie pulled as much of the workload as possible; and there was Manny in the kitchen full-time. There was still too much for them.

Adriana was prepared to stay the night. They hadn't reached the cohabitation stage, but she had a drawer of the dresser for herself and some of her professional clothes in the closet which she only needed to break out if she was following up on news with public figures like politicians. She wasn't given that chance often by her editor at the media office.

"I got you a fresh glass of water because I'm pretty sure you've had that one sitting there for two days." Adriana pointed to the water glass on the Ursula's nightstand.

"You know me so well." Ursula was drying her 3C hair curls with a baby blue towel. The fruity aroma of her shampoo created an aura around her. Instead of blowing it dry, she waited for it to be only damp and twisted a loose braid which reached the top of her back.

As they lay together in bed, Ursula scrolled through the social networks. Nothing stood out to her and she was exhausted.

"Screw this. I'm beat." She plugged her phone in, turned off the ringer, and left it on the nightstand.

"You want to talk about what happened?" Adriana's arm was snuggled around her. She rested a hand top of Ursula's wet head.

Ursula recapped the events of the SOAR meeting. She reaffirmed that she felt ignorant for suggesting a tracking device on a bear right before hundreds were going to be slaughtered.

"It wasn't a stupid suggestion. It's sweet that you want Walker to be free roaming and part of the community."

"I sense a 'but' coming."

"But, I agree that he should be caught and relocated to a preserve. I think that's the safest option. Plus, then he could be seen by a veterinarian and get the right kind of care. He'd get fed regularly. He'd have a good retirement."

"Something about it doesn't feel right to me. I know that sounds absurd and I can't explain it. I have this feeling in my gut."

All Ursula wanted was a solid night of sleep, but her mind wasn't ready to settle down even though her body was. Ideas bounced around her head.

"Don't you think animals in zoos are sad?"

Adriana reached her hand over to Ursula's and entwined their fingers. She looked at the beautiful colors of tan and dark brown alternating in stripes. Her manicure was ruined by closing up the shop. It was the sort of thing she noticed that Ursula wouldn't.

"I think the zoos have come a long way. They aren't tiny cages anymore. They have nice habitats that are supposed to mimic the natural environments. I know we don't agree on all this stuff..."

"No, you still eat meat." Ursula's interruption wasn't harsh, merely a point of order.

"And you still cook it for me and your customers. My point is people aren't always going to agree even if they're on the same side. A zoo is a much better option if you want to keep the bear safe from hunters. Maybe he'll be depressed in a confined area. Who knows? But he'll be alive and he'll have people to take care of him."

Ursula wasn't about to start an argument over meat — not at that moment. She did still cook it for people, but tried to ease her conscience over it by purchasing sustainable and hormone-free supplies. It was the biggest change she made to the store operations when she took over. There were times when she still felt like it was her family's store. Her maternal grandparents eventually retired then passed on handing it down to her mother and father. When her parents died in a plane crash going from Haiti to Cuba, Ursula was all alone with the exception of aunts, uncles, and cousins. She was too busy to ever visit them. She was dating someone when she became the owner of Applegate's Country Store, but that was not the type of "forever" situation. She had to stand on her own two feet, finish college, and get shit done.

Back then lawyers circled like vultures and it disgusted her that she was willing to go down that road. Settlements were made to all the families' survivors in a class act lawsuit. She kicked that boyfriend to the curb when he began making plans for her share of the settlement money.

"You know what? Maybe there's some way to build a compromise that would be right for an animal like Walker." Ursula loved her fantasies about saving the world no matter how unrealistic. Adriana had to reel her back to reality.

"What do you mean?"

"Not a zoo and not shipping him off to a preserve that's far from his home. Maybe we can crowdfund to build one right here in his home area!" Fatigue couldn't keep Ursula from dreaming of the best life possible for someone, even if that someone was a disabled black bear.

"I don't think you're being realistic, sweetie. Something like that could take a million dollars just to get it set up. Then there would be annual budgets. A small skeleton staff would need to be paid because you can't run on all volunteers. There'd be veterinary expenses and how many vets do you know work on wildlife like bears?"

Ursula pushed herself up from Adriana's soft chest.

"Stop trying to crush all my dreams. You do this all the time! People have to have big plans. Museums and zoos exist. Wildlife preservations exist. If I want to find out how they did it, how they got started, and how they keep up funding, dammit, I'll do it! Musky Park isn't far, but it's not a great place. It's way too small and rundown."

Adriana slid herself up the bed to sit with her back straighter against the headboard. The pragmatist in her told her that building a multi-million dollar preserve with dozens or hundreds of acres of land was batshit crazy. It made more sense to capture Walker and take him to a place that already existed even if it meant he had to leave his known territory and be confined to a tiny enclosure.

"Mira, I love your enthusiasm. I love how fiercely you care about the world around you. All I'm trying to do is keep you grounded in the real world. You told me there isn't much left of that settlement from your parents' deaths. You don't have the personal fortune to make what you want happen. And unless you have friends I don't know about, none of them are billionaires either."

"This is important to me. If we can't stop that hunt in four weeks, Walker will be a target. So will a thousand others. I want to save as many as I can in a responsible way — so they don't starve to death from over population, but not because humans destroying their habitat find them a nuisance for tossing garbage cans around."

"You have a good heart, Ursula Applegate. That's why I love you."

"Maybe we shouldn't talk about this anymore. I'm tired. I need sleep and have to get up in five hours."

CHAPTER THREE

The computer beeped and hummed to life. There was no point in turning on the television morning news because at that time of day it was all about weather, traffic, and sports scores. Ursula's commute consisted of walking down stairs. The weather didn't matter — Applegate's almost never closed. The violence of most sports turned her off and there was no way Mid-Atlantic news would be covering the Women's National Volleyball of Haiti in the Caribbean Nations Championship. Checking social media was the easiest thing to do for Ursula to catch the biggest headlines of the day and make sure all was well with the SOAR accounts before work.

Boffo was the site she went to for news. Other sites were more about people's family photos, memes, and unvetted stories that were passed off as news. Boffo listed ten trending topics which could be sorted by region. Fourth down on the list was #BipedalBear for the New York region. She clicked and felt a mix of love and tremendous burden.

National news channels reported that locals in the Rockaway, New Jersey area had spotted what appeared to be a bear walking on its hind legs; although many people speculated that it was a person in a bear suit. One of the posts embedded a video from a correspondent. It was dated the previous night. Somehow Ursula failed to see it after the SOAR meeting.

The news of the bear must not have gone viral until sometime overnight. Affiliate stations across the country had the same video.

"This is Monica Lord reporting live from Rockaway, New Jersey where there have been reports of a black bear walking upright. We know bears in circus performances are trained for such behavior, but this particular bear lives in the wild. More specifically, he lives around this neighborhood at least part of the year."

The video cut to lesser quality footage shot by someone on a cell phone. The bear walked through a cul-de-sac minding its own business. It went through the front yard of the person holding the phone. The image shook as a blur of the home's interior flew by. Then the camera was outside, possibly on a porch, and the bear cautiously approached. It paused, deciding whether to walk passed the human or not. After a few seconds, it proceeded to walk through the backyard and continued into the grove of trees behind the house.

"Walker."

"Something wrong?"

Adriana entered the small living room. She was wearing navy pants and a white blouse typical for her business casual dress code. Ursula paused the video when she heard Adriana come closer.

"Watch this."

Monica Lord's voice continued over other amateur videos posted online. "The residents of the area don't seem to mind this bear walking among them, however there is concern about the state-sanctioned bear hunt which has been met with controversy since it was reinstated. We were able to locate the citizen who shot this video and asked him what he thinks of this unusual bear."

A white man, probably in his thirties and already balding but trying to hide it by shaving the rest of his head, was lit by the news camera's mounted light. It made him look sickly and shiny with nervous sweat. The banner text below said he was Martin Donovan.

"Uh, yeah. We all know this bear. He comes around a lot. Digs through the garbage bins sometimes."

"And does it always walk upright on its back legs?" Monica Lord asked from off camera.

"Yeah, mostly, for sure. I seen him go on all fours sometimes, but he don't stay that way long. He's got something wrong with his front arms so maybe it hurts him to walk normal."

"You think it's been injured before?"

"Maybe. No one knows for sure. Maybe he was born that way. I guess that could happen. But he don' bother anybody. People around here like seein' him."

"I understand the residents have decided to name the bear."

"Yeah, we call him Walker because of how he walks like a person."

"What do you say about the people who think it's all a hoax and really a person in a bear suit?"

Martin chuckled. "Well they haven't met him then. It's definitely a bear. A real bear. I swear to it."

The camera returned to the correspondent, Monica Lord, who had a look of uncertainty on her face. If she preferred to believe it was a Bigfoot hoax, she wasn't the only one.

Ursula scrolled through more of the micro-posts on Boffo.

> *"Mother Nature is pissed & raising an army.*
> *Captain Bearmerica!"*

> *"No way that's real. Nope."*

> *"That poor thing! What's wrong with its hands?"*

And the posts continued on a roller coaster of pity, amusement, and denial.

Her stomach wrenched tight into a knot when she saw the more aggressive posts. "He's gonna make a nice trophy. I'd stuff him and put him in my living room."

Adriana stood up from her hovering position over Ursula's shoulder. "Goddamn! These are national news stations!"

"So you're concerned about the exploitation of Walker all of sudden?"

"No. They scooped the story. I've written about this kind of charming, small town quirk for the last five years and it never gets national attention. Now people with cell phones go viral and New York and Los Angeles pick it up!"

Ursula closed the browser window and shut down the system. Her head shook in disbelief, but Adriana didn't notice.

"I have to go to work. People expect their coffee to be ready."

"I may end up working out of the store today too. I'd like to interview people about Walker and the bear hunt in better detail than Monica Lord from New York City. You don't mind, do you? There's just no point in my driving all the way to Newark if the story is right here."

Ursula figured she didn't have a choice in the matter. If she told Adriana no it would end up in a fight that she didn't have energy for. She half-shrugged a shoulder conveying a cross between, "Whatever," and "You'll do what you want anyway."

Before heading down to the store, Ursula picked her hair and tied it up into a ponytail short enough to be an adorable pom-pom on the crown of her head. She tied a folded up bandana around like a pin-up girl from the

1940's. Luckily, she was graced with bold, tapered eyebrows that didn't require a lot of maintenance. She put on some mascara and a glossy camel colored lipstick that was supposed to last for hours. It never did, but after the morning rush crowd, she couldn't possibly care any less.

"What do you think of this outfit? Do I look too unapproachable?"

"You know everyone in this town anyway. Why are you stressing out? Don't you interview people all the time?"

"Yeah, but I interview people I'm trying to impress like state senators or a police detective. That's not the same as trying to be relatable. Approachable has its own fashion."

"I have no idea. I'm going to work. See you when you get there." She silently added, "To harass my customers," inside her head.

CHAPTER FOUR

Applegate's Country Store was part diner, part shop for faux antique decor and Town of Frankhurst souvenirs which were mostly of the fishing themed variety due to the river and lake. There were only eight small tables which could be pushed together to seat parties greater than four.

The regular and decaf coffee brewed in thirty-cup urns. Ursula saw that a stack of fresh tea towels was already set out and the mugs were lined up like little ceramic soldiers. She got angry with Adriana often enough, but she did appreciate how much she helped keep the store running smoothly.

After fishing and hunting slowed down, the Christmas shopping would take over. Ursula wished that by then, she had enough profit to hire more help than the two part-timers, Kylie and Tayleigh. Not only did Tayleigh have an unfortunately terrible name which was a portmanteau of her parents' names, Taylor and Leigh, she had a slacker work ethic to match. "White people," Ursula thought when Tayleigh interviewed for the position. "They mock our names all the time."

The earliest of the morning crowd consisted of local police officers, fishermen, and corporate types who had grueling commutes into New York City. Ursula got to know all of them.

Officer Morris has a pair of six-month-old twins that kept him looking for all the overtime he could get. Cal and Toby were best friends with competitive streaks about who caught the biggest walleye. Monday through Friday, Jen walked from her apartment above the ice cream parlor to the train platform (there was no station in Frankhurst) to get to Penn Station. And the man who was always on his phone and never made eye contact worked for one of the huge pharmaceutical companies; Ursula surmised that much by his side of a conversation about trials and drug accountability.

One of her least favorite people came in at eleven for lunch. Travis Iver worked for a road construction company that was contracted by the utility services. He ordered a cheeseburger with bacon.

"Make it rare. You know I like to hear it moo."

Ursula smiled at almost every customer. Not Travis. He constantly made comments like that to rile her up.

"To go, I hope."

"I was gonna, but looks like there might be a table opening up over there."

"To go." It was not a question this time when she said it.

"Aww, Ursula. Ursula, Ursula, Ursula. You know you love when I tease you about your misguided save-the-animals B.S."

"If I loved it, Travis, then why did I dump your ass for constantly slaughtering innocent wildlife and being an all-around horrible human being?"

"It's not like you aren't making money off meat." He reached over the counter and stroked her upper arm. She pulled back as quickly as her reflexes allowed.

"If I thought operating a vegan restaurant in this town would survive, I'd change the menu by tomorrow."

The bell above the door jangled. Peter Medvedovich walked in looking his usual handsome, burly self donned in a red flannel shirt, jeans, and boots.

"And keep your hands off me." Ursula gave the warning softly, but made no attempt to whisper or keep anyone else from hearing her. She didn't care if other people knew Travis was an ass. He had been getting whatever he wanted his whole life because his daddy was a dairy farmer who had a lucrative contract with a major brand.

Ursula noticed Peter approaching slowly. Travis tried to be nonchalant about following the direction of her gaze, but she knew his hackles sensed someone getting closer.

"Everything okay, Ursula?"

"I'm fine, Peter. Thanks for asking."

"Maybe you should wait over there for your order." Peter's head nodded in the direction of the bench seat along the front window.

"I think I'm fine where I am. What're you gonna do about it?" Travis kept leaning on the countertop with his arms.

Even though Peter's right hand functioned rather well with ways he learned to adapt, that definitely was not all that made up this man of such virility and strength. He looked up at Ursula. As if she knew some plan had formulated in his head, she gave him an affirmative nod silently. Peter's leg swept across the front of Travis' shin making him lose his balance and his face planted into the counter. Ursula reached across and grabbed him by the collar.

"Don't come back here until you learn some respect. Get the hell out of my shop."

Travis rubbed his jawline and scowled before cracking a smartass grin.

"You'll regret that." Since he looked from Peter to Ursula, it wasn't clear which one he meant to warn. Probably both.

Everyone else in the diner had quieted down to soft murmurs and bowed heads as they witnessed the spectacle.

As Travis walked passed Peter, he intentionally collided with his shoulders. He sneered and leaned into Peter to speak. "Gimp." He said it with the firmness and bravado of all schoolyard bullies who weren't used to being called out on their shit. He exited and the crowd of customers resumed their buzzing conversations. Half of them with their faces down and texting. Ursula realized it too.

"Oh goddamn. I hope no one got that on video."

"He had it coming."

"Yeah, he did, but I don't want the police showing up and arresting you for assault and battery. Now what can I get you? On the house." Her smile was genuine and radiant. Her eyes spoke lyrics with their gaze and soft blinks.

"I'm waiting for Rona actually. We'll take a table whenever one opens up. No rush."

"Coffee?"

"Got any herbal tea?"

That was not a typical request of her customers. She told him she'd see what she had around and said it would be a couple minutes while she checked on all the tables since Tayleigh was one of the people too busy texting.

Adriana entered from the back door carrying her large bag containing her necessities and her laptop. She saw how busy Ursula was and that there wasn't any place for her to sit and work.

"Swamped, huh?"

Ursula found a couple random bags of tea to offer to Peter, lemon mint or orange spice. She practically ran into Adriana on her way through the narrow space behind the counter.

"Uh, yeah. I'm sorry. I don't have time to linger."

"Okay." Adriana's look of disappointment wasn't missed on Peter who was only eight feet away, but Ursula didn't catch it. She could hear it in her girlfriend's voice and it was enough to make her feel guilty.

"Look, I'm sorry. I just can't hurry paying customers out the door."

"Naw, but he can." Tayleigh prodded herself into the conversation and filled Adriana in on the tussle between Peter and Travis.

Peter looked away not wanting additional attention for his violent outburst.

"Really? He beat up your ex?"

"Barely. And you know Travis. He's a dick. He was asking to be thrown out." Ursula saw a customer gesturing in the air. "Tayleigh, you better bring Mr. Blake his check and focus on your work instead of gossip."

"Fine. Whatever."

"It seems like now might be a bad time for me to try interviewing people if they're riled up about a skirmish. Or, maybe that'd be more interesting." The gears inside Adriana's brain sped up as she considered the possibilities.

"Please, don't. I take back my offer. I can't have you do that here. At least not now. I'm busy. People are upset. Please, go and get your story somewhere else."

Adriana mimicked Tayleigh with her, "Fine. Whatever," response. She pulled a scarf out of her bag, quickly wrapped it around her neck causing her hair to frizz, and walked out the front door without kissing Ursula goodbye.

Before the door closed, the bell jingled again and the sun glare bounced off of Rona's shiny black hair. She slid her sunglasses to the top of her head and looked around.

Tayleigh was near one of the tables at the front delivering a check for the couple that hadn't spoken a word to each other the whole time they were there. As she twirled around to saunter to the cash register, it looked like she was putting on some kind of show for Peter's benefit. She was nineteen and going to community college with the big dreams of most girls that age from Frankhurst — she was hoping to escape. A gorgeous older man who stood up for damsels in distress though — that kind of man might be worth sticking around for.

"Ro!" Peter called out from a table that had opened up against the wall.

Ursula was behind the counter with her arms filled with dirty plates to put into a bin for the kitchen staff which was Manny the cook and herself when she was in between other things. Before carrying the overstuffed bin to the dishwasher, she waved to Rona. She tried to acknowledge everyone who came in, but especially people she liked. Rona may have been extreme, but she was passionate. Plus, her caring side shows through every time Peter was around.

The lunch crowd wasn't as great as it should have been. A little drizzling rain started and a lot of people chose delivery food so they wouldn't have to leave their offices. The fishing fanatics came in for the early breakfast no matter what. Ursula could see the people on the sidewalk through the front windows. A few had umbrellas up. Others had their caps or hoodies.

A cluster of four men around the cigarette receptacle caught Ursula's eye. It was Travis and his hunting buddies. She stayed lost in her thoughts, berating herself. How could she have ever dated such a shitty human being? It wasn't just the hunting hobby either. She always made a point of stating that hunting for food was different. Travis and his boys had gotten meaner and more aggressive about the competition and trophy of the animal. Best bow. Best shotgun. Biggest rack. Even who had the best dog and truck.

Then New Jersey reinstated the bear hunt in which Ursula saw no purpose. Few people saw black bears as a food source in the modern normative world. It was mostly about trophies. Making the pelts into rugs or having them taxidermied and put on display (usually in an upright pose making it look like they were attacking someone despite being routinely afraid of humans). There was no sport in murdering bears in their dens, luring them out, or plucking off a baby cub as it tried to keep up with its mother. It was never about food or self defense. The bear hunt was about people being annoyed because their garbage cans were tossed.

Ursula saw one dead on the interstate on night coming back from Adriana's place. It horrified her to see the bloodied remains of a two-hundred pound beauty in the road's shoulder. She told herself, it would serve a purpose: it would feed the turkey vultures and maybe a coyote. Mother Nature had her own cruel cycles for survival. Humans were greedy and took advantage of that harmony.

"Hey, do you mind if I take a smoke break?" Tayleigh snapped Ursula out of her memory.

"No, it's quiet now. Go ahead. I can manage the four tables left."

Tayleigh smiled towards Peter as she bounced her way out the door. Her game of young naive seduction worked better on Travis' friends who fell for her, "Gotta light?" means of breaking into their circle.

Ursula picked up the spray bottle of cleaner and a towel. She wiped down the two tables that were empty. The antique clock above the counter said it was half past one. She desperately needed a break. Kylie was due to come in at three and take over once her husband, a teacher, was out of work for the day and could take care of their kids. Tayleigh kept her cigarette break to ten minutes and got back inside immediately; she must have sensed the mood of her boss.

"Ursula?" Peter called over.

The table where he and Rona sat was Ursula's favorite spot in the diner. There was an oil painting of her grandmother above it. It made the whole place like it was being protected or watched over. Sometimes, Ursula didn't appreciate the sensation at all when she doubted herself like when she repainted the mint green interior to a warmer sage with cream trim.

"Hey, you two? Is everything all right? Can I get you something else — maybe some apple pie?"

"Tempting, but no."

Seeing that they had finished with their food long ago, Ursula could tell something was keeping Peter and Rona inside.

"You know, I can't thank you enough for taking care of Travis before, but you don't have to babysit me. I'm okay. Looks like his goon squad left anyway."

Rona reached across the square wooden table and gave Peter's forearm a squeeze.

"My baby bro, the hero." It may have been the first time in days Rona smiled. Maybe weeks.

"Only by thirty-three minutes, old lady." He smiled back.

"Wait... thirty-three minutes? Does that mean..." Ursula looked from one to the other.

"Yeah, we're twins," Rona said as she sat upright in her chair and hung an arm over the back.

"That's so cool!"

Rona looked around checking on who was still left within listening distance. She invited Ursula if she could take a minute to sit with them.

"We have to ask you something." Rona kept her tone out of earshot of Tayleigh who delivered the last two lunch table checks.

***

Peter squirmed a little in his seat. Ursula hoped it was nervousness and not something in his lunch making him uncomfortable.

"I'm all ears." Ursula pulled over a chair from another table.

"Is your girlfriend Adriana Garcia? The writer from the *Jersey Express* website?"

"How did you know? I'm sorry I didn't get the chance to introduce you formerly. It was busy and Travis distracted me." Ursula hadn't even thought of introducing Peter to Adriana when she came into the shop hoping for a place to interview people about the bear hunt.

"I recognized her from her profile picture. I follow her feed." Peter hoped that didn't sound as creepy out loud as it did in his head. He looked at Rona. In return she tilted her head like she it was an arrow pointing to Ursula. Go on, tell her, she silently conveyed.

"Guys, what is it? Did you want to ask Adriana something? Now that it's dead in here, I can text her to come back."

Rona had an easier time speaking to people than Peter. It was common for her to speak for him or for both of them.

"Our aunt is running for state senate. We noticed you have her campaign poster in the window."

"Devora Zhukov is your aunt?"

"She is. She raised us." Rona saw that Peter was already looking down at his deformed left hand, but she also knew it wasn't self pity making him sad at that moment.

"Oh. One of the party volunteers came in here one day and asked to hang that up. I read over the sheet of her positions and was more than happy to post it. One of her top causes was putting a moratorium on the bear hunt and her first one was making healthcare for small businesses more affordable. She sounds like an angel to me."

The twins offered to help arrange a meeting between Adriana and their aunt if it would mean bringing more attention to the facts about the hunt.

"It's not only the black bears, you know? The small game hunts last year accounted for the deaths of six-thousand-seven-hundred foxes and seventy-eight coyotes. People have to be shown the real data and understand the effects."

"I'm with you there. Although, to be honest, Adriana is after the bylines of the stories and how many hits she gets; she's not covering it because she cares."

"Even better. Unbiased media." Peter looked from Ursula to Rona. He approved of the idea even more.

"When you see that the numbers of rabbits used to be hunted at nearly eight-hundred-thousand in a season and now they're down to seventy-seven-thousand or less, it's because humans are wiping them out. Not predators." Rona spouted facts with ease. To Ursula it sounded like she should be the one to be interviewed, not Devora Zhukov.

"Where did you get this information, if you don't mind me asking?"

"From the state's DEP website. It's public information. I'm not skewing anything."

All of them agreed that a thorough story about the real hunting numbers wouldn't look like the information was made up by SOAR or any other animal rights organization. Ursula confessed to them that things between her and Adriana had been a little rough.

"I don't know if she'd be willing to take a story suggestion from me. She does not like to be told what to do with her work since she already has editors doing that job."

"Please, Ursula?"

Rona's facts were convincing, but it was the melted dark chocolate eyes of her twin that brought Ursula on board with the plan.

"If your aunt knows the facts and figures as well as you do, I'm sure it would entice Adriana. She'd get more life out of the story talking to candidate than talking to citizens a lot people see as granola-crunching whackjobs."

Tayleigh went back to the kitchen and came out without her apron but with her blood red jacket embroidered in black roses and her knock-off Michael Kors handbag. She said she signed her timecard and would be back tomorrow. Manny was finished for the day too. They didn't serve dinner at Applegate's, so if you went in after two o'clock, all you could do was shop or enjoy ice cream and soft drinks. Milkshakes were popular year round. It was just enough for one other person to handle all on their own so Ursula could do the bookkeeping, her SOAR work, and get to bed early.

Rona, Peter, and Ursula made sure they had the correct numbers and emails for each other from the SOAR contact list. They agreed to work on arranging the meeting between Adriana and Devora and hopefully have it set up that week.

CHAPTER FIVE

Ursula left the shop in Kylie's capable hands. By the time she checked the invoices of the supplies, entered the cash register totals of the first shift, and calculated the modest part-time pay of Tayleigh, she needed a break.

She turned on her television to check the New Jersey and Pennsylvania news. She barely paid attention to it while scrolling on her tablet to catch up with social media and international headlines. It was September 11th though so the threads were predictably awful.

By eight o'clock, she hadn't heard back from Adriana which was strange. They didn't keep a specific sleepover schedule, but it was always Adriana staying at Ursula's since she worked six or seven days a week and Adriana could work remotely. The store was closed on Wednesdays, but that didn't mean Ursula wasn't working. There was always something to do: deep cleaning, restocking, placing orders, and even doing small repairs.

The television news showed a woman with brown and grey streaked hair wearing a business suit and black trench coat. The chyron beneath said it was state senate candidate Devora Zhukov. Ursula searched for the remote control and found where it had fallen inside her shoe on the floor. The little vertical bars at the bottom of the screen scaled up as she pressed the volume button.

Devora stood in the glare of the camera's lighting while everything around her was dark from autumn's early sunset. There were people amassed behind her chanting and yelling.

"...and the DEP's kneejerk reaction is nothing short of irresponsible." Devora's final words of the sound bite were all that Ursula was able to catch live.

Boffo was buzzing with the hashtag #bipedalbear and #Walker. The threads were mostly shares of the New Jersey region, but like before when Walker was first revealed by the national news, it would be viral by morning.

> *"Walker, the black bear commonly seen around the Denville and Rockaway, New Jersey areas of Morris County, was tranquilized by state environmental officials and will be moved to captivity."*

> *"Controversy surrounds Walker, deemed harmless and disabled by the residents of the area."*

> *"Animal rights activists can't agree on whether Walker should be contained in captivity temporarily during the NJ bear hunt or for the rest of his life."*

> *"The bear would likely starve to death due to its injured front paws."*

> *"If activists claim Walker can fend for himself, it should be fair game to hunt him."*

The posts were devastating. Ursula couldn't believe what she read. Walker was captured. Why hadn't Mick, Peter, or Rona contacted her by now? Although this kind of news explained where Adriana probably was. Chances are she wasn't too far away trying to get the story for the *Jersey Express*.

Ursula entered "@ExpressGarcia" into the address bar and it took her directly to Adriana's professional work stream. Sure enough, Adriana had posted several pictures of the bear lying in a truck bed tranquilized with his tongue sticking out.

Other videos and photos posted by people on the scene included the entire capture. Walker was clearly trying to flee humans approaching him. He must've known they weren't the neighbors who peacefully let him walk through their yards. Ursula couldn't contain her heartbreak as she watched. She sobbed, tears freely dropping onto her chest.

Her text message notification finally alerted her, but it wasn't Adriana. It was Rona and half the words were misspelled. She must've typed in a hurry or while driving — dangerous but the sort of behavior Rona would do. She begged Ursula to come to Adams Township where Walker was captured. It was urgent.

Ursula texted Mick Hoffman to see if he and other members of SOAR were at the scene too. He replied confirming that he was there during the entire thing because he and other club members who supported capturing Walker and relocating him went ahead and convinced the Division of Fish and Wildlife that it was the best option.

Her tears switched to anger quicker than turning on a light. Mick and his clique went ahead without a group vote and contacted the state officials. How could they? There were valid points made to allow Walker to remain a free animal. While she did support getting him healthcare from a big game vet, she didn't want Walker to end up confined in a cage.

The night air retained some of the damp warmth from earlier in the day, but it looked more like midnight than eight-thirty. Ursula texted while speed walking to her car.

"Why did you do this? At night? Were you trying to hide something?" she wrote to Mick. Everything was a disaster. If they couldn't show solidarity, there was less of a chance of them being taken seriously. They had to present a united front with agreed upon mission statements and objectives. Mick and his cohorts went rogue. It was unacceptable.

She pressed the key fob, slid into the seat, and buckled up. She popped the phone into the dashboard holder and watched as the hands-free mode icon displayed in time with the engine growling to life.

"Call Mick."

He didn't answer. Brushing her off when she was supposedly not only an active member of SOAR, but also one of their key public relations staffers? She couldn't believe the brass balls on their leader.

"Call Rona."

Thankfully, Rona picked up. She sounded hysterical and even more filled with rage than Ursula.

"I have to talk to you! I have to tell you something! Please hurry!"

"Can you just tell me now? I'm on my way. It'll take me thirty minutes to get to North Road."

"I can't tell you over the phone. It's too important!"

"I'll be there as soon as I can. Can you tell me anything? Is Walker all right? Have you talked to Mick?"

"No and yes. I was here before Mick. I saw the whole thing. He's hurt, Ursula. He's hurt!"

"Mick?"

"No! Walker! Those bastards shot him while he was trying to escape them by going up a tree! He fell from the branches!" Rona's voice screeched more than talked. She sounded helpless and furious. She had every reason to be.

Ursula was surprised at her own blubbering reaction when she saw the news, but Rona was far beyond her own grief. She wasn't holding herself together. The extreme response seemed out of character from the little bit Ursula knew of Rona. She thought this was a woman who had all the confidence in the world. She was passionate and outspoken, but never came across unhinged until that phone call.

Things weren't making sense. For Mick to get such rapid response from the state officials had to point to something bigger. Some SOAR members definitely had the money to bribe underpaid civil servants. It would have taken more than that. It would've gone higher up. Jane Doe processing papers could be bought off for probably a few hundred dollars, but not a division head or department commissioner. That would cost a whole lot more.

She didn't have time to think intently about those possibilities. She had to race to Rona and make sure she wasn't hurt too. The protests could sometimes end up that way. Not to mention, Ursula didn't have money for bail.

"Please don't do anything stupid, Rona." The call had already been disconnected, but Ursula had to vocalize it.

The asphalt was damp. Tires clung to it, but not as well as Ursula wanted them to. She had been meaning to save up for a new set for the front wheels. The back ones weren't even street legal, but she wouldn't need an inspection for another ten months.

"Please-please-please," she kept muttering to herself.

The exit ramp was sharp. The yellow sign warned to take it at twenty-five miles per hour. Ursula was at forty-five and praying that her guardian angel could do more than watch from overhead. She needed a divine intervention and so far, so good. Her car didn't flip over the guard rail upside-down onto Route 80 below. Another four miles and she turned onto Buckingham then through the S-curves. She cleared the next three miles at record speed and squealed the tires as she made she left onto North Road.

Spotlights from the roof racks of volunteer firemen's pickup trucks shone over the sight. Police had patrol cars lined up. People from the area had heard the news and showed up to gawk. Others, like Rona, showed up to protest. There weren't too many who agreed with Rona and Ursula that relocation was not in Walker's best interest. On paper, it sounded pleasant, but the animal should have had rights to live unimpeded. Word on the internet broke through fast and as soon as Rona began posting that Walker, the already disabled bear, had been abused and further injured by state employees, the cops knew hell was going to rain down.

Protesters from different environmental groups were represented and easily identified by logos on their hats or sweatshirts. Greenpeace. PETA. The Human Society. And of course, there was SOAR. The local club that had made a promise to the citizens and wildlife of the Skylands region that they would keep animals from being abused.

State Police were on the outside border of the scene keeping anyone new from entering. Municipal cops and the state park rangers were mulling around the mob with the DEP officials. They were inside one of the state wildlife reservation areas which was one of the sections for legal hunting during the specified dates. The activists thought it was a shame that Walker had been going through there and spotted so easily.

Ursula pulled off into the weeds and parked. She needed a way passed the police at the entrance road. The parking lot ahead wasn't normally well lit, but with all the extra lights it was easy for Ursula to spot Adriana's SUV. She texted again and prayed for another miracle.

"I'm here on North. Can you get me in with your credentials? Please! It's urgent!"

"I can try. Brt." Adriana didn't think she'd have any legitimate way to convince the police that yet another member of the press was needed. With journalism on its deathbed, most reporters were also the photographers and copyeditors; and there were no fact checkers anymore. Everyone pulled triple or quadruple duty. You didn't get to call in a story anymore while someone else made the words pretty and got it out the next morning. Except for more in-depth features, everything was live.

The state troopers always had the most professional appearance. Their uniforms were sharp periwinkle blue coats and dark trousers with the notable bright yellow stripe down the leg. The ones at the blockade of wooden horses were as crisp as usual. They also looked to be in no mood for cavorting and small talk. Ursula definitely would not be able to schmooze her way in without Adriana's press card.

"Ma'am? You can't stand there," one of them said.

"Um, okay. I just have to wait for someone. She's already in there. She's with the *Jersey Express*." It was a gamble whether mentioning a reporter would give her some slack or create more friction.

The troopers heard the clacking footsteps behind them. They turned their heads as Adriana approached showing her hands were only carrying a phone, her bag slung diagonally over her torso. She went up to the one with the least fierce expression and smiled. Her hip jutted to the side. Her head tilted the same way.

Ursula couldn't make out what they were saying to each other. Her stomach churned. The terrifying drive out there in the dark at a way-too-fast speed had already squeezed the bile inside her gut.

It took a minute, but then the officer looked at her, nodded his chin upward and moved the wooden horse's end about a foot for her to squish through. She thanked him a bit too zealously and grabbed Adriana by the elbow to scurry into the mix.

"What the hell is going on?"

"You're welcome, by the way."

"I'm sorry. I'm grateful. I really am. But I got these urgent messages from Rona. Mick is here doing God knows what. The internet will be viral with the story in time for the morning news."

"Don't I know it! The news vans arrived already with crews and I'm out here by myself for the *Express* trying to bust my ass and get people to talk to me."

They came to the crowd where protesters demanded that the ranger who tranquilized Walker be immediately suspended or fired for injuring the disabled bear. There were as many people from the press as angry citizens.

"Ursula!"

They looked and saw Rona waving her arms from behind another set of cops who had formed a line with their batons and arms.

"I'm with the *Jersey Express*," Adriana brazenly said to local cops blocking Rona. "I need to interview this woman. Can you let her through?"

"No way, ma'am. But you can go to that side." The cop smirked.

Apparently Adriana used up all her sexy Puerto Rican charm with the state troopers. This guy was not seeing her for the Jennifer Lopez doppelgänger she fancied herself to be.

"Fine." She and Ursula went through another blockade.

Rona grabbed Ursula by the arm and practically dragged her to a quieter spot. People were being cordoned off from a particular area. It was where a truck was parked and the gate down.

"Right over there! Look! He's in that Ford! Those monsters. I can't believe they hurt him. I think they want him dead. I bet the state is angry Walker has become internet famous, but he's the perfect imagery for why we shouldn't have this disgustingly vile hunt anymore!"

Ursula took Rona by the shoulders and forced her to make eye contact.

"Slow down, okay? We're here. Adriana is working on the story. If anything nefarious is going on like a plan to get Walker out of the picture, we'll find out. I promise you."

"Just look at him!" Rona was tall, but even she had to stand on her tippy toes to get a glimpse of the black furry body lying limp in the truck's bed.

Ursula tried to see, but couldn't get any vantage. She caught something in a microexpression that flashed on Adriana's face.

"What? What do you know?"

Adriana hesitated. She knew what she had would only upset them more and judging what she could about Rona, one more straw would break the camel's proverbial back.

"Tell us!" Rona demanded.

"I have video and pictures. I was closer than the protesters. You're not going to like it."

Some of them were similar to media files Ursula had already spotted on Boffo threads. Others were better in the sense that Adriana was allowed to be unrestricted. She had only posted a small peek online. The rest of her pictures showed the ranger who made the shot. There was an entire sequence of Walker falling from the tree and rangers and cops walking over to him. They used a crane to lift his pathetically drugged body. His eyes were sad and showed confusion. It was as if he was trying to ask them, "Why?"

CHAPTER SIX

There was nothing more they could do that night. Adriana had to stay up and draft the story for the *Jersey Express*; Rona said she was going home to her aunt's house; Ursula headed home and needed sleep even though it was unlikely to come to her. Right before she left, she walked over to Mick Hoffman to give him a piece of her mind.

"I cannot believe you orchestrated this without a vote by the members. How the hell did you manage this so quickly anyway?" Ursula had always wondered if it was their age difference that made Mick unable to see eye-to-eye with her. Boomers versus Millennials was the new Foreman versus Tyson. Maybe he honestly believed what he said and followed his gut like she did they weren't on the same path.

"I appreciate your concern, Ursula, but I would have had a majority of board members votes, so the way I see it, I took justifiably quick action on behalf of SOAR. Walker was in danger of being another target of the hunt in a few weeks. There wasn't time to waste."

She watched him walk towards the parking lot. He stopped to talk with people wearing identification badges on their jackets. From that distance, she couldn't tell which agency they were. Mick had friends or at bare minimum, connections in the right places to get Walker captured.

Home was the ideal place for Ursula to sift through the cavalcade of thoughts. The cotton sheets were cold when she climbed into bed. She laid on her side, fetal, and wrapped in the soft squishiness of her Grandmother's antique white duvet. Her body told her one thing — get sleep. Her mind, however, was screaming into a void. She couldn't stop questioning herself. Maybe Mick and the others were right. Maybe Walker would have a decent life in captivity. Maybe she and Rona were being too radical in their views. She and Rona could consider this a compromise to the alternatives.

When she became vegetarian, people made fun of her constantly. Somehow during that time, she dated Travis Iver who mocked her and excused his behavior as "only kidding."

She had gone with Travis once to deliver a whitetail deer to the processing shop. Holt's Treats was an interesting business: during the warm weather it was a popular ice cream stand; in the fall and winter they processed game for hunters. In the parking lot of the ice cream stand, temporary walls of tarps formed the dressing spot. Ursula waited in the truck with the engine going and heat on. They were there to pick up the buck Travis took down.

The blue tarps were only put up after complaints from people driving who saw the reality of where meat comes from. The crisp breeze made the tarps billow. As they separated, Ursula saw enough of a deer being cut open that she felt her stomach contents start to come up. She opened the door for an immediate smack of cold air to keep herself from puking in Travis' truck. After that, she wondered exactly how awful the insides of factory processing plants must be and never took another bite of meat again.

When she told her decision to Travis, he and his family and of course his dopey friends took every opportunity to ridicule her. He would do things like move his face closer to hers while taking a bite. Or he'd try wafting bacon under her nose. Frequently, he'd moo right before biting into a burger. There were only so many times she was willing to hear him say he was only joking when it came to his asinine behavior. Enough was enough and she kicked his ass to the curb and told him to grow up.

There was a time when Ursula understood how hunting was considered a sport. There were "targets" and people liked to brag about the biggest *This* or the most *That*. Then she got to know Travis. Luring. Trail cameras. Deregulation. Bigger bag limits per permit. It seemed that it was more about superiority than food.

***

Irritating. Annoying. Disturbing.

It took some time for Ursula to realize what the hell was going on. Her phone vibrated on the nightstand. The clock read twelve-oh-five. Had she overslept and Manny was looking for her?

Oh hell no. It was midnight and Rona was calling. It went to voicemail. Ursula closed her eyes.

Brrzzzz. Brrzzzz. Brrzzzz. Brrzzzz.

"You've got to be kidding me." She reached out, her hand flopping around to find the device responsible for ruining another night's sleep.

"What!" To hell with being cordial. She had to get up earlier than most people.

"It's Rona. I'm sorry, but I couldn't sleep. I really need your help."

"Were you arrested? I don't have bail. Call your aunt." Ursula was about to hang up and roll back over, but Rona pleaded more.

"I can explain. I will explain. But, please help us."

"Us? What's going on?"

"I'll tell you if you meet me in person."

Ursula argued that it was the middle of the night and she had a business to run. She hadn't known Rona for long and didn't know her as well as an urgent midnight call would normally apply to a friendship. Dire circumstances were the only explanation — unless Rona happened to be a drunk jerk calling for something stupid.

"What? Where? I have to be back here to open my diner."

"I'll come over to pick you up. I'm only fifteen minutes away."

So much for sleeping. Ursula pulled on her jeans and layered herself in a camisole, long sleeve shirt, and a thick hoodie. She braided her hair in a matter of seconds and pulled on a knitted hat. Based on her assumptions of things that people could do in the middle of the night, she didn't think dolling herself up was necessary. One thing that was — hot coffee. She popped a K-cup into the coffee maker and added enough water for her travel cup to be filled. After adding a little almond milk and snapping the top in place, she was ready to face Rona and her cryptic matter.

The single street light at the edge of the road lit the parking lot behind the buildings. Ursula took the long strap of her bag and shifted it over her head to cross her body. The walk across the pavement, regardless of how peaceful Frankhurst was, made her hyperaware. The scent of the leaves dying on the trees flowed through the current of the nippy air. Rona pulled into the lot without bothering to signal to the empty road. Her window rolled down before she came to a stop.

"Come on. Get in."

Ursula climbed into the passenger side of the sedan and didn't wait for an invitation to put her travel cup into one of the holders. She buckled herself in the seatbelt — no way to know how a hysterical person drove.

"You want to tell me what the hell is going on now?"

"Not yet. When we get there."

Ursula shook her head and watched the cross streets zip by her window.

"Get where? Can you tell me that much or am I an accomplice of my own kidnapping?"

Rona turned the wheel to make a right onto Irvington Street and followed it to the highway. She didn't take her eyes off the road. That was probably a good thing. Eye contact with her passenger could send them into a tree or worse. She drummed her long fingernails on the steering wheel.

"I'm not kidnapping you. We're going to Musky Park."

Musky Park was short for the Musconetcong Animal Park and Education Center. It was a long name for rather small and bleak zoo. Throughout the building were formerly alive animals, now stuffed and on display. Some of them looked like the taxidermists were high when they made them. There were rooms for lectures in the main building too. The veterinary facility was a separate building at the rear of the park away from view so customers never had to see a tranquilized or dead animal carried inside.

"Let me guess — Walker was taken to Musky Park."

"You guessed correctly. Ding, ding, ding. Give the nice lady a prize."

"Okay, listen to me. I love Walker the same the way you do. I think he's an innocent, yet wild creature who deserves to live his life his own way. Tonight though, I've been questioning whether Mick isn't right that the bear would be better off captive. He may live a lot longer than in the wild as a disabled bear."

"Trust me. You do not love Walker the same way I do."

"What the hell is that supposed to mean?"

Her question lingered in the air, unanswered.

"You missed the entrance." Ursula tried to get a read on Rona's expression, searching for a clue to understand her better. Nothing came to her.

"Well, they're not exactly open. We can't go through the main entrance."

"Oh dear god. You think we're breaking in there? Are you insane? That's rhetorical. Don't answer that. Clearly, you are."

Rona knew where to find the service road employees of the veterinary facility used. There were a few lights turned on above the doors, but it appeared to be the only lighting around. The wall around the park turned it into a creepy abandoned military style outpost in the dark of night. It resembled the Waco, Texas cult compound torn apart by the National Guard in 1993. Fortunately the inside of this place was filled with adorable animals held captive and not human ones.

"This is like some damn horror movie, Ro. I don't know what you're thinking."

"There aren't any cameras back here in the vets' parking lot like there are in the main one for customers. A lot less lights too. We can park on the edge. I remember seeing a line of oak trees right... around... here!"

Rona pulled the car across the grass at a surprisingly appropriate crawling speed. She parked them behind the trees and got out before Ursula had time to get her composure together.

"So do we need, like, bolt cutters and ski masks or something? Because I didn't pack that stuff in my purse."

"No. Follow me."

Rona led the way along the wall and pointed out where there were security cameras, all of which were facing into the park not on the exterior. Ursula followed along, but her inner dialog continued to warn her that they'd be mauled or arrested before sunrise. She wasn't sure which was worse considering that an all-white police force arresting a black woman was one of her worst nightmares. Sandra Bland was forever in her memory.

"There's a part where the ground slopes with a tree on the inside of the wall. It's one of the weak points of the perimeter I found." Ursula picked up her pace moving through the shadows.

"Perimeter? Weak points? How do you know this? Walker was only brought here hours ago."

"I've spent a lot of time outdoors. I know little details about the whole landscape including parts of New York state and Pennsylvania."

They turned a corner and came to the incline. There was a huge drainage pipe with bars covering the opening. The slope was steep next to it and lined with cement bricks. The surface was smooth making a climb seem impossible. The wall stopped there and resumed at the top where it wasn't as high. On the far side of the hill, the wall was back to its tall height.

"It's tricky, but as long as you find even the smallest lip in the block edges for your hands and feet, you can grab hold and scale up."

"I have never gone rock climbing in my life!"

"Luckily, this is not that high. You'll be fine." Rona made sure her own bag was secure and took a bug-like pose on the rocks.

"Aren't you worried about breaking your nails?" Ursula was being glib. She knew the answer. Nothing short of guns pointed at them would stop Rona on her crusade. "I can't believe I let you talk me into this."

Rona scaled ten feet to a wider foot hold. It was enough for her lean sideways and look down at Ursula. She stretched her left hand down while her right gripped for dear life.

"Just get a few feet up and reach my hand. I can pull you up."

Ursula's athletic, competitive side began and ended with volleyball which she had not played in years. Her muscle tone was strictly due to her hard work at the store being on her feet for long periods of time and carrying heavy plates or boxes of supplies. One might be shocked how much lifting gallons of mayonnaise and ketchup can do for biceps and core strength.

She tried to mimic Rona as best as she could. Ursula's fingers grazed her fearless leader's. She grunted and gasped.

"I can't do it. I can't reach you!"

"Yes you can!" Rona shifted her foot another inch and bent her knees as much as the small ledge would allow. Her knees were spread apart to keep her center of gravity as close to the slippery blocks as possible.

Ursula tried again and again. She looked down. It wasn't that far, but she didn't want to have to start all over.

"Gimme a sec. Let me rest."

After what seemed like a surreal high speed minute, Ursula reached up to Rona's hand and their fingers were able to hook each other. It wasn't much to secure Ursula, but it was the best grip they were going to get until she was several inches higher. Rona's hooked fingertip strength impressed Ursula. It was like she was made of steel — a crane lifting her up to safety.

"How did you do that? How much time do you spend at the gym?" Ursula was flummoxed. She had no idea anyone other a master like Bruce Lee could have such power in the smallest appendages.

"Bro, do you even lift?" Rona's attempt at divergent humor didn't land the way she hoped. Ursula's face showed all her skepticism swell back up the way it was in the car.

Rona led the way up to the top which was slightly easier for Ursula. This time Rona was prone on the ground and able to reach down for a solid hand-over-hand grip. She hoisted Ursula up with ease and shifted herself back onto her knees.

Ursula looked into Rona's eyes and searched for any clues to explain what had just happened. The chocolate eyes pierced back through her. It wasn't a staring contest. Their blinking became soft and relaxed. Something was there behind those eyes, but Ursula couldn't solve the puzzle. She shook her head and snapped herself from the unexpected trance.

***

Rona hopped to her feet. They delayed long enough. She stood at the wall and jumped straight up to reach the tree branch that would lead them to the other side. She swung her feet up and over, dropping her top half down like a trapeze artist.

"Come on. I got you."

Ursula couldn't argue after what they'd been through already. She realized where a lot of her doubt manifested. Every day for years, she was the one in charge. She was the boss. She was responsible for everything in her life from the moment her parents were killed — that meant their business, their building, the staff, and herself. She gave orders. She was not used to taking them. She rarely had a break. All this time, she believed people like Adriana who called her stubborn; but there at the edge of an animal park, she realized what was inside her. It was more than being a respectable adult. It was leadership. Sometimes, it made her seem too tough to be around.

She met her match with Rona. On the car ride, she felt the shift of giving up control to someone she hardly knew. It was quite nearly unbearable for her. At the top of that hill, that uncomfortable feeling evolved into mutual admiration. Respect: so few people earned it, but Rona definitely had won her over. Ursula no longer saw her as crazy. She watched her as they ran that perimeter and scaled that concrete barrier together. Rona led her, guided her, and used her strength to help her. Her pursuit to free Walker wasn't radical environmentalism. Her motivation was magnanimous. Ursula could see that Rona would put her own life on the line to help someone she cared about — even if that someone was a disabled bear. She finally felt like their mission was feasible because she was with someone who believed in her.

Her new friend hung from a tree branch upside-down waiting. Ursula smiled and ran into a leap to grasp Rona's wrists. In no time, both of them were on the branch.

"Thank god I remembered to zip my bag or I'd be leaving evidence all over the place. I did not expect to be climbing walls and trees when I left my house."

"How do you feel about it now?" Rona turned her head away to see what obstacles were in their way down into the park.

"I'm glad you came to get me. If I'm going to be arrested, I'd rather have a friend with me." Ursula looked down at the touch of Rona's hand reaching back to hers as she gripped the branch.

"Are you ready to break some laws?"

"Wait! How will we get back out? Even if we open the place where Walker is being held, what do we do then?"

"I promise, I have a plan and I will keep both of you safe."

It was time to fully put her trust in someone. Trusting Adriana had never been challenged this way. Even her relationship from Travis never built to this level of physical safety. If anything, with Travis it was the exact opposite.

"The first thing we need to do is take out the cameras along the top of the wall." Rona dropped her feet onto the wide brick surface and crouched to get her focus. She stood up and walked along it like it was no different than a sidewalk.

Ursula copied her friend. She crouched to make sure her footing was secure. Then she made the mistake of looking down. A new kind of fright burst into her mind: the possibility of falling into an enclosure. She didn't have a map or program guide telling her where they were or what was below in the darkness.

"Unicorns," she whispered to herself. "It's a den for happy little unicorns with rainbow manes." She crawled the first twenty feet. "With sharp, spiral horns on which I might impale myself when I fall to my death. Death by unicorn. Sounds great."

Rona looked back. "Did you just say there are unicorns?"

"I'm talking to myself."

"Unicorns aren't real, silly girl. But we are over the cassowary enclosure. That's why there are so many trees here and a tunnel for them to go inside where it's warm and tropical in a special greenhouse."

"Cassowary? That sounds like something from a fantasy book about magical teens."

"They're birds from Australia. They look like blue ostriches. Mostly harmless except for the disemboweling and eye gouging."

"The *what* now? Pecked to death by Big Bird sounds a lot worse than impaled by a unicorn."

Ursula looked down again and begin to doubt her newfound trust. "Screw it," she told herself. Standing up, she readied her balance and walked behind Rona.

When they came to the first camera, Rona was about to rip it off the hinges.

"Hang on. Do we really want to vandalize and cause thousands of dollars in damage on top of the multiple laws we're breaking?" Ursula dug into her bag and pulled out a tube of Darkest Desires lipstick, the darkest red could be before it was black. She handed it to Rona.

"Excellent thinking." Rona took off the top, swiveled the base, and proceeded to reach over and color the camera lens with the lipstick.

They followed along the top of the wall taking out six more cameras from operation in a way that could be cleaned with soap and water.

Rona stood tall and smelled the fragrances of the air. Some not so pleasant. To Ursula it mostly smelled like scat, hay, and wet dog.

"I know I've asked you trust me a lot so keep in mind what I said. I will protect you and Walker no matter what. Promise me if anything happens, you'll keep going forward and release him."

"No. No, I will not promise that! You are a human being. We'll protect each other if it comes down to it. Both of us are getting out of this alive and with all the body parts we came in here with. You got me?"

"Okay fine. We jump down over there." Rona pointed to a spot where the drop down didn't look so terrible.

CHAPTER SEVEN

Ursula knew people adept at parkour could handle a jump from that high, but she wasn't her former athletic self. She didn't know what would happen to her bones in her late twenties. Heck, even the most fit person could land badly and break a leg. Then, what? She'd be trapped in a fenced-in pen where a bird could peck her to death or maybe a lion would shred an intruder. She loved animals, but didn't necessarily want to be killed by one.

The thump on the ground told her that Rona landed without incident. Every crunch on dry leaves worried Ursula. The sounds could be Rona's feet or something's paws. From across the park, she listened to the nocturnal birds cooing and cawing.

Musky Park was small as far as zoos go, but they had over forty outdoor exhibits and ten indoor exhibits. Ursula remembered visiting there on a school field trip. Her favorite thing back then was the intricate indoor cave for the bat exhibit. There were windows so people could see into the spaces lit by black lights. The long tube shaped hall kept the human visitors on a clean floor instead of stepping through guano.

"Are you coming or what?" Rona didn't bother to whisper. Apparently she didn't care about whether she woke up the animals.

Ursula decided a better way to get down would be to lessen the fall. She sat on the wall and rolled over to her belly. Slowly, the weight of her body pulled her down and her armpits with bent arms were holding her up. She shifted her weight to the left so the right hand and fingers could find a hold and then did the same for the left. She only had to drop six feet from there.

"Come on," Rona called.

Ursula's fingers let go. Her feet hit the ground, but she was too close to the wall to find her center of gravity and balance. She fell backward onto her ass.

"That better have been mud I just sat on."

It wasn't.

"Think of it this way, you're masking your human scent."

"Fantastic." Ursula started to get up when Rona offered her a hand. She felt her butt and it was covered in the squished wet, thick pudding texture of shit. She unzipped her bag again found two crumpled napkins to wipe some of it off, but she didn't want to put the soiled napkins back in her bag so she stuffed them in her front jeans pocket which would be getting a severe laundering. She could hold onto the napkins until she saw a garbage bin. No reason to add littering to their list of crimes.

A low growl cut through the air. It was too dark to see where the source of it was. Ursula prayed it was something on the other side of a fence. Her own heartbeat resonated so loudly inside her body that she couldn't parse the different noises around her.

"Ro?"

"I'm here. Don't move yet."

Ursula heard steps moving closer. The growl was low, but closer. All she could see was a black mass of something creeping towards them.

"Ursula, don't be freaked out."

"How can you say that? I think a wolf is about to kill us."

"Trust me. Here — hold onto these for me."

Ursula turned to her right and saw Rona, naked with her purse, clothes and shoes in her hands shoving them away.

"What the hell! Rona, what are you doing?"

"I asked you to trust me."

Ursula took the clothes. Her own feet were frozen in place. She tried to keep her movements to a minimum. The growls were indeed a wolf. A large gray wolf of about a hundred and fifty pounds.

"It's not hungry. They're regularly fed. But it's probably pissed off that we're in its territory."

"And you took off your clothes to what? Hypnotize it with a burlesque dance?"

Cracking. Crunching. Peeling. Sounds that were definitely not from the wolf got Ursula's attention. She turned her head and watched in horror as her friend's human body ripped itself apart to grow and transform. Ursula didn't know what to do. Running wasn't happening. She couldn't move at all. She watched Rona's face and body grow a thick blanket of black fur as shiny and luxurious as her human hair had been. Ro's body continued to snap and pop making her hunch forward to all fours which were now enormous meaty paws with gigantic claws.

Ursula's breath stammered while she shook in place hugging her friend's clothing into her chest. Moans and growls spewed from the beast. Even the wolf kept its distance, but lowered its shoulders and snarled not knowing what to make of this.

A two hundred pound black bear stood there looking back at Ursula. She assumed she was dreaming or she really had fallen off the wall and smashed her head, because there was no way Rona had transformed into a freaking bear.

The new Rona had heft yet grace. She walked between Ursula and the wolf. Growl met with growl. Barks and roars. Rona stood up on her hind legs displaying the majesty of her bear form. Her size was enough to make the wolf back off slowly, a few steps then a few more. It realized a physical confrontation wouldn't be worth its time and walked back into the shadows of its lair.

Still petrified, Ursula waited until her brain engaged with some kind of logic and a plan. Rona lowered back to all fours and walked over to Ursula. She came within a few feet and waited for a sign.

"Ro? Jesus. Is that really you?" Ursula held tight a few more seconds before reaching out her trembling hand.

Rona approached slowly so as not to scare her friend. Her nose made contact with Ursula's palm. She lowered her face and allowed Ursula's hand to stroke across her snout to the top of her head.

"What the holy effin' hell is happening? This isn't happening. This isn't real. I'm in a coma or something."

Rona came closer and rubbed up against Ursula's legs like a monstrously huge cat would. She licked Ursula's hand as a gesture to show that this was real. It was in fact happening and she was not suffering from a head injury.

Ursula's arm dropped the pile of clothes. She used both hands to run her fingers over the thick animal fur. No one would believe this. She couldn't even believe it.

Rona lowered her head and moved the clothes with her nose towards Ursula. It was her way of saying, "Hey, don't forget these."

"Oh. Yeah. Okay. I guess you want me to put these in my bag like you told me to before you turned into a freaking bear. Okay. I got this."

Ursula crouched down and found a stone under the clothes. It was probably a hundred carats if Ursula had to guess. Its opalescence shimmered as she turned the cabochon around in her hand. The setting looked antique, maybe even ancient. Ursula put it in her bag first to make sure it was safely zipped inside a pocket then shoved in Rona's clothes.

43

Good thing she had the habit of lugging an oversized bag everywhere. When she accomplished the bear's orders, Ursula waited to see what was next.

Rona walked over to the gate for the enclosure. She let out another roar, pulled back an arm, and swung at the keypad lock. It flew right off and burst into pieces when it hit the ground.

"Well this explains how your hands were able to lift me up without any problem." Ursula pushed on the wire gate and it opened easily.

There were only a few lights at a dim level along the path. Unless the other animals there could become human and tell the zookeepers what happened, their break-in should be hard to solve since they masked the surveillance cameras.

Rona stopped in her tracks. She smelled the scents on the air again like she did as a human on the wall. She waited and listened for more sensory information. She led them passed the concert pavilion. The bear exhibit was the next one after that. Ursula remembered them having a black bear and an Asian sunbear in captivity all those years ago.

They walked towards the fence and a black bear was already there waiting for them. The sign on the post stated the exhibit contained two male black bears, Wilt and Dwayne, who were sons of the previous female bear born in 2013. There was no mention of the sunbear.

Rona and their greeter exchanged groaning sounds. Soon, the other male came over and joined the odd Wonderland party. The brothers on the other side of the fence were obviously lacking the distinctive deformities of Walker. Ursula could only assume this foreign conversation was Rona asking where he was.

Unexpectedly, Rona let out a roar that did not sound like polite conversation. It was anger. She stood up and yelled with menacing rage. The brothers took a couple steps back, but didn't leave. Whatever she said, they weren't afraid of her.

"The keypad is right over there." Ursula's voice stammered again. She tried to believe that her wild animal friend wouldn't hurt her, but Rona was terrifying when she wanted to be. The lock was only a small obstacle. She wanted to get inside that enclosure and that meant Walker was in there too.

This time, Rona not only swiped the keypad lock into bits, she also gripped the wire fencing and pulled back, peeling it away from the posts. Ursula jumped back. She was nearly sliced by the sharp shredded metal. Before she knew it, Rona was running inside the exhibit leaving the male brothers at the gate to eye Ursula.

"Ro? Ro! Am I supposed to... come in... there... with these... guys?"

The strangers made no move of aggression towards Ursula. She hugged the fence post and slithered around it. The bears followed Rona without getting too close.

"Ro? Where are you? I'm scared to death here."

The glint of moonlight bounced from the shadows. Rona's eyes. Ursula could tell and ran to her. It was one of the darkest parts of the exhibit, but Ursula's eyes began to adjust. She saw Rona's massive form and then saw Walker on the ground.

Rona moved her face all over him like she had with Ursula. It was her bear-speak for, "I'm here and you'll be okay." They exchanged quiet purrs and other sounds Ursula had only heard from tall, hairy science fiction characters.

"What's wrong with him? Why isn't he getting up?" Ursula didn't know how she'd translate any growls from Rona. "Can you please change back, Ro? I'd like to talk in English if possible. Human English."

The spectacle was unpleasant as Rona reversed her transformation. It was the noises that made Ursula's stomach flip-flop. Cracks. Snaps. Gurgles of fluids. Groans that told her it had to be a painful process. Guilt overcame Ursula for asking her friend to go through that for her sake.

Naked in the shadows, unashamedly on her knees next to Walker, Rona hung her head. She placed a hand on the bear then looked back at Ursula.

"Walker isn't just a bear. He's my twin brother Peter."

CHAPTER EIGHT

"I should have known." Ursula couldn't take her eyes off of Peter, lying there in his pathetic condition. She finally put two and two together. The bear had crippled hands and so did Peter. Rona was overly protective of both. It all made sense now. Not so much made sense, since she couldn't believe her friends were actually bears, but she saw the connections. The twins being so cautious for each other; their volunteer efforts to stop the bear hunt; Peter's injuries; and their general distrust of others.

"Can I have my clothes now? It's chilly without my fur." Rona stood up showing off her flesh which was amply covered in dirt and raw scars.

"Oh, right. Sorry." Ursula unzipped her bag and handed the whole thing over to Rona.

Rona pulled on her thick socks and underwear. She hooked her bra and pulled her black turtleneck overhead then layered on the grey flannel shirt. When she pulled her jeans up, she stuck her hands in the pockets, not to straighten the fabric, but looking for something.

"Did you see a shiny white jewel?"

"Yeah, I forgot. It's gorgeous. I zipped up in the inside pocket." Ursula pointed to the inside of the bag. "Is that a family heirloom? It looks old."

46

Rona found the stone safe and secure. She tucked it into her jeans pocket for the time being in order to lace up her boots. Ursula took her bag back as it was proffered.

"It's older than I really know." Rona took the stone back out so she and Ursula could look at it. "I don't need it to transform, but it protects me when I'm human and helps me heal unbelievably fast. And now, I'm going to see if it'll help bring Peter out of his doped intoxication."

"Look, I can't wrap my brains around all this, but I gotta ask. If that stone helps heal, why are his hands deformed?"

"Valid question. I usually keep the moonstone on me. Peter doesn't mind the transformation process and his body hair and facial scruff cover a lot of his scars. When his left hand got caught in a snare trap, he tried to use the other to free himself. Both ended up damaged, but the left was beyond repair. He couldn't get to me in time to use the stone. His right arm has some ulnar nerve damage limiting the use of some fingers but not all of them."

They needed to see if the moonstone would work on clearing the tranquilizers out of Peter's system. Like modern medicine, they wondered if there were interactions since they had no idea of knowing what else the veterinarian gave him.

"Will this mess with any antibiotics or anything else?"

"Headaches, nausea, aching joints, rashes, hair loss, impotence, infertility, blindness, sneezing, dizziness, and uncontrollable bowel discharge." Rona saw Ursula fight the bile she was about to spew. "I'm kidding. It's not like the FDA has approved trials on it."

"I'll get you for that one. So do it already. Make it work before those big guys come over here and pulverize us."

Rona sat on the ground so she could cradle Peter's head in her lap. She placed the moonstone on his heart and covered it with one hand while the other delicately stroked his forehead.

Ursula couldn't understand what was spoken. It was almost like a song. There was cadence, but not quite a melody. And Rona wasn't using words so much as tonal vibrations through throat singing. The notes ranged from high to low as Rona kept her body still, but allowed her head to sway ever-so slightly. It was mesmerizing.

There was a small patch of blonde hair in the middle of Peter's black furry chest. The moonstone was on top of it like a tiny planet surrounded by a field of wheat. Ursula had only seen things like this in books and on television. She didn't know what else to go on as a basis for what she saw. She expected the stone to radiate a glow and levitate on its own. The chanting kept going for more than a two minutes. She didn't know if she was allowed to touch Peter or Rona during it so she bent down and sat as close as possible without interfering.

Coming from the other side of the darkness, a sensation hit Ursula. That prickling at the back of her shoulders and neck told her someone was watching and coming closer. The two male bear brothers, Wilt and Dwayne, were closing in. Rona had better hurry. Maybe the real bears were coming to watch the show, but on the other hand, they might be looking for victory over two measly humans. Ursula believed that they would be more scared of people and the thing to do is make a lot of noise to spook them away. All that advice was about encountering bears in the wild. These two were born and raised in Musky Park. They could have had instincts running through their veins that they didn't know what to do with.

Ursula turned her attention back to Peter. The cloudy vapidness cleared from his deeply mysterious eyes. He showed more signs of movement in his hands and feet, or rather paws. Rona ended her chant. She lifted Peter's head from her lap and slid her body out from underneath him. She leaned down and kissed him on the head then backed away further.

Peter shifted his body placing weight on his back legs and right forearm. He rested a moment on those three points before standing erect, his usual "Walker" way. He towered over the women yet looked so sweet and adorable. Ursula couldn't understand how anyone would ever fear him or want to hurt him. Thinking of people like Travis, though, she knew they were out there looking for a story to tell and a trophy for their living rooms. Those people refused to see him for the gentle soul he was.

"Why hasn't he transformed back into Peter?" Ursula got close to Rona trying not to bring unwanted attention from the real bears only fifty feet away.

"He's always Peter, but I understand your question. We need him as Walker the bear right now. I have to transform back too. It'll be easier if we have as much strength as possible to break out of here."

"You got us in here as a person. Why can't you stay this way so I can talk to you?" Panic grew in Ursula's chest. An annoyance of tinnitus pierced through her head. It always happened when she got too stressed out.

"Don't be scared!"

"I'm not scared of you. I'm scared of them though." She pointed to the other set of twins getting closer. Only forty feet now. They seemed to be taking their time to assess the situation.

"He can't do too much harm to them with his hands. He needs to use his height, weight, and jaws while his feet keep him steady."

Peter let out a powerful roar warning the other males to stay back. They hadn't bothered him before while he was all alone, but his companions had suddenly made him much more interesting to them.

Before she had the chance to debate tactics, Ursula got a face full of Rona's shirts; she was stripped down in seconds. Ursula knew she was responsible now for the clothes and the jewel. It also made her realize that if Peter transformed back into a human he'd be buck naked. As much as she wanted to savor that thought, she had to get her own ass into gear and pack up Rona's stuff. The moonstone was again secured into the inside pocket first.

The ungodly sounds penetrated through Ursula's ears and stopped the ringing. She wished the tinnitus had waited until Rona was finished. Her friend emitted more growls and snarls as bones cracked and popped. Cries of agony howled out as her skin stretched. The shape of Rona's face elongated into a snout while her teeth grew into fangs that could kill if necessary.

Rona and Peter understood each other so well — the product of being twins and being heavily involved in each other lives. Rona didn't waste time. Just as Ursula learned before, this was a woman who charged through life regardless of danger. In her bigger and stronger bear form, Rona took off after the males and tried to chase them away. It didn't work. They engaged in a brawl. Peter stayed at the rear of the melee until one of the brothers was thrown to his feet. He bent over and clamped his jaws at the bear's throat.

Ursula wondered if there was a limit to what the moonstone could do. It had already been used in a ritual and from the way things were going, there would be more injuries to heal.

The largest among the bears was one of the male twins, Wilt. He had over a hundred pounds on Rona's form. He drove into her with his head and she lost her footing, flying backward. He reached his enormous paw overhead and swung it down to her face.

"No!" Ursula's scream was nothing compared to Rona's howl.

Blood dripped from the side of Rona's head. She rolled over to all fours and sprinted to get distance between them. When she turned around, she saw that the smaller male, Dwayne, had shaken Peter off and smacked him aside.

Ursula yelled out again. "Hey, dummies! Over here!" She jumped up and down waving her arms. She knew a bear could outrun her, but she had to try something to save her friends. She bolted to the damaged gate and slid through. She looked back and saw all of them following her, the Medvedovich bears at the rear.

Her legs burned as she ran at full speed down the pathway. She knew she couldn't risk slowing down to look back again. She reached an area of benches in the grove next to the pavilion. She jumped and missed the lowest branch. Growls grew closer. She let out a grunt as she jumped higher than she ever could have in a volleyball tournament. Her hands made it and she gripped the branch to hoist her legs up like she had seen Rona do earlier.

The bears took the bait and headed for Ursula in the tree. Rona's vision took in the whole area before she locked eyes with Ursula's terrified gaze.

"Ro! The cassowary! Get the lock!"

Faster than even she thought possible, Rona was at the gate of the bird's exhibit and smashed the keypad lock to pieces. She ripped the wire gate off its hinges as she had done to the bears' den. She charged through the exhibit to the door that lead inside to the warmer area.

The curious cassowary peaked out to see what was happening. Its blue head looked like something Ursula had only seen in alien movies with a lot of special effects. The enormous bird was none too pleased at the disturbance.

The bear brothers immediately stopped their stalking of Ursula. The commotion of Rona's destruction made them think twice about which situation deserved their attention. The bizarre behavior of another bear won their attention.

Peter waited patiently as the brothers followed Rona into the cassowary exhibit. Rona snuck around as best as she could as a large black bear, mostly by using the darkness as cover. She and Peter met next to the tree Ursula climbed.

Ursula watched from overhead as Rona stayed on all fours next to the tree and Peter used her as a stepping stool to get higher than his right arm could reach. Rona carefully stood on her back legs to prop up Peter even more. It was exactly the right height for him to use the strongest part of his upper arm to hoist himself up to the branch. Ursula climbed another branch higher to make sure there was enough room and hopefully not too much weight.

Meanwhile the cassowary propelled itself towards the bears invading its space. The bears had spent their entire lives in captivity, mostly in that exhibit. The only regular contact they had with other animals were the peacocks and peahens allowed to roam freely and whatever outside wildlife managed to explore their space. Usually it was nothing more than squirrels and small birds. The scale of the cassowary startled those bears and they stopped in their tracks. The bird squawked and screeched through the September night to warn them that they had better back off. They were male bears who already engaged in a battle which they won.

The feathery black orb body moved across the grass on its skinny, but deceptively powerful legs. The smaller brother, Dwayne, stayed back, but the larger one still wanted to fight. The bird's blue head bobbed like a cobra waiting to strike. First, a roar. Then the bear stood tall for a few seconds to show off his own power and hulk. When he lowered back down to all fours, the cassowary's head protracted so quickly, the bear had no idea what happened. It pecked and pecked while he backed away. He turned and the bird pursued until both brothers were out of its home. The bird seemed awfully proud of itself as it headed back to the more tropical comforts of its indoor habitat.

Ursula, Rona, and Peter watched as the other bears ran back towards to their own damaged den. The tree branches fortunately supported the roughly six hundred and fifty pounds of extra weight. They climbed down, grateful to finally feel a modicum of safety. They still had to solve the problem of breaking back out.

CHAPTER NINE

Rona morphed back to her human form and got dressed again. She checked over Peter's injuries which were healing but not as rapidly as her own. The drugs in his system must have had an effect on the moonstone's abilities.

"Your face is pretty mangled." Ursula couldn't believe all they had been through and it was nearly two-thirty in the morning. She thought she knew what exhaustion felt like on her body after years of work with almost no days off. The adrenaline and terror made the physical exertion so much worse than ever before.

"I'll heal. It's fine. Now we need to get the hell out of here. Alarms have probably gone off and I'd bet the staff and police will be here any second."

"Hey, Bear-Girl, I thought you said you'd break us out of here?" Ursula had been assuming the night would end up with all of them in jail. The moment of pride for taking action faded and she was back to being worried about the realistic possibilities of needing bail, losing her business and her home, and destroying her life. It wasn't like she could explain her devotion to a cause and out Peter.

"Don't call me Bear-Girl."

"Fine. Were-bear. Just stay furry and crash through a door or something. We have to bolt! Now!"

"Were-bear is worse. It's derogatory."

"Shut the hell up. I'm taking over this mess. Follow me." Ursula took the path to the pavilion and looked around to see where the rest of the security cameras could be. There was a display in front of the pavilion area with a map of the park. She traced her finger around it while plans formulated in her head. "I got it!"

Ursula said she needed Rona to transform again and apologized for the pain it would cause, but they needed her strength. Plus, any cameras catching Walker the bear walking around with another bear might look like the resident brothers broke out of their enclosure and Walker was along for the stroll. Only expert eyes of the zookeepers would notice how much smaller Rona's bear form was compared to the males.

She ordered Rona and Peter to break into the offices and find a staff uniform for Peter so he could transform to his human body. After that, the humans Peter and Ursula would go with Rona in her bear form back to the wolf den to escape the way they came. They'd need Rona's muscle for that part. She'd be better equipped to help Peter climb the wall and the tree to get back to the outside of the perimeter.

It was a solid plan that neither Rona nor Peter could debate. They got to the administration building without any problems. The other bears had had enough fighting and stayed in their exhibit. The cameras caught Walker and a bear on all fours exploring the park as Ursula planned. Then the team of unusual activists heard the sirens.

"Hurry up. Hurry up." Ursula muttered out loud to no one. She looked around and saw the peacock on a picnic table staring at her. "What?" Unlike the cassowary, he had no response and kept to himself.

She finally saw Rona and Peter, now a human and dressed in a brown uniform with a cap on his head, running her way. They darted back to the wolf's lair and hesitated.

The chatter of nearby police officers and voices from their radios broke into the inner sanctum of the park. The trespassers had only seconds to go before they'd be caught.

"Shit!" Ursula saw the wolves come out of the shadows. There were two of them.

"How did you get passed them before?" Peter hadn't been filled in on the details of the break-in.

"Your sister. She kicks ass," Ursula looked at Rona, "even if she is reckless."

Rona could understand English in her bear form, but didn't have the capacity to reply with a snide, "Told ya so." She got between the wolves and the humans and stood up as she had before.

The wolves stood there and let their keen senses feed them information about this strange pack. They decided to keep watchful eyes on them and stay within a distance Ursula found frightening. She loved animals, all of them, but they were so much scarier in the dark.

Rona was going to act as interference but realized she didn't need to. The wolves weren't going to attack them.

"Ro, change back. You need to climb up this wall and hoist Ursula. You'd be better at it than me." That wasn't the plan. Peter expected his sister to argue, but there wasn't any time. The cops were coming closer and for the moment, that felt more dire than wolves.

She roared her displeasure at that decision, but began her process anyway. Ursula quickly pulled pieces of Rona's clothing from her bag and helped her get dressed. They were nothing like a well-rehearsed cheer squad lifting someone high in the air, but Peter and Ursula managed to shove Rona up the wall to the top. Ursula climbed onto Peter's shoulders and reached up for Rona who deftly hoisted her up.

"Freeze! Don't move!" The police officer had a gun drawn on Peter. He worked his way into the wolf enclosure unaware that the lupines were watching every step. He reached for his radio and called in that he found the intruder. Singular.

"He hasn't seen you guys," Peter said not turning his head up to show that he was speaking to the women and not to the wolves.

The growls started. The wolves had reached their limit of being disturbed in their home base. That's when the officer finally heard them and his eyes cautiously panned to the right.

Peter stood there with his arms up. Getting shot with a tranquilizer was enough. He didn't need a startled cop shooting him with bullets too.

CHAPTER TEN

The municipal police officer took his gun off Peter and directed it at the wolves. Human footsteps thumped in rapid succession along the pathway. The cops had their guns drawn. Animal handlers arrived on the scene with tranquilizers and bear mace ready.

"Booker, what's the situation?" A sergeant boomed from behind the crushed gate.

"One intruder. And I don't know how many wolves, sir." The patrolman hesitated taking his eyes off the wolves. He was relieved when the lead animal handler entered the den.

"Three gray wolves," she said. "They're all females. We'll take care of them. You can take him." Two other animal handlers followed her into the exhibit. They must have not have had time for uniforms, but wore Musky Park hats. One was armed with a long pole with a looped choker at the end; the other armed with meaty treats to lure them to the moderately disguised door leading to a room where they could be managed away from the public eyes or other interference.

Officer Booker cuffed Peter and read him his rights charging him a litany of offenses: trespassing, vandalism, and breaking and entering.

"We'll be able to come up with more when we get you back to the station," the sergeant said. "I'll have to check with the park administration, but I bet your little escapade here endangered some animals too so you can brace yourself for even more charges. I hear that one bear is rather special to this town." He holstered his weapon, smirking at Peter.

The officers were ordered to divide up and search the park for the missing bipedal bear they couldn't find. One of the zoo employees went with them, prepared to tranquilize Walker again if they did find him.

"Sir?"

"What is it Booker?"

"If and when we find Walker, where will they put him and the other bears?"

"That's the park's problem. They own the two. Fish and Wildlife will get to decide about Walker. He was only going to be here temporarily from what I understand."

Booker kept a grip on Peter's arm even though he wasn't resisting. They passed the gift shop and guest services building. They kept walking towards the administration building which housed the staff offices, locker room, and two conference rooms.

"He got hurt last time they caught him." Patrol Officer Carl Booker was unsure how to show his concern for a wild animal when priorities were always placed on human lives.

Peter kept quiet and listened. He observed in case they said anything he could use to his own advantage.

"Your point being?"

"Nothing, sir. Just that I hope they can wrangle him without hurting him is all. He's already disabled."

"He's still wild and probably scared. That makes him more dangerous now than when people spot him walking through their yards."

Sergeant Anthony McElroy, Mack to his friends, had already calculated multiple ways the night could turn out. One of those possibilities was that Walker would be shot and killed in order to save people. He wasn't broken up about that. No matter what happened, he'd know what to say to make sure it was understood clearly that the events were the best outcome for all involved. Good headlines and pats on the back from the town council might be just the thing to finally get them to promote him. It was a small town. There wasn't exactly much room for growth. He was depressed thinking that he'd still be a sergeant by the time retirement rolled around.

They arrived at the administration building and pushed Peter into the hallway.

"The small conference room," Mack said.

"Why that one, sir?"

Mack shoved Peter up against a wall hard and pressed on his turned head.

"Because small confinement generally makes people more uncomfortable and willing to talk sooner. We'll take him to the station once we have a status report. We can't question him here. We'll want it all on the record."

"Then what can we do here, sir?"

"Verify his identification. Call that in and find out if there are any outstanding warrants." He pushed harder on Peter's head. "God, I hope there are. It'd just make my night."

Peter did not have ID on him since he had been taken to Musky Park as Walker the bear. Despite cartoons and comics, animals don't normally exist with fashionable vests and neckties though marsupials are fortunate enough to have large pockets. Still, they don't use them for wallets.

They got him into a room and shoved him into a chair. It wasn't supposed to be comfortable and his hands cuffed behind him made sure of that.

"Peter Medvedovich," he said when Booker asked his name.

"Spell that."

"M-e-d-v-e-d-o-v-i-c-h."

Booker wrote it down in his notebook. He left the sergeant to babysit. Booker exited to call in the name to dispatch without Peter listening.

"Russian?"

"Born here."

"Hrmmm." The sergeant remembered the Cold War clearly even if his arresting officer was too young to recall it. Of course by 2016, they were in a new iteration of it and people didn't quite know what to do.

Booker came back in and announced that there was nothing on Peter Medvedovich. Not even parking tickets. He's had zero infractions his entire life.

"Interesting." Mack took a seat at the head of the table with Peter at the end of the long side. He rested an elbow up on the corner and let his posture slip to something more casual. He looked at Peter's face searching for a big revelation. Peter broke eye contact and looked around the room.

Mack's voice exposed that he had been a smoker for over two decades. He took out a toothpick and gnawed on it. The sergeant had his own demons. Maybe it wasn't that long since he kicked the habit.

"So, Medvedovich. If you've been such a good boy, why would you risk everything by breaking into Musky Park and trash the place? And I am curious how you ripped those gates down without a truck and tow cable."

"I'll wait to speak with a lawyer."

"Sir? I don't mean to interrupt but there is something." Booker didn't dream of taking a seat at the table. He had too much nervous energy to sit anyway.

"What is it?" He looked up at the officer.

"The press is here."

Mack's expression conveyed his annoyance with the news.

"Let me guess... Garcia?"

"She's one of them of, yes. Should I tell them to wait at the municipal building for an official statement?"

"I'll take care of it. You watch him. He lawyered up."

Adriana Garcia and four other members of the press had been given permission to enter the park to take photographs. Park officials didn't have much to say, only that Walker the bipedal bear was unaccounted for after an apparent break-in by a man with no prior record. When questioned if he was some kind of animal rights extremist, officials had no information to share at that time. The man was found alone trying to escape through the wolf enclosure. He had caused thousands of dollars of damage to gates, fences, and electronic locks. Other than the one bear missing, none of the other animals had been harmed or needed tranquilizing.

The status reports came in from the people searching the park grounds. There was no sign of Walker or other intruders, Peter heard them tell Mack. That meant Rona and Ursula escaped or at least hadn't been found on their way to the stashed car. It was enough that he had hope they were safe.

"Time to go, Russian." Mack ordered Booker to take Peter back to their headquarters at the municipal building. They were in the same building as all the town administrators, but had a separate parking area and an entrance with a metal detector.

At the police station, Peter's restraints were changed to hook him from one wrist and then to a bar secured on a wall. He used his phone call to reach Rona on her cell. She said that as long as he was physically all right and not being abused, he could sit tight and wait for morning when she and their Aunt Devora would have better luck finding a lawyer. They never needed one for criminal defense before.

"Where are we?" Ursula's heartbeat was still faster than normal. She thought Rona would have taken her back home. Ursula texted Adriana from the car and didn't get a response. Yet one more thing to worry about.

"We're at my aunt's house. I live here with her. Peter lives in the studio apartment above the garage. Aunt Devora will know what to do. She has the best contacts and I don't really speak to anyone outside of SOAR or grad school, half of which are kind of unreasonable jerks anyway."

They parked in the circular driveway in front of the house. Rona didn't bother locking the car. The next closest house was over a mile away. Devora owned a considerable amount of land just shy of ninety acres.

Peter agreed to keep his mouth shut until morning. He wouldn't talk to the press either. They didn't groan too much since it was the middle of the night and people wouldn't be reading posts for a few more hours.

Adriana and the others had enough to make a short news story out of it which would end with a statement that more would be reported as it's learned.

Adriana looked at her phone and saw the texts from Ursula. For two years, she consistently heard how important it was for Ursula to get to bed early because of her business. Yet, something cryptic went down and Rona needed a friend and she was willing to sacrifice sleep for that. A text like that only enforced Adriana's suspicion that Ursula was afraid of commitment or painfully not interested in committing to her. She replied back that she was busy on a breaking story anyway.

CHAPTER ELEVEN

The sun wouldn't be up for five more hours. In the darkness, Devora's white house loomed like a giant ghost in the middle of the woods. There were electronic candles in all the front windows that made each set look like demonic eyes staring Ursula down as she approached behind Rona.

There was a sign on the front porch written in a beautiful script that said, "Ursa Major" and had an illustration of the constellation. Rona caught Ursula reading it.

"There's one on the side of the garage where Peter lives that says Ursa Minor."

"Cute."

Rona's keys clattered against the hard wooden door. Ursula wanted the help from Devora, especially since she had connections, but she wanted to be back in her bed even more. She texted Manny and the girls asking if they could run things at the store for her. She knew it would take hours before getting replies. The silver lining, if she dug deep to find one, was that if the staff could manage without her in this emergency, perhaps she could start taking occasional days off for leisure.

The house's architecture was like an old Colonial manor. They entered in a foyer where there was a central hallway and rooms to the left and right. Before them, a wide staircase that curved around the bottom few steps to the wood floor. Nothing was ostentatious. The design and decor were enough to be pleasing to the eyes, but not overdone and gaudy. It was upper class modest without being intimidating.

"I'll show you to the kitchen. You could probably use food and drink after that shitshow."

Rona lead the way down the hall. The kitchen was in the back of the house. It had windows overlooking the property and doorways to the cellar and dining room. She made Ursula peanut butter and jelly and took a hard apple cider from the refrigerator. Simple, yet perfect. It was exactly what Ursula needed. She savored the respite. She fought the urge to drop her head on the table and fall asleep while Rona went to wake her aunt.

Devora somehow managed to make being awaken in the middle of the night glamorous. She had what Ursula considered "grown up pajamas" meaning an actual matching set of pants and top with a shiny robe. Her slippers were practical — thick and insulated — and looked like designer label. Her hair matched Rona's black locks but longer with enough grey to show she wasn't embarrassed by age. They had the same eyes, just like Peter. Deep, rich, hypnotic. The kind of eyes that made it nearly impossible to look away.

Introductions were made quickly in order to get down to the crisis at hand: getting Peter out of jail.

"I'll call Cynthia Steinberg in the morning. She'll know what to do." Devora filled a tea kettle and put it on the gas stove to boil. "Now, Ms. Applegate, I understand you've been let in on our secret."

"Call me Ursula, please. And yes, I've learned about Rona and Peter. You're saying you're a were-bear too?"

"That's an offensive term."

Ursula hunched her head into her shoulders. She thought Rona had been joking before when she said it was a pejorative. She apologized immediately.

"We're volkolaks. It's the form of lycanthropy for bear shapeshifters. Wolves usually get all the stories in folklore, but there are other kinds of lycanthropes." Devora hadn't spoken out loud about this ability to a human before. Revealing such knowledge, as Rona had, put everyone at great risk during a time when all bears were being targeted.

"I had to tell her. You get that, right?" Rona pleaded.

"It's too late to debate that now. She knows and we have to figure out what to do."

Ursula didn't like the sound of that. "I'll keep your secret. I swear! Don't hurt me."

Rona and Devora looked at each other then back to Ursula at which point they burst out laughing.

"She's not threatening you. Chill."

"No, I'm not. I try to live a peaceful life. Most of us do. Rona here, she's the one that has more spunk and tends to land in trouble."

"So there are more volkolaks than the three of you?" Ursula was relieved that she got to keep breathing as hard as that was for the moment. Her heart came down from her throat as she calmed down. She needed to be able to get oxygen to her brain to fully comprehend all this news. Part of her still thought she was dreaming.

Devora explained that there are volkolaks all over the world from Asia, Africa, and Europe to the Americas. Their own ancestry came from Russia. As humans, they immigrated to the United States and made new lives. It sounded like the same immigrant story as anyone else up to a point.

"My father was killed by hunters here in New Jersey and my mother was captured and taken to a zoo in California last we heard." Rona's sadness was clear as was her motivation for stopping the hunt.

"I'm so sorry. I didn't know how close you were to this type of activism."

"Good. I guess I was able to keep our secret from everyone else. I almost lost control in that SOAR meeting." Rona admitted it wasn't the first time she came close to blowing her family secret wide open in front of people.

Devora turned around and pulled some things from a cabinet. She mixed them together in a glass measuring cup. She opened another cabinet and took out a large mug then retrieved a sieve which she placed over it. Rona kept talking about how important it was to stay hidden. Ursula was only half listening, intrigued by what Devora was concocting. It didn't look like any ordinary cup of tea.

"You know what would happen. We'd be subject to torture, tests, vivisection with no limits. And I'm absolutely sure the governments would want to weaponize us as a kind of super soldier program. Ursula? Ursula?"

"What? Yes, I agree. People can be terrible. What's going on over there?" She mouthed the last part of that. Rona raised her eyebrows and shrugged that she didn't know.

"What's going on is that I'm making something I hope works. It hasn't been used in probably a hundred years. It's a mixture of osha root and kinnikinnick charged with a small moonstone." Devora poured the hot water into the measuring cup holding the ingredients. She waited ten minutes then poured the infusion through the sieve into the mug.

"What's this supposed to do to me? Make me forget about volkolaks?" Ursula looked at the mug with a combination of skepticism and fear.

"The opposite. It's supposed to give you the ability to see us for who we are. Since I've never had to take it or use it, I'm not sure what that effect will feel like for you."

"Can I ask what's in it first?"

Devora told her the short list of ingredients. She added more details about the moonstone and how it came to her possession.

Like the stone that Rona keeps on her at all times, the much smaller cabochon moonstone Devora used was far more precious than any antique to them. Both were jewels passed down through the generations going back to Russia.

"But I've seen moonstones for sale in a lot of places. That one shop in New Hope has a whole tray of moonstone jewelry," Ursula said.

"Ours have been charged through sacred ceremony. Our ancestors used a lot more of their special gifts than we do. We've gotten lax, I'm sorry to say." Devora took the stone out of the mush left in the filter. She rinsed it off with the goose-neck faucet and well water of her kitchen sink.

"So it's magic? Like spells and witchcraft and sorcery?"

Rona intercepted that question. "Witches exist, but we're volkolaks. We have our own abilities. Maybe you'd call it magic. To us, it's just how we live."

There was no time like the present, Ursula told herself. She looked at her reflection in the liquid. Her hands were warmed by the cup as she lifted it up to her mouth. Her eyes were closed. She took a breath and swallowed more. The others watched in silence. When she was finished, she kept her gaze down at the empty mug before finally looking up, curious about what Rona and Devora would look like through her new vision.

"You look the same. It didn't work."

Rona threw a hand up displaying her impatience, a move with which her aunt was familiar. Devora told them to give it time. She didn't have any information about measurements or the lunar cycle or how long the reaction would take to kick in. It was a matter of hoping for the best.

"Whether this works on you or not," Devora said, "I appreciate all your help in trying to save our kin. I know Peter and Rona appreciate it too."

"And first thing in the morning, we'll see what the official charges are against him and see if there's a bail hearing," Rona said.

"I don't know about volkolak biology, but ladies, I desperately need rest before tackling all that. When I do, I'm going to call Mick Hoffman and rally the SOAR members to show up at the town hall demanding Peter be set free on his own recognizance. There's no way they're going to be able to convince a judge that he tore those enclosures apart with the condition of his hands. They'll have to let him go on trespassing charges and explain the disappearance of Walker some other way."

"Come on. I'll drive you home." Rona put her jacket back on and grabbed her keys.

"Thanks for the um... refreshments." Ursula waved to Devora while she followed Rona towards the front door. Once they were in the car, Ursula apologized again to Rona about what happened to her parents. As an adult orphan, she knew how much it sucked to not have them around.

"I know my mom is alive though. She's out there somewhere. Every time I've brought up investigating it and tracking her down, which shouldn't be that hard for us, Aunt Devora tells me to drop it. She thinks it would only upset me more and cause me to do something drastic."

"You mean like break into a zoo and rip apart exhibits until she's freed?"

Rona smiled. "Yeah, like that."

***

Slumber was within reach. Deep, precious, restful sleep. Or so Ursula wanted to believe when she walked through her bedroom and pulled the blinds closed. She peeled out of her clothes which made her think about how many times poor Rona had to strip down and redress in front of a stranger and her brother in one night. Rona definitely was not fazed by it though. She had to be used to it if this was normal since birth. Ursula pictured baby cub versions of Rona and Peter and it made her smile.

She enjoyed a brief, hot shower to wash away all the dirt from their expedition. Before nodding off, she checked her texts and was relieved that Manny and Kylie were going to handle everything downstairs. She sent a quick note to Adriana letting her know she was home and safe and would catch up with her later.

Ursula slept until nine when the phone vibrations on the nightstand roused her. There were a string of texts and a few missed calls. The most unexpected of them was in Adriana's thread. She said she was going to the police station where she heard about the SOAR protesters and hunters going face to face.

"Oh that can't be good." Ursula scrolled with her thumb to read all the rest of the messages. Mick sent out a blast begging everyone who possibly could make it to get to the municipal building to free Peter. He and Dolph had materials to make signs.

A quick change into jeans and a sweatshirt with the SOAR logo on it and Ursula went down the back stairs to the employee entrance of Applegate's. She helped herself to coffee and a blueberry muffin (made fresh by Dream Girls Bakery) and made sure everything was in acceptable operating mode.

"We've got everything under control," Kylie said. "Manny is kicking ass in the kitchen as usual and I recruited a friend of mine to help me out this morning since Tayleigh never replied."

"I don't know what I'd do without you. I'd give you a big fat bonus if I could. You might have to settle for a computer printed certificate that says Employee of the Year."

"Hey, I'd put that on my resume." Kylie dumped more dirty dishes into the bin that needed to be walked back to the sink.

"Resume? You plan on leaving me?" Ursula was only kidding. She knew a young woman like Kylie still had dreams and ambitions. "Let me take that back for you before I go."

"Where are you going?"

"There's a protest at the police station to free Peter Medvedovich. You probably remember him. He's the guy who helped me with Travis the other day. I told you about that, right?"

"Yeah. That's nuts. What do you mean, 'free' him?"

"He was arrested last night for breaking into Musky Park. They think he freed Walker the bear. Anyway, I gotta book it over there."

Ursula dropped off the dirty dishes and filled the dishwasher. Manny assured her that everything was fine. She trusted him even if the United States government didn't think undocumented workers deserved a life. He'd been working for her family for over ten years. He had sweet kids and a quiet wife who came in every so often so Ursula could see why he worked so hard six days a week.

The parking lots were filled and news vans hogged up whatever space they could muster. Frankhurst hadn't been newsworthy... probably ever, Ursula thought. It was a hell of a sight. The cops had all hands on deck from the look of it. They had wooden horses set up to create a walkway to the police department entrance. One side of the division had the animal rights activists; the other side had individual hunters and those who were also members of the Frankhurst Gun and Bow Club.

The hot travel cup warmed Ursula's hand. The other one stuffed into her sweatshirt pocket fondling an old tissue and coughdrop she had left inside it. Her eyes scanned the crowd and the scene as a whole.

She spotted the familiar mud-covered matte black body of a pickup with the three-inch lift. It belonged to Travis Iver. Ursula was in no mood to have another run-in with him. He would most certainly be filled with rage towards Peter and would use his loud mouth and townie connections to push for steep charges and punishments. Travis and his family knew all the local cops. His brother and father worked for the town public works.

The news vans were from New York stations and the only New Jersey station. This far north in New Jersey wasn't usually covered by the Philadelphia affiliates. Stringers were getting interviews from both sides. Frankhurst's finest had nothing to say yet. The police chief ordered them not to speak to the press at all because he would do it when he was ready. Not even Sgt. McElroy could comment on the capture and subsequent disappearance of Walker the famous bear.

Ursula waited for Adriana to finish up getting quotes and sound bites from Miriam Vanderwal before approaching.

"Peter Medvedovich is a sweet and gentle young man. He wouldn't hurt a fly. There's no way I can believe that he caused the damage to Musky Park. I can't say why he was there at night, but I simply cannot believe it was to harm any animal or property."

"Thank you, Ms. Vanderwal." Adriana clicked the button on her audio recorder and noticed Ursula standing there. The greeting wasn't what anyone would call warm.

"Hey, I'm sorry about last night. Rona had some family problems, as you can see. She needed a friend and I don't think she has many."

Ursula kept thinking about how much trust she could find in Adriana. She considered telling her about the volkolaks. It was the sort of secret that couples should share with each other even if one promised never to tell another soul. Couples were supposed to be an exemption.

"You can make it up to me by introducing us and then getting me an 'in' with Devora Zhukov. I understand that's Rona's aunt?"

"Yeah, she is. I was at her house last night. Rona and Peter both live there. Is she here?"

Adriana pointed to where Rona was standing and shouting at the top of her lungs. She said Devora was inside the building because she was allowed time to speak with Peter. The last thing that family needed was Rona getting arrested too.

"I have to see if I can more quotes."

Adriana had a job to do. As the controversies surrounding the bear hunt grew, she became more determined to make a name for herself beyond being a freelance stringer covering lousy municipal council meetings. She wanted to work her way into a staff position. She longed for things like vacation days and sick days — those mysterious fringe benefits that used to come with journalism jobs thirty years ago.

The previous year, Adriana got to have a byline on the article when one of the SOAR protesters, Jon McHugh, age fifty-two, was arrested for civil disobedience; he proudly spent a week in jail. Adriana figured he was that type of person who looked forward to being arrested for protesting.

If either SOAR or the hunters got especially riled up and did something like throw objects or even violate the barriers, there would be more arrests which meant another shot at the front page of the county section of the website. She wanted an ample collection of sample stories for her portfolio where it wasn't only a research role. Seeing "by Adriana Garcia" with a link to an author's page mattered immensely.

People were tired of standing outside even if was a balmy sixty degrees for September. A few hours passed. The hunters' smirks of joy got more devious as the activists yelled louder. It fed them with energy. It was a relief to everyone when Sgt. McElroy came out the door.

"Listen up! Chief Martinson invites all of you into the council chambers for a statement and questions. Once we reach capacity of the room, the rest will be forced to stay outside for your own safety due to fire ordinances. Have anything metal removed and ready to go in the bin for the scanner. The Frankhurst Police Department thanks you for your cooperation."

Thankfully, the process was not nearly as bad as going through Newark International's TSA checkpoints. Officers had hand-held metal detector wands and moved the line at a reasonable speed.

Once inside, Ursula found Rona and asked for an update. There was no new information yet. Rona had to wait for Devora to provide that. Devora arranged for Cynthia Steinberg to represent Peter just as she promised. Unfortunately due to the court schedules, Ms. Steinberg didn't get there until after eleven-thirty. She didn't spend much time with Peter or Devora. She got the facts, her retainer by check, and went to meet with the judge and prosecutor to get some of the charges dropped.

Devora did whatever she could to keep Rona and Peter out of trouble. They were adults, but she cared for them as a parent since before they needed her to fill that role.

"Cynthia is going to take care of the more serious charges. She's hoping to get a lot of it dismissed since he has no priors and there's no way they can pin the vandalism on him. We don't need to stay for this circus. Peter was brought to county lockup after they processed him and he talked to Cynthia. The police have released his mugshot to the media unfortunately."

"I'm sure that's something they have to do for protocol if anyone asks for it. Freedom of information and all that." Ursula had plenty of that embedded into her brain from two years of dating a reporter.

"I don't want to leave. I'm staying." Rona's stamina and tenacity seemed like an endless font.

"Fine. Stay out of trouble." Devora looked directly at Ursula. "I need to talk to you anyway about that tea I made you last night." She kept it vague in case any of the people nearby overheard.

Ursula and Rona said goodbye to each other and promised to text with updates. Adriana was among the first inside the council chambers so Ursula texted her a goodbye too.

"Let's go back to my shop and talk. When Adriana gets out of there, she would really like to interview you for the *Jersey Express*."

"I won't say much. Cynthia warned me not to, but since she's your girlfriend, I'll at least listen to her questions before dismissing her."

It wasn't a long walk, but since Devora had her car in the parking lot, they drove back towards Applegate's.

***

Applegate's wasn't as bustling as it normally would be. Seemed to be that everyone in town found the protests more exciting to watch. Ursula wanted to stay and hear and the police chief's statement, but she knew she'd hear all about it in time.

Devora pulled into a parking spot on the street and fed the meter. She pointed to the campaign sign in Applegate's front window.

"Thank you for that, by the way. It's good to have some support. I don't think I'm too popular around here."

"I like what you've said and what your stances are." The door set the jingling bell above it in motion as Ursula held it for the state senate candidate. "And, you are welcome to host a rally right here at Applegate's anytime you want. I mean, we don't have a lot of space, but it's yours if you need it."

"I think I'll take you up on that. I'll ask my assistant check the calendar."

"Who's your assistant? Do I know them?"

"Yes, you do. It's me when I get home and sit at my computer and on occasion, Rona when she's not too busy with homework." Devora's smile was bright enough to lift some of Ursula's sadness.

Ursula gave the store a cursory once over after showing Devora to a table. Tayleigh had finally come in to work. She had swapped shifts with Kylie after all.

"Boss, Manny says we need someone to make an emergency run to the bakery." Tayleigh didn't offer to do it herself. Running out of bread or rolls was a true emergency in a greasy spoon, even one as tiny as Applegate's.

Ursula shouted in the direction of the kitchen pass-through window.

"Hey, Manny? Which one your sons is old enough to drive?"

He leaned over from the cutting station. "Tony."

"Well, if you can get Tony here, he can take my car and do the bakery run. I'll pay him for his time."

"Si. I'll call him now."

If his kids were anything like him, Ursula knew she could trust them with her life not just her ten-year-old car. She heard Manny praise all of kids. They had good grades, played soccer and baseball, and his youngest son was active in the school drama club.

Ursula fetched cups of coffee for herself and Devora. She brought them over with a small plate holding two Jersey size (meaning enormous) black and white cookies.

"This is a decadent lunch for me. Beats the hell out of a small field green salad." Devora carefully snapped off bite size chunks of the cookie. Her fingernails ended up with some of the thick frosting on them.

"Look, you should know, Manny and his wife are undocumented. I'm not saying that to rat him out. I'd preach from a mountain for them. They're good people. Their kids were all born here in New Jersey. But if you do host an event here, I don't want you to be surprised if someone digs that tidbit up and accuses you of being lax on immigration."

"I am lax on immigration. He's here. He's a hard worker and has roots. He's made a life."

"I read that you said something along those lines in a statement. That's one of the reasons I like you and have trust in you — for a politician." Ursula winked. She also understood Devora's plight. Applegate's was the only shop on the block that had her campaign sign in the window. Others were displaying her conservative competitor's signs, Rodney Jones.

"I didn't want to talk about my campaign. I needed to tell you that I dug through some of my grandmother's old things and I believe I know what went wrong with that tea I made you."

Ursula listened carefully as Devora explained that she found a folded up letter with a photo inside from her great-grandfather to his daughter. It was however written in Russian purposely to make it unlikely anyone who stumbled upon it in the states would know what it said. Devora believed it to be the instructions for the bear root ritual that would give a human the ursine vision.

"Can you translate it?"

"Only a few words, but it shouldn't take me too long if I feed it into the computer and use a translation tool. It's not ideal. Nuances can make or break a ritual. It's all I can do without having easy access to another Russian volkolak who speaks the language."

They agreed to be patient about the process. They had more urgent matters like getting Peter freed from jail and keeping Rona out of it.

Forty-five minutes later, Adriana walked in the front door already pulling her laptop from her bag while she balanced her recorder, notebook, and phone in her hands. Devora gave her a brief interview from the perspective of candidate Zhukov, who wants to halt the bear hunt, rather than as Aunt Devora whose nephew is the prime suspect in the Musky Park break-in. Adriana's face showed her disappointment. She wanted the quotes to be juicy and emotionally dramatic, not political and about the environment. Still, she thanked Devora for her time and asked Ursula if she could stay there to upload her story.

"You can go up to the apartment if you want to avoid the distractions."

"No, I'm fine here." Adriana's thanks didn't come across quite sincere enough for Ursula. The bug up her butt about Rona appeared to be keeping Adriana short-tempered.

By the time Ursula was in bed, early even for her, she had seen Adriana's story on the *Jersey Express* website. It didn't please her, but it was fair reporting. Adriana talked to both sides of the controversy. The gun club hunters came out sounding far more level-headed and reasonable than they were in person. The photos showed the SOAR members holding their signs emblazoned with some sweet photos of the wildlife and some tragic photos of the wildlife killed. Peter had taken all those photos the year before.

The notification on her tablet chimed to alert her to a new message. It was from Rona. She said that Devora had the translation of the bear root ritual ready, but didn't feel safe emailing it.

Ursula rolled her eyes then reprimanded herself. It wasn't that ludicrous to think about hacking in everyday life; and Devora was running for political office so there were possibly people looking for gossip or scandal. A magical spell written from the email of a candidate would look like front page news to invasive reporters eager to call a woman a witch, a Satanist, or mentally unstable.

She wrote back to Rona and said she could drop off the translation, but they weren't going to stay up all night again. Rona agreed and kept her promise.

"Does this have to be prepared by a volkolak or can I do it myself?"

"She didn't say. But I guess it would make more sense to have one of us around to test the effects."

Ursula looked through all the ingredients and checked them against the list on the page.

"There's one missing. Adder's tongue?"

"Shit. I'm sorry. I didn't notice that." Rona immediately pressed the icon with her aunt's avatar on her contact list. "She said she knew that one was missing and wanted to talk to you. Here."

Rona handed the phone over to Ursula. The conversation was brief and frustrating from the look Ursula gave to Rona. She thanked Devora for all her research and time then hung up.

"I have to go find this adder's tongue or whatever. Part of the ritual means I have to wait for a new moon and harvest this weed myself for it to work best."

"I never heard of adder's tongue before." Rona looked worried.

"Me neither. It ain't happening tonight anyway. We can check the internet some other time and get information on where this stuff grows."

"One more thing. Here." Rona handed Ursula Devora's moonstone amulet. "She said you can borrow it."

The gemstone was precious to the Medvedovich family. Ursula was paranoid that she would lose it or break it somehow. After Rona left, the pearl white stone sat on the nightstand next to Ursula's bed. She had the weirdest dreams that night. She was surprised when she woke up in the morning to find that she wasn't covered in fur with a long snout and cute stubby tail.

Her bizarre situation demanded a divergence from her routine. She took the time to look up adder's tongue on the internet and learned it was also called serpent's tongue. The plant requires a damp environment like wetlands. It was not the sort of plant one could easily find in a flower shop.

Fortunately, Ursula was in northern New Jersey where wetlands were relatively close. She was a bit relieved considering the plant could have been a dead end and only found in Eastern Europe or farther. She was not about to take another full day off and gallivant through marshes without a plan. How could she ask anyone for help? If they were to ask her why on earth she was scouring Jersey for this plant, she had no answer. To make the situation even more confusing, the pictures online weren't consistent. Some pages showed a yellow flower that looked like a lily; other pages showed the leafy fern part. She had no idea what she specifically needed.

The more Ursula dug into the internet, the more she realized why it would be important for someone to stay with her if she ingested it. The wildflower could be used an emetic. The suggested use was externally as a poultice for skin ulcers. If she ingested it, she may end up vomiting. It would not be pleasant and she assumed expelled herbal cocktails would void the ritual.

There were also other factors. The plant species lists were filled with multiple classifications. The translation said "adder's tongue" but that came back with results of: _Erythronium americanum_ (Northern adder's tongue), _Ophioglossum pusillum_ (yellow trout lily), _Erythronium albidum_ (white trout lily), and _Erythronium propullans_ (dwarf trout lily). Plus, as she discovered earlier, it could be colloquially referred to as "serpent's tongue."

It was only five-thirty in the morning. Too early to text Kylie and ask if her boyfriend still worked for the garden center on Route 46. She put it in the back of her mind and headed down the back stairs to the business.

She flicked on half the lights and stopped dead in her tracks. She was filled with rage before having any seconds to be afraid. Her front windows had been spray painted with graffiti! She couldn't make out what it was until she ran towards the front, unlocked the door, and bolted to the sidewalk. It took up half of the window. WALKER in bright red with a bullseye painted over it. Ursula didn't care if she woke the whole neighborhood. She took out her phone and waited for police dispatch to answer.

"Travis Iver! I will hunt YOU down and castrate you! You son of a bitch!"

"Nine-one-one. What's your emergency?"

CHAPTER TWELVE

A patrol cop stopped by and helped Ursula checked for more damage and to see if anything had been stolen. With Frankhurst being a relatively quiet town, the officer gave her predicament more attention than she expected. He told her someone else would come by later for photos of the scene.

Ursula had so much energy brewing inside her that she needed to keep busy. The cop didn't act like the case could be solved. Frankhurst wasn't corner to corner in traffic cameras. Theft certainly occurred but ninety-nine percent of the time, it was petty larceny - shoplifting. Once in a while someone had a stolen credit card and could be caught.

The initial panic subsided. Ursula had to check the rest of the shop. Fortunately there was no damage to the rented out office space on the second floor's facade. The kitchen was in good shape. Manny never slacked. Ursula was always able to find annoying projects to do like scrub all around the fryer. Before pulling on rubber gloves and diving in, she texted Adriana and Rona with the news.

The morning crowd gawked on the sidewalk. Some people hesitated coming in for their orders. It did not take long for Ursula lose her patience after hearing, "Geez, what happened?" for the tenth time. She would force a smile and reply, "Oh probably just some teenagers who think they're hilarious and want to get on the internet, ya know." She knew that was a lie.

Adriana showed up with a photographer from the *Jersey Express*, also a freelancer of course.

"Oh, *Conejito*, are you okay?"

"Yeah, I'm just great." Ursula had a hard enough time faking her morning enthusiasm with paying customers. She wasn't going to use up her personal energy resources to mask her rage when speaking to Adriana.

"I left Mark outside to take photos. He'll probably only be a few minutes. Then he'll probably want some of you behind the counter and next to the window looking annoyed." Adriana pointed to Ursula's face. "Just like that. It's perfect."

"You came here for the story? I thought you came here to provide some comfort. Lend an ear or a shoulder to cry on. Maybe even offer to help me out here. But you came for the story?"

"I thought that's why you told me so early in the morning. I had to wait a reasonable time before seeing if Mark could meet me."

Ursula's heart mixed like a blender full of fury, sadness, loneliness, and disappointment.

"Why are you mad at me? My job is important to me."

"My home is important to me!"

Ursula never saw her work at Applegate's as a regular job. She never even worked a regular job. It's a family business and she's been there since she was born. She learned how to ring up customers, bus the tables, and show people to their seats before most kids stop believing in Santa Claus.

"If you don't want to be in the pictures just say so."

"That's not... I'm not..." Her exhale was forced, more than a sigh. Ursula needed to calm herself down. Count to ten. Exhale. The photos wouldn't hurt. Get it done and over. Once the police finished with their part, she and Kylie would be able to start washing it off.

Ursula excused herself and made sure all the salt, pepper, sugar, hot sauce, and ketchup containers were filled. It was something done normally before customers arrived, but there was nothing normal about her day so far.

"What the hell?" Kylie arrived and got to see the damage even though it wasn't her shift. She walked up to her boss and reached her arms around her for the hug that should have been offered by Adriana. Kylie was a good person. She matched maturity levels with Ursula and provided the stability in front of house service that Applegate's needed; Tayleigh was not nearly so capable.

Ursula told her exactly what happened and her suspicions about Travis. Kylie agreed to help scrub the window as soon as they were allowed. She went above and beyond even offering to ask her boyfriend,

Mason if he could come by and pitch in since he didn't have to work until later.

"Thanks, but I have no idea when I'd need his muscle." Ursula had met Mason many times. She liked him. He seemed to treat Kylie well and if he didn't, she'd be protective. "Hey, does he still work in the home center in the garden department?"

"Yeah, why?"

"I do need him, but for something else. Can you ask him to come by if he has the time?"

Kylie pressed Ursula for details about what she wanted Mason's expertise for, but all Ursula would tell her was that she was looking for a particular plant. If telling Adriana about volkolaks was off-limits, then Kylie couldn't know either. Ursula trusted her to run the shop for a day, but not with a global secret about lycanthropes. She stood for the photos as Adriana wanted before a small kiss goodbye.

Ursula worked through her morning by rote. She stopped looking people in the eye when responding that the police would be working on the vandalism case and no, she can't say who did it. Her certainty in the matter wasn't going to open her up to more nasty threats, more violence, or worse — a slander lawsuit.

For all of Travis' bravado, he was still well-liked by the community. His only run-ins with law were as a teenager and charges were never filed. Travis, his brother, and their friends had plenty of noise complaints against them from those high school years. He never quite grew out of it.

Ursula was not about to get into more crosshairs of the Iver family. Having them painted on her home was enough. She found it rather miraculous that it wasn't also covered in racist garbage. Somehow he showed that much restraint. She wished she could prove Travis' guilt and make people see him for how he genuinely was.

Around nine-thirty, McElroy arrived. He was also the detective but normally never corrected anyone calling him sergeant. It was a small town. There was a fair sampling of citizens that remembered the days he was still called Anthony instead of Mack. Though folks who implanted themselves from eastern Jersey pronounced it "Ant-nee".

Mack took the staff one at a time and questioned them. No one could overhear the interviews, so Ursula explained that Travis Iver was an ex-boyfriend who disagreed vehemently on her political stances such as the bear hunt.

"He's part of the gun club and was there at the protest yesterday wanting to see Peter Medvedovich charged with crimes."

"Why would he want to see that?"

"They had a disagreement right here the other day. Peter helped me kick Travis out."

"I see."

That was the best lead so far and Mack knew it. The perp had to be someone pro-hunting of bears otherwise there was no significance to Walker's name being in the sprayed bullseye.

Mack asked if he needed to speak to the girl who worked in the afternoons. Ursula knew Tayleigh was unlikely to be much help.

"She's in at twelve-thirty if you want to speak to her." Ursula kept her opinions to herself about Tayleigh having a crush on Travis or one of his friends, maybe all of them. It didn't matter to Ursula as long as they kept out of her shop.

"All right. My next step is to canvas the block. Talk to the other merchants and see if any of the residents in the apartments saw anything, but considering the time frame, don't expect much."

Gee thanks, that's so encouraging, Ursula thought.

"Uh huh. Maybe you can make some official police fliers for people to hang up letting folks know we're looking for information." She didn't have any inclination to offer a reward since the damage was minimal.

"Sure. I'll take that into consideration." That translated into a polite rejection of her idea.

"Can we clean it off now?"

"Yes, ma'am. I have what I need. Oh, in case you didn't know, the easiest way to scrape that off is with a razor blade." Mack took a toothpick from the container near the cash register and stuck it in the corner of his lips.

"Thanks." *No mansplaining needed*, she thought.

Ursula wrangled cleaning supplies and a step stool so she and Kylie could start on the window. She couldn't get Travis out of her mind. She wanted to though. She wanted to think about anyone or anything besides him. Instead, her spirit darkened when she heard his voice.

He whistled. "Aw that's a shame. Who would do that?"

"Get away from me, Travis."

"Your crippled friend isn't here to save you now. But, come to think of it, I hear he'll make bail today." Travis walked up close to her step stool. He put a hand on it while his eyes scanned her body until looking at her eyes.

"Where'd you hear that?"

"Word gets around."

"I believe I asked you to leave."

"It's a public sidewalk."

Kylie was frozen in a blend of anxiety and fright, but Ursula was not. She lifted up her foot and stomped her rugged hiking shoe onto Travis' hand. He clenched his jaw trying his best not let out a sound.

"That's twice people from this little business have assaulted me. I just might have to do something about that now." He held one hand in the other and flexed his sore fingers several times.

"You go ahead. I've got witnesses that you keep harassing and stalking me."

As Travis turned and walked away, Ursula was sure she heard him mumble something. She asked Kylie if she heard anything, but she said she couldn't make it out. Ursula didn't doubt her own ears as long as they weren't ringing with tinnitus. She definitely heard him mutter the N-word under his breath like a coward.

"He's such an asshole."

"You actually dated that guy?" Kylie knew the answer, but couldn't believe it. Travis was not Ursula's type, especially considering that Kylie has only known her to date women.

"It was a long time ago. I was young and stupid. At the time, I thought he would be fun to be around."

"I never knew you were into guys too. Not that it matters. I just didn't know."

"Now you know."

"Cool."

The scraping took hours, but the window didn't look so bad when they were done. At the start, Ursula was worried she'd have to cover the whole thing until it could be replaced. Before they packed up the cleaning supplies, Ursula needed someone's opinion and since Kylie was there, she would do.

"Hey, let me ask you something. You've been with Mason how long?"

"Three years, believe it or not. Why?"

"If someone asked you to keep a life-changing secret, would you let him in on it since you're a couple?"

"Life-changing? Jeez, I don't know." Kylie stood still to think about it. Her eyes drifted up to the overcast September sky. "I guess it depends on what you mean by life-changing. I wouldn't tell if it was going to hurt someone. But if it was life-changing in a good way, like good news, maybe like being pregnant or something — I guess then I would tell him."

"Hmm. Thanks."

"I take it you have a secret you're not telling Adriana?"

"Oh, uh, nah. It was just hypothetical. Let's get back inside. If you don't want to work today, I can cover you and count this as your shift."

"I did this as a favor. I'll stay."

Ursula let out a deep breath from her belly which made her realize exactly how tense Travis and Adriana made her. "Thank you."

"Mason should be here soon to talk to you about that plant. He texted that he's on his way."

Ursula thanked Kylie again as they headed through the shop to the kitchen to put things away in the cleaning supply closet.

***

It was mid-afternoon and Ursula took a much needed break from Applegate's. Before she went back upstairs to her third-floor apartment, she asked Kylie to send Mason up when he arrived. If he asked too many questions, Ursula didn't want her reactions witnessed. Plus, even if it was only going to be five minutes, she needed the solitude only her apartment sanctuary offered.

Two chimes alerted her to new messages on her phone. One from Rona and one from Adriana. It gave her pause that she should somehow feel guilty about opening Rona's message first. *Nonsense*, she tried to tell herself. Adriana wouldn't know that her message was opened after Rona's. And if she did, what kind of lunacy was that? Ursula couldn't believe she was having such emotionally insecure feelings about her relationship. She liked how things were, but Adriana had made some recent bad choices the way Ursula saw it. Those choices flew red flags up in her mind and waved around like an airplane was about to crash into a tarmac.

"My aunt is getting Peter out on bail at three. Can you want to be there?"

Ursula had been let in on the volkolaks' secret, but it didn't hit her until that moment that they pulled her into the family.

She looked at the screen and noticed there was something strange about the format of the message bubble. Then Ursula saw that it was a group text sent to SOAR members.

"You are thinking too much of yourself right now." Ursula told herself out loud. "You are not the center of everyone's universe."

She opened a new text window and wrote back to only Rona letting her know she got the invitation, but that she was busy meeting with someone who knew more about special tea ingredients. Rona shouldn't have to think too hard to crack that code.

Adriana's text message was a link to her post about the Applegate's vandalism. Ursula clicked it and decided it would be better to view on her computer's large screen. She opened up the parent company's website and navigated to the *Jersey Express* section. It wasn't front page news even in the local subsection. She found it in the crime section though.

"Well you can definitely tell how pissed I am," she said gazing at the photo of herself in front of the graffiti.

Scanning the article didn't warm her heart. At the bottom was a disclaimer that the author had a personal relationship with Ms. Applegate. It wasn't that Ursula minded the protocol to reveal such a thing, but she wasn't told and it made it look even more like preferential coverage. Ursula only agreed to the article because she saw the bigger picture: to bring more attention to the hunt for Walker and other bears as trophies.

Mason arrived giving her the opportunity to think about something else other than her troubled romantic life. Ursula led him to the couch and offered him some water. She apologized for not having much, but she wasn't used to entertaining guests after serving people all morning.

"Don't worry about it. I drink water all day. It's perfect." Mason waited for her to return from the kitchen with a glass of filtered water.

They got the small talk out of the way and Mason was fired up to get into this special request.

"You don't strike me as a person with an interest in plants. I noticed you only have that lucky bamboo over there by the TV and I'm guessing that was a gift. Am I right?"

"You have a good eye and great instincts. One of the other merchants on the block gave me that when I took over the business after my parents died. I do not have a green thumb."

Ursula told him that she was hoping to find out where adder's tongue grew in New Jersey because she needed to collect some personally.

"And you said can't just buy it in a store or online?"

"Nope."

"Is this for like a religious thing?"

What the hell. Why not? That sounded more believable than the real reason.

"Sure is! You're good."

"Ahhh. I see. You're a witch! Kylie didn't tell me." He beamed with his cheeks slightly reddening.

"Umm. Yeah. I'm a witch. Well, sort of. My family is from Haiti so it's not Wicca or whatever. It's vodou."

"Voodoo? Nice."

Oh dear gods, Ursula thought. He probably believes there will be a goat sacrificed or something.

"It wasn't something my parents did, being well-immersed in American culture instead. Catholic of course. But my grandparents, from what I understand, before they came here, were practitioners of the old ways. It was their thing. Ya know, a secret though here in the states. You can't let people get the wrong idea." Her laugh came out more maniacal than nervous. She internally scolded herself to keep it together.

"Okay! Let's see what we've got. Do you mind?" Mason pointed to the desk and computer which was in sleep mode. Ursula gestured for him to take a seat and do his thing.

She admitted that she tried solving the problem herself before calling on his expertise. "I did try searching online but got confused. There are different types of this plant and I don't know which one is the right thing I need so I figure, maybe I should try to get whatever is out there."

"I see. The thing with adder's tongue is that isn't not about the location being difficult for you. I believe it's only around in the spring. The summer heat destroys it."

"Crap!"

"But here, I'll show you a map of where I think you can check next year."

Ursula didn't think the season would be the hardest part of the bear root ritual. It wasn't a lack of patience that drove her disappointment either. She had hoped that she would have the whole ritual completed by the time the bear hunt began in October which was only a few weeks away.

Mason also filled her in on the old European ways the plant was used. The juice was extracted from the leaves and mixed with distilled water then used to heal skin wounds. Another way was to grind up the plant into a mash and apply that to wounds. He did warn her that when taken internally, if the dose was even a little bit too strong, it would cause vomiting. That part she already knew and gave her trepidation. It would be worth it though to see the volkolaks.

"Do you have any idea why the plant has a snake's name?" Ursula had been stumped from the beginning on why a bear related ritual would involve a plant named after a snake.

"It is also called serpent's tongue, but my guess is it's because of the shape of the singular leaf and the stem. Or maybe it's because of the vomit and adders are vipers who can spit venom. I'm not a hundred percent sure on that."

She only asked out of curiosity. The whole ritual was a bust now. She wouldn't be able to make the concoction in time.

"Look," Mason said, "I can tell you're not happy about this. But, if there's any way you can use the dried version of this gathered and packaged by someone else, I have a suggestion."

"Anything at this point."

"There aren't any botanica shops around here that carry this kind of stuff, but there are plenty in the more urban cities like Newark and Camden. Take Manny or his wife Elisa with you in case you need someone who speaks Spanish."

"Maybe I'll have to. Thanks for all your help."

"Sorry it wasn't better news."

Mason tried to pry more information out of her about the purpose of the ritual, asking whether it was a love spell or money spell. She told him it had to be kept secret. The look on his face said he was more satisfied with an enigmatic answer than a real one.

CHAPTER THIRTEEN

Travis' information was correct. Peter Medvedovich was going to make bail. The SOAR members gathered again. They met in the same place at the lower police and court entrance of the municipal building. This time they didn't have to yell at anyone; the hunters weren't there. Some of them still held their signs calling for the hunt to be canceled. Mostly, they were there to watch Peter come through the door and cheer for him. It was far less of a spectacle than when he was taken into custody.

Adriana Garcia was the only member of the press there. The story wasn't as hot and wouldn't be again unless there was a trial. As it turned out in this case, there wouldn't be.

Rona pushed the door open first. She was followed by her twin brother and their Aunt Devora. Everyone wanted the chance to hug Peter or pat him on the back. He was bombarded by their questions. "How did they treat you?" "Was the food terrible?" "Are you hurt?" "What happens next?" He pleaded with them to give him a moment to enjoy his freedom.

"Okay! Okay! Let him speak. Let him speak." Mick shouted.

"Thanks, everyone. Your support has meant so much to me. Honestly, I'm so sorry if I cast a poor image of SOAR and would understand if you wanted to kick me out of the club." Peter's sincerity shocked and basically confused everyone.

"Kick you out? My man, you got us attention about the bear hunt. You showed the people how important Walker is to us that you'd risk your neck breaking in there. We got some press out of it."

Mick looked over at Adriana. His smile momentarily disappeared thinking about how she also gave the Frankhurst gun club press and plenty of space for quotes.

"If you're sure?"

"Let's take a vote, shall we?" Mick knew it wasn't a formality and wouldn't be recorded in any official minutes, but it was the show of solidarity that counted. "Everyone who wants Peter Medvedovich to stay in SOAR as an active member and official photographer, say Aye!"

All of them shouted, "Aye!" while Adriana snapped a photo from her DSLR camera.

Ursula opened her phone and quickly snapped a few shots of the celebration to post to Boffo and the other social media sites. The best news wasn't actually about Peter being released on bail. He was released because the only charge that would stick was misdemeanor trespassing. The prosecutor saw Peter's malformed hands and despite musculature, didn't see how he could be capable of tears fences apart without machinery. He had to pay a fine and was free to go.

"This calls for a celebration! Pie and coffee at Applegate's sound good to you guys?" Ursula wanted to support the volkolaks and mend any bridges with the rest of SOAR before they were accidentally burned to the ground. She walked over to Adriana and personally extended the invitation to her as well.

"I don't think there's a story in a group of people eating pie."

"I'm trying to offer an olive branch. Are you coming or not?"

Adriana agreed to meet her there. She had to drive her car over so it wasn't sitting in the visitors' parking lot. She had a "press" placard on her visor, but only took advantage of it when parking was difficult. She was being cold towards Ursula on purpose and she knew in her heart they couldn't move forward without moving through their current problems together.

"Do you want a lift?"

Ursula watched Peter, Rona, and Devora climb into a shiny silver Lexus. Had to be Devora's car. Ursula had been in Rona's and suspected Peter was as no frills about his transportation as she was. She turned back to Adriana and nodded.

They didn't have much time to talk in the few blocks it took to get back to Applegate's.

"I feel like you're keeping something from me. I don't want to jump to conclusions, but something is up since you started hanging out with Rona. Are you cheating on me?"

"What? No! She's a friend. And probably straight. I don't actually know. We never talked about it."

"Then what's going on? Why don't you want to spend time with me?"

Ursula wanted to have that conversation. It needed to be addressed, but they only had seconds. It wasn't the best time to get into it.

"There is something I want to tell you, but it'll have to wait until later. Right now, we need to go be thankful Peter is all right and support him."

Once inside the store, Ursula grabbed her apron and began heating up apple pie. Adriana helped out by getting scoops of ice cream onto plates and delivering them to the tables.

Jon McHugh took a bite and rolled his eyes towards heaven. "Are these made with apples from the Gates' farm?"

"I believe they are. The pies come from Dream Girls bakery. Anyone need a sugar-free slice?" Ursula saw two hands go up and prepared slices from a different apple pie. She cut herself one from that too. She preferred the less sweet version.

"I won't be able to fit into my suits if I keep eating here," Devora said.

As a woman moving up through political ranks from committee volunteer to planning board to her current run for state senate, she had to watch her figure in a way her male counterparts never did. Women in politics — or any field — were publicly criticized on their attractiveness. A male senator could look like a creature from Stan Winston Studio and no one would care the same way. Men were elected young and then managed to keep getting elected. Good looks definitely helped, but modern times were slowly opening up the definitions of beauty standards.

Devora didn't dream of the presidency, but she had fantasies about running New Jersey from the governor's office. One of her anchor platforms was to make the state better for handicap accessibility in a wider approach. Many businesses supported the adjustments for wheelchairs, though not all when you took a good look; and Devora had watched Peter adapt to his new life with one hand that he couldn't use and the other with half of its abilities. There were challenges that needed to be addressed in this state beyond ramps and garbage service entrances. There was dignity to restore and Devora vowed to make that happen.

"I guess we can't exactly talk here with all these people." Adriana had the last bite of her pie impaled on the fork. She slid it around on the plate in the melted ice cream puddle, back and forth in a figure eight.

"No, but I do have to go ask Devora something. Do you mind?" Ursula was standing up before Adriana had the chance to answer.

Rona and Peter noticed Ursula coming closer. They thanked her for the little party and all her support.

"Devora, I was wondering if I could steal you away for a minute to ask about that recipe again and your family's secret ingredient. Don't want anyone to overhear that." Ursula was hit more nervous and fake laughter. Rona shot her a look of curiosity. "I figure as the head of the family, you'd be the one to talk to. If you have a minute."

Rona's expression eased up. Ursula looked over to Peter and felt some of her anxiety melt away. As far as she knew, volkolaks didn't have magical powers of hypnosis, but whenever she allowed herself to look into their eyes, she was captivated and then soothed.

SOAR members grew louder as they consumed more coffee and tea. Victories didn't come often. They allowed themselves time to enjoy this one. The war wasn't over.

In the back of the kitchen, the "office" was a wide ledge mounted from the wall with stacked trays for invoices, shipping lists, and orders. A clipboard of timecards hung from a nail above them. The ridiculously outdated computer system, a relic by technology standards, sat there always turned on because it was so slow to boot up. Ursula did her work upstairs unless she forgot to do something like print out a check for a COD.

Without preamble, Ursula blurted out her request. "I have to tell Adriana. She knows I'm keeping something from her. She's on the verge of breaking up with me because she knows something is between us."

"No. Absolutely not." Devora shook her head. Her voice had the firmness of Ursula's mother when her mind was set. It was a voice that Ursula knew meant a debate was out of the question, but that didn't stop her from trying.

Ursula continued to plead her case. She kept her voice hushed, but it was animated and emotional. She even surprised herself. She loved her independence. She didn't think she would fear a break up at all. It would be just another relationship that wasn't meant to be. She didn't picture herself happily married and eating holiday dinners around a long table filled with family. It was the lying and covering up that made her freak out. Not the fear of Adriana walking away.

"First of all, you're the first human in a long time to be allowed in like this. Secondly, and probably even more critical, is that Adriana is a journalist. She will out us the first chance she gets. I'm not going through that. I'm not taking my family into hiding on some mountain."

"She's always supported me though even when she doesn't agree with me. Like this bear hunt — I don't think she has much of an opinion on it, but she knows it matters to me so she's covering it."

"Oh, you can't be that naive. She's covering it because it's news. Politics, social activism, the continued debate about the Second Amendment and the First, by the way. All these things intersect here. She cannot know. Don't make me regret trusting you."

"She needs to have trust in me too. And I don't often show her that I trust her. I know how huge this is. I know what's at stake. I love your family. I love the ridiculous dangers that Rona will go through to protect Peter. I love how he is quiet and talented and makes me feel like everything will be okay as long as he's around."

Devora cocked her head. "Wait a minute. What? It sounds like you have interest in Peter and Rona more than Adriana. I don't know if it's some kind of crush on Peter or what exactly, but you should hear yourself. You're only looking to share our story with her for selfish reasons. If you had presented a better case, maybe explaining in some unbelievable way that her knowing our secret would benefit us and not you, just maybe then I would have considered it."

Ursula's lips didn't move but her mind kept trying to make her apologize. Devora wasn't wrong. Her motives were selfish. She wanted to tell Adriana as a way of showing that they had something worth salvaging. Her head lowered, her eyelids dropped down to mask the pain she would see in Devora's face. She let down someone who had faith in her as a person, in her humanity.

"You're right," Ursula whispered. Her gusto was gone. "She can't know. But I do know her pretty well after a couple years and believe me, if she suspects anything, she's like a shark smelling a drop of blood in the ocean. She'll keep searching for it."

"Then it's your job to make sure that doesn't happen. I don't want to have to fight her off."

Ursula wasn't wholly certain what type of fighting Devora meant whether publicly through the press and image of her campaign, or physically. She had seen what Rona could do. Devora was older, perhaps stronger. Certainly more careful and cunning than her niece. She was not someone to go up against.

"I'm on your side. I promise."

Devora excelled at smiling in front of people no matter how insincere. It came with the territory. Ursula barely managed to look neutral.

"Everything okay?" Adriana could read the tension in Ursula's facial muscles when she returned.

"Yeah. I just had to check on something for Devora. I had offered for her to use this place for an event if she ever needed the space. She said she'll consider it."

"Doesn't sound like the sort of thing that upsets you and you're upset about something. But I guess I'll never know." Adriana stood, grabbed her purse, and threw down a ten dollar bill. "For the dessert."

***

Mick Hoffman intercepted Adriana on her way out of Applegate's. He thanked her for the work in getting their statements out to the public.

"Just doing my job." She reached for the door again and he put a hand on her arm. She looked down at it, brows furrowed, then her eyes met his and he released her quickly.

"Sorry. Um, I was just wondering if you would be interested in a more in-depth feature on Peter Medvedovich. He's a nice guy. Talented photographer. Now that he's been freed from the false charges, I think people might be interested in his life."

"I'm more interested in Devora Zhukov. How involved is she with SOAR?"

"Devora? Not very. She shows up to support us because she's against the bear hunt too, but she's not even a member of SOAR like Peter and Rona. She probably doesn't want to appear too extreme to the voters." Mick looked like he had regrets about sharing that theory.

"Well, thanks for suggestion. I have to be going."

"Will this be in an article tonight or maybe tomorrow?"

"That's up to the section editor." Adriana shifted around Mick and pushed through to the breezeway to the exterior door leading to the sidewalk.

Before Adriana reached her car, Ursula texted her and asked if she would come over to her apartment that night. They needed to talk and figure out how to move passed the roadblock in their relationship. Adriana wanted to lash out and let the pettiness insider her crash through. She wanted to reply that if Ursula wanted to meet, they could do so at Adriana's apartment for a change. Instead, she knew why it was important for Ursula to be home near her business. She agreed to go back there at eight. Applegate's closed then — small town pastry counters don't need to be open that late in the fall unless there's a community event.

"It wouldn't be so inconvenient for us to have a face-to-face conversation if we lived together. After two years, I think it's time." This wasn't the first time Adriana brought up the subject of cohabitation.

Ursula came out of the kitchen with two glasses of filtered water which she set on coasters on the coffee table.

"It's not about how many years it's been. It's about whether both of us feel ready for that step — and I don't. You know that. We went through this a month ago."

"I'm gonna need something stronger than this." Adriana picked up the glass and went through the kitchen to find a bottle of anything else, as long as there was alcohol in it.

"You do not need anything stronger for this conversation. If anything, you need to be clear-headed and fully present."

"Don't you dare police me and my moral choices!"

"Why not? You police me all the time! And Rona, who you don't even know. You throw around wild accusations. You act like a jealous teenager. I think I have some right to ask you not to get drunk right now because it's not the time."

Since the door to the jealousy over Rona was opened, Adriana proverbially took the bait and walked right through. She admitted that she was jealous. There a new, hot woman around in Ursula's life. A woman with shared interests in animal activism. A woman who was capable of convincing Ursula to stay out all night and then take a day off work which she hadn't done as long as Adriana had known her. This "Rona person," as Adriana called her, had some kind of hold over Ursula.

"She does not have a hold over me!"

"Then what is it? Is it really that you're using her to get to Peter? Is it Devora? Do you have a thing for a woman that much older?"

"Oh. My. God! No! You sound like a crazy person right now."

Adriana pressed on with theories and accusations. No, Ursula wasn't secretly dating Rona, Peter, nor Devora behind her back. No, they weren't blackmailing her or threatening her in any way.

"Then what the hell is it? Tell me!"

"They're volkolaks! Okay? Dammit!"

Adriana looked puzzled. She held the tumbler of Irish Cream on the rocks to her lips and stops abruptly without sipping it. Her head tilted to one side.

"They're what?"

"Volkolaks."

"Is that some branch of Russian spies?"

Ursula explained that while they were Russian in ancestry, they were not spies of any sort. She was caught in a tug of war where she was in the middle of the volkolaks and her girlfriend. She had already said the word. She couldn't think of a way to back pedal. Maybe she should have said they were spies. That would be more believable.

"Well? I'm waiting." Adriana stood in the threshold between the kitchen and the living room.

Ursula struggled to find the words. She stumbled over every sentence she began.

"I promised I wouldn't tell anyone. Not even you. That's what I was talking about with Devora downstairs. I can't tell you any more. I shouldn't have said anything."

"Uh... you absolutely will tell me more. You'll tell me what the hell a volkoraptor is."

"Volkolak. They're not dinosaurs."

"Then what are they? Or who are they?"

The beans were spilled. Ursula had to continue. Now that Adriana had heard the word volkolak, there was nothing to stop her from opening her phone and a browser window to search its meaning.

"They come from a line of people who can become bears. Or maybe they're more bear than people. I don't exactly know the details. What I do know, is that I broke a promise."

"You expect me to stand here while you lay on some bullshit story that your new friends are werewolf-bears? Were-bears, I guess? Is that what just came out of your mouth?"

"They don't like the term were-bear. It's offensive."

"Oh, it's offensive! Sure." Adriana rolled her eyes and wondered if it wasn't Ursula who had ingested the alcohol. Or perhaps, she hadn't been counting how many glasses she had and was dreaming all this nonsense.

Ursula wanted to release all the anxiety making her shake, but her body wasn't crying. She wasn't able to do anything else. The guilt was overwhelming.

"I trust you enough to tell you. You can't tell anyone you know about this. You can't talk to them about it. At least not until I've figured out how to tell them that I've told you."

"You're insane. Maybe this is some kind of nervous breakdown because you're so overworked, so exhausted. I'm worried about you, Ursula. You need medical help. Like, right now. I'm not kidding."

"I don't need professional help. I'm not crazy. I'm not losing my mind. I am exhausted and overworked. That much is accurate."

Ursula could not convince Adriana that she wasn't making this all up in order to avoid another discussion about living together. Adriana left in a fit of confusion and disappointment thinking that Ursula invented some cockamamie story to get her off her back.

"Volkolaks? She can't be serious? She expects me to fall for that?" Adriana talked to herself the whole drive home to Harrison.

She powered up her laptop as soon as she got home. She whipped off her daytime outfit and swapped it for cotton shorts and an oversized t-shirt. The drinks weren't sitting well in her stomach. It wasn't the little bit of alcohol content; it was the disgusting amount of cream.

She shook her head before allowing her fingers to type v-o-l-k-o-l-a-c-k-s into the search bar. The first line was a spelling correction to remove the "c" to "volkolaks." Adriana's right hand moved to the touch screen and scrolled down. There were results. She didn't expect to find any because she didn't expect Ursula to have come up with such a bizarre tale. The publicly sourced encyclopedia didn't have anything about them. A click led her to an ugly website that looked like it was written in 1998.

The content she scanned was interesting. Too bad it was against a purple star field background with visible table borders. There was a section in a lower row that listed references. All of them were things out of

Adriana's comfort zone. Role-playing games (she had to look to see what RPG meant). Video games set in fantasy worlds (she had heard of one of those). Cosplayers (another thing she had to research and ultimately impressed her when she saw the skills). No mention of anything out of historical mythology and folklore though.

Ursula had to be losing her mind. Adriana grew even more concerned. At first she was being flippant suggesting that Ursula was having a mental breakdown, but she sounded so sure of herself when she spoke. She believed these volkolaks were real.

In order to save her girlfriend's mental state, Adriana formulated a plan to prove that volkolaks were not real. That they were a figment of Ursula's wonderfully imaginative, but fragile mind.

She clicked through the page of search results until she landed on the message boards of one of the games. They only allowed validated gamers to enter some of the areas. There was a public section she was able to read. The categories had some of the same unfamiliar words as the other website: Cosplay, Fan Fiction, Fan Art, Monster Guide.

A monster guide sounded like the right place to begin. Someone out there must have given some information about volkolaks and their origins. What she wanted was a properly cited research paper.

Inside the monster category, there were threads of posts. So many posts, Adriana thought she'd lose her own mental grasp on reality. She didn't think people actually spent their time in these fantasy worlds to this degree. It always seemed like a joke about nerd culture and stereotypes of gamers who couldn't separate fact from fiction.

The cryptids thread looked like a promising place to begin. It was the exploration of animals or creatures with unsubstantiated claims to their existence. She found threads about Bigfoot and yeti; mermaids and sirens; sidhe and fae; vampires; lycans/werewolves; zombies, necromancy and the undead; ghosts and spirits; boogeymen; and finally a miscellaneous category.

"I can't believe I'm giving any energy to this nonsense. I must be losing it too."

CHAPTER FOURTEEN

Applegate's Country Store was fairly dead on Wednesdays. Ursula had plenty of catching up to do on her paperwork and supply orders. She hated that part of the management role. She preferred to be up front talking with people from Frankhurst and knowing things about them like when the woman with the gold cross necklace came in it meant she was running; or if kids offered to shovel her sidewalk for ten dollars in winter, it meant there was no school. Time cards, paying bills, balancing the checking account — all that sucked.

Her email was filled with responses to Mick's original post about needing weekly meetings until the bear hunt. Since Ursula had offered for SOAR to use Applegate's on Wednesdays at seven in the evening, she would have to prep refreshments. The real incentive was that on a laid back evening, she could serve coffee and desserts and put a few bucks into the till. Mick liked the idea and he and the officers of SOAR willingly signed a contract between SOAR and Applegate's for private catering for four weeks. As a non-profit they were exempt for any sales tax which made the job even easier for Ursula. She wouldn't have to add the income to her monthly tithe to the state.

Ursula heard the back door open and the sound of rubber soles cross the linoleum of the hallway by the staircase to her apartment and passed the door to the kitchen used for deliveries and taking out the trash.

Ursula had her back turned while she taped a sign to the inside of the front door. "Closed for private event." She opened the door and taped a second sign on the actual outside door which was separated by the cramped breezeway. She had a third sign for the front window under the turned off neon "Open" sign.

"Need any help?"

Ursula turned and felt a wave of relief as she saw Peter standing there in his jeans and flannel shirt. A blue one this time. As always, his camera was in a bag slung over his solid, lean body.

"I think I have everything under control. Can I get you some hot tea? I brought some herbal ones that I had in the apartment. Just for you."

His shyness began to crumble when he was around her. He had given Travis that smackdown which he deserved. Then Peter sacrificed his own freedom for Ursula and Rona, taking the fall for the Musky Park break-in.

"Dealer's choice then." He walked to the counter and rested his elbow and weak right arm on it.

The cups were sage green to match the interior paint of the walls. New mugs with white lettering were among the upgrades Ursula made. They were thick and could handle some amount of drops to the floor depending on the force with which they fell.

"Unlike your aunt's tea, this will not grant you magical powers, but maybe the lemon and honey will provide some comfort after your ordeal."

"I managed okay. It wasn't as bad as you might think. It was only county lock-up."

"Which you were sent off to because you were saving my ass. And Rona's ass of course. You two seem to do anything for each other."

"We do. We're twins."

"So it's true what they say? There's a special bond that only twins have? Do you know when she's gotten herself into trouble before she calls?"

"Yeah in a way. Both of us have always been like that. Knowing when the other one is in a desperate situation. Not that it happens often. It might be hard to believe, but Rona is not routinely criminal. Mostly, she runs her mouth and that's what gets her into trouble."

Ursula didn't know why Peter showed up so early for the meeting, but she enjoyed standing there talking to him alone without the distractions of Travis, customers, or police.

"Since I learned about this whole family secret you guys have, I've had a million questions go through my mind."

"I knew this was coming sooner or later. No, I do not steal picnic baskets or stick my hands in honey pots."

The betrayal resurfaced in Ursula's gut. She felt such warmth and tenderness from Peter, but she betrayed his whole family. She hated herself.

"It's not that big a deal if another human knew about you, right? I mean, more than one person can keep a secret."

"You know the old saying: three can keep a secret if two of them are dead."

He could quote Benjamin Franklin too. Ursula was a sucker for literary minds. It was one of her weaknesses. Intelligence and honesty. Peter had shown her both. She fumbled for how to tell him that she told Adriana about his family and that there were other volkolaks living among humans around the world. She was almost tempted to take the easy way out and pretend she didn't do it.

Peter ran through the same list of potential problems that Rona and Devora had told her. Humans had a need to feel superior to every living thing. Humans would want to perform experiments and put other beings through torture; and they would say this agony was an evil necessity in the name of science. Humans would want to turn someone like Rona into a weapon if they saw what she could do.

"Why are you asking this? We told you the dangers before."

"I know. I know. It's just so um... hard for me to absorb everything. You have to understand where I'm coming from too."

"No one else can know about us, Ursula."

She couldn't look into his eyes when she told him. "I told Adriana. Last night."

His brows furrowed. His eyes appeared darker if that was possible. The hairs on his face bristled. For a split second, Ursula was worried that he would lose control of his bear side and attack her like some hybrid in comic books. But Peter was not Dr. Jekyll and his bear side was not Mr. Hyde. He wasn't a being split into parts. He was a whole being who felt a range of emotions just like anyone else.

She apologized repeatedly and begged for forgiveness. She tried to convince him that it wouldn't be any problem at all because Adriana thought she was having a psychotic episode and needed to be taken to a hospital.

"I swear, Peter. I swear, she didn't believe a word of it! And I'm fine if she thinks I'm mentally unwell. Your safety is more important to me than that."

They were interrupted by the sound of SOAR members parading through the back door and down the hallway. Peter walked away from her, leaving his tea on the counter. He took a seat by the front window and stared out into the twilight sky ignoring passersby on the sidewalk looking in at him. Humans weren't capable of peace. Peter knew it. He had spent his life trying to show them they could try harder and be better for this world. They let him down all the time. He was disappointed in himself for believing one of them could be trusted.

Ursula worked through the distraction mulling in her mind. She could pour coffee and serve pie without much brain power to attentiveness. She watched Rona enter from the back door. When Rona lifted her hand and waved, Ursula's panic struck her like being hit by a truck. On instinct, Rona saw where Peter was sitting and saw the look on his face too. She dropped her hand and lost her smile. Rona took the seat across from Peter. A moment later, she gave Ursula a look that could have shot laser beams clear through the space between her eyebrows. Rona was out of her chair and across the room faster than it should have taken.

"How could you? How could you do this?"

Ursula apologized again and again. People around were beginning to notice that something was wrong. Rona wouldn't make a scene. Not in front of others. But Ursula was afraid that Rona would want some kind of revenge.

"Please believe me. Please, Ro, I didn't mean it. It blurted out. Adriana was hounded me about keeping something from her. She thought I was having an affair with you or Peter. She knew I had a secret. That's one thing about her and why she's great at her job. She keeps digging until she knows the truth."

Rona managed to refrain from grabbing Ursula by the collar and dragging her body over the counter. However, her fingernails started to rake through the countertop when she noticed it would cause attention. As far as she was concerned, her family was in more danger than worrying about the hunting season. Rona walked back to Peter. They exchanged a few words. Other people showed signs of curiosity. They could tell something was off. Rona stormed through the tables and left by the back door. Peter stayed and Ursula had no idea why. He should hate her too.

Mick called the meeting into session. Everyone had been served so Ursula was able to leave her spot behind the counter. She so badly wanted to sit by Peter and feel like everything would work out. She needed everything to be okay.

"Ursula? Ursula, an update?" Mick caught Ursula in her trance, lost in her thoughts.

"Oh, yeah. Engagement is up on Boffo and LifeLook. The posts with photos get the most views and shares." Everyone waited for her to say more. "That's it. For now."

"Okay. Brief reports are fine. Sounds vaguely similar to last time. So, make sure you have plenty of Peter's photos then. Keep the buzz going. Jon, do you have anything to add from the PR perspective? Any response to direct mail?" Mick turned his head to find Jon McHugh at the table to his right.

Jon put down his fork, finished his bite, and stood. "I've limited our direct mail list to people who are registered Democratic voters. Not to choose sides, but they're more likely to be supportive in our efforts while the rest are in the gun lobby's pocket. For online campaigns, my suggestion is to make sure all the photos have our SOAR watermark and offer a variety of photos so it doesn't look like all the posts are automated or recycled."

"No problem." Ursula didn't bother standing from her spot close to the dessert case.

"Peter, can you make sure Ursula has new content for the posts?" Mick said.

"No problem." He didn't stand or bother to look at Ursula either.

CHAPTER FIFTEEN

The computer screen illuminated Ursula's face while she stared at the search page. She wanted to type, "How do you fix friendships after you've been a selfish ass?" Instead she thought about how she could prove herself to the volkolaks.

It was going on eight-thirty and normally she would have begun her nightly routine: shower, moisturize, go through social media and schedule some posts, then maybe watch some TV or read before falling asleep. Instead she searched for the closest root work supply store to see if any were still open late at night in the middle of the week. She scored when she spotted Saint Martha's Botanica. It was located in another suburb, Ahsënèsink, New Jersey — one of the towns that voted to return to the Lenni Lenape name after it had been another colonizer's name for two hundred years. Most residents never bothered to use the accents on the letters. The shop information online said they were opened from ten to ten.

Ursula arrived at nine-thirty and found the proprietor behind a low counter with display cases. She was glued to LifeLook, one of the social media platforms. She turned her head and greeted Ursula. Her voice was warm and friendly, but she appeared bored or tired.

The store was more spacious than most small retail shops. The wall opposite the short counter was lined with clothing racks of Persian,

African, and Indian wraps and clothing; they looked authentic rather than the knock-off Boho chic lines found in mall stores.

The back wall was filled practically to the ceiling with bookcases showing off a variety of candles in different sizes, colors, and shapes. There were adorable sculpted brown- and black-skinned fairies on fishing line hanging from the ceiling throughout the whole store. In the elaborately decorated front window, a statue of Oya stood three feet high with the long folds of her skirt flowing around her. Her arms outstretched and one hand holding her iruke. Ursula wondered which path the proprietor followed considered how many different types of faiths were presented by the shop's name and contents.

The woman turned around and moved smoothly behind the counters like she was on a conveyor belt. That's when Ursula realized she was in a motorized scooter.

"Are you looking for something specific?"

Ursula walked over and saw a sleeping dog behind the counter in the corner of the front window and the wall, easily mistaken as part of the scenery.

"Aww. Someone is ready to close up."

"That's Matilda. She wakes up when I need her. I'm Chinue."

The older woman reached her brown arm over the counter to shake with Ursula. Her wrists were covered in jingling bangle bracelets. Her fingers were adorned in more than wedding jewelry. Her hair was wrapped in a colorful iro woven with metallic gold thread sparkling through fields of dark red and orange.

Ursula introduced herself before unloading her reason for shopping so late at night. She didn't know how to spell it all out that she was in need of a plant in order to see shapeshifters.

"The plant I'm looking for is out of season, I'm told. It's called adder's tongue. Do you know it?"

"Ah, yes. Serpent's tongue. I don't get requests for that normally."

Bulk jars of dried herbs and berries were kept behind the counter. Some more commonly used ones were pre-packaged into small plastic zipper bags with handwritten labels stapled on them for hanging on pegs of spinner racks in the middle of the floor.

"I'm not even sure if I'm asking for the right thing to be honest. I don't know if a dried version would work. I was told I had to..." Ursula thought about how Adriana reacted and how she, herself reacted when first told about the supernatural elements around them.

"Had to what? Grow it yourself? Pluck it from the ground while naked under a full moon?"

"Something like that."

Chinue let out a bold "Ha!" She moved a few feet forward and reached up to a shelf. She struggled, but eventually her fingers pulled out a jar close enough to grasp.

"That is how you know a man wrote the spell. Naked. Please. Women use their bodies in magic all the time and it's been demonized, sure. But a lot of religious practices ended up falling into men's hands and men made the rules."

"Yeah, that's honestly why I never felt comfortable in any religion. I was raised Catholic, sort of. I stopped going a long time ago."

"Oh, they talk about the divine feminine mother, but God forbid, a woman rise to the same level of power as a priest or bishop or Pope. It's like the world would end, you know?"

"Exactly!"

Ursula relaxed the more she talked to Chinue. It felt validating and satisfying to hear another woman speak things she had always felt inside. She learned that Chinue was from Nigeria and had worked as an elementary school history teacher for many years before following her passion to open a store in 1982. She hosted spiritual circles for women once a month and taught workshops on world religions and divination techniques. She was also the author of two books on the subject. She had a sister named Star Turner who owned and operated the second branch of their operation in Riverside. People didn't often realize the shops were related, but Chinue and Star are equal partners, each managing a shop. It was better for their budgets and resource management that way.

"You said your sister is in Riverside?"

"That's right. Star's Blessings."

"I think I've been there. I think that's where I had a palm reading years go. What a coincidence."

"There are no coincidences." Chinue winked and smiled.

"I don't want to keep you past your closing time. Do you have the adder's tongue?"

"How much would you like?"

Ursula had no idea. She didn't want guess too little and have things go awry again. She asked how much it was and decided to take three ounces. That should be more than enough. It was dried bits of leaves and stems.

"Tilly, get that for me?" Chinue pointed to a low shelf a few feet in front of her scooter. Matilda rose from her padded resting place and fetched a bag containing the small plastic bags used for the hanging herbs.

Ursula watched the precision of Chinue's hands. Chinue scooped the herbs onto a piece of paper on top of a scale then folded the paper and poured the contents into the plastic baggie. She asked Ursula if she needed any other ingredients while ringing her up.

"I don't want to hold you up. It's ten o'clock already."

"Tilly, the sign." Chinue pointed and the dog obeyed. She walked over to the front window and pulled on a cord that turned off the Open sign. "If you're a paying customer, I'm open for you. Now what else?"

Ursula asked about the power of moonstones. She had questions about whether the size mattered or if they had to be handed down through families in order to be a viable tool. Chinue told her that what most likely mattered was that the stones were charged with energies of a particular ritual. If she were inclined to buy her own stone right then and there, she would need to know the charging ritual before using it for her purpose. As for general use, a stone can be charged several ways: left out in the full moon for three nights; cleansed with salt water; cleansed in moving river water; covered by salt in a dish and left under the moon. She cautioned using heat because certain gems were too fragile and could break.

"I was just curious. I have the stone I need. I wanted to know the significance."

"When you're ready to learn more, look up our workshop schedule on LifeLook. I'd love to have you join us."

Ursula thanked her for all the help and the invitation. She said it was difficult for her to commit to things because of her own business which Chinue respected.

The late night drive and excellent conversation certainly beat marching through wetlands in search of adder's tongue during a dark night. The volkolaks' ritual she was going to perform was created by the lycanthropes of Russia. Ursula kept arguing with herself whether or not advice from a Nigerian woman would apply to her situation. Was all magic the same? Did intention matter more than ceremony or vice versa?

"Shit. What happens if the spell works but not the way I want?" There was no one else back at the apartment to answer her.

The translation was inside the kitchen drawer where she left it so Adriana or any other visitor wouldn't see it. She concentrated on the memory of Devora's steps in assembling everything. She found a sieve in the utensils. The measuring cups were in another drawer. The tea kettle always sat on the stove burner.

She talked herself through it. "Osha root. Kinnikinnick. Adder's tongue. And the moonstone. I can't believe that's everything. I've written brownie recipes that are more complicated than this."

Ursula read through Devora's notes for what felt like the hundredth time. Ideally, the ritual should be performed during the new moon, but she didn't want to wait. That was two weeks away. It was less than forty-eight hours until the full moon. But the volkolaks were upset with her right now. She needed to do all she could to protect them as soon as possible.

Chinue told her something crucial about the moon phase. Ursula wasn't sure it would matter to her at the time, but it was beginning to make sense. Chinue said the moon was in Pisces which was a time when people would feel more driven by their emotions, in particularly to help others. She told her it was also the right night to address healing friendships. Ursula hadn't mentioned anything about a falling out with friends.

CHAPTER SIXTEEN

The moon's nearly full face shone through the tree outside Ursula's living room window. She held the mug of bear root tea in both hands, looked down at her reflection in the infusion, then back to the moon's face.

"Tell me what to do. Give me a sign." She was out of her element. Catholicism had plenty of ritual and ceremony in its liturgy, but Ursula hadn't cast her own magical spell before. Blowing out birthday candles and making a wish somehow didn't seem equivalent.

Were all magic spells witchcraft? She had so many questions. She doubted herself every second. Maybe she should wait until the correct phase as Devora instructed. She put the mug down on the accent table under the window. Photographs of her parents and grandparents covered almost the entire surface and everything there desperately needed to be dusted.

She picked up the photo of her grandmother holding her as a baby. She was little brown angel dressed in an antique Christening gown for her Baptism. Grandmère as she was called, never looked happier.

"What would you have done to protect people you care about?"

Ursula worked through her thoughts to find the answer. Her grandparents left everything they knew to come to the United States from Haiti. They believed life would be safer, better. They weren't seeking riches. They were seeking sustenance. They wanted shelter that wouldn't be ravaged by hurricanes every late summer. Ursula hadn't been told much, but she remembered hearing that the people there always helped each other out. Her grandparents and their neighbors knew everything about each other's lives and their kids. They helped repair any damage or teamed up to deliver food to people who needed it more. Ursula contemplated her own actions. She was raised in a place that was always overflowing with people, but also overflowing with love and safety. She took it for granted until the day she was all alone in that apartment.

The selfishness in her happened naturally. She wasn't blaming her family for it, but it grew there because of her security. Ursula had been believing that helping out animals was noble and good for the planet. Then when her friends, sure they're volkolaks, needed her for protection she blew it. What would Grandmère do?

She would figure out how to make it right.

If the ritual failed again, she had enough ingredients to do it one more time. She didn't want to fail. She wanted the universe to provide a sign that it was the right thing to do and that it would work as expected. Now that Adriana knew about the volkolaks, the third dose of the infusion should be given to her if it would help course correct the major mistake Ursula made.

The pounding on her door scared the crap out of her. She almost dropped the picture, but managed to place it back on the table. *Thump thump thump!* Whoever it was, they were determined to get her attention. She left the infusion by the window and went to answer the door. She peeped through the hole and saw Rona and Peter. Was this the sign she was waiting for?

She slid the chain off and unlocked the door to let them in. Ursula tried to show them warmth in her greeting, but Rona's take-no-shit personality dominated.

"You did something truly horrible to us! And we're here to finally get it all out on the table which we couldn't possibly do in front of people downstairs."

"I want you to. Please. Come in and sit or stand or pace. Whatever. Punch me in the face if you need to, but not with your bear strength."

Ursula led them into the living room and again offered for them to sit. She let Rona rip her a new asshole without interrupting. She deserved their anger and longed for their forgiveness.

Peter knew his twin sister well enough to let her get everything out of her system before trying to voice his own disappointment. His anger was more subdued than Rona's. It was however, still anger. Peter wasn't a push-over the way a lot of people judged him to be.

"You finished?" He looked at Rona.

"Yeah. Fine. Go ahead."

"By telling Adriana, you put all of us in danger. The best we can hope for is that she doesn't believe you. How can we ever trust you again, Ursula?"

"I'm glad you asked. I haven't been able to think about anything else since this happened. And I'm trying my damnedest to make it up to you." Ursula walked around them to get to the mug she had left on the side table. "I want to do the ritual. I want to have the vision to see you, all of you, so that I can help protect you."

"You've had the ingredients. You even have Devora's moonstone. No one is stopping you." Rona had been feeling that Ursula would do the ritual anyway. She was there now. Ursula hadn't completed it yet. If she wanted to, she could stop her, but that wouldn't solve their problems.

"I know. But I'm glad you're here. I messed up and I don't want to do this without knowing you want me to have this kind of power. And, I swear on my life, I will use it to try and protect you from the hunters."

"How exactly?" Peter loved to spend half his time in bear form. Ursula's logic was lost on him.

"Okay. For example, you refuse to go into hiding during the weeks of the hunt, right?"

Peter and Rona nodded in confirmation. They didn't think they should have to hide. They believed firmly that the real solution was to stop the hunt all together.

Ursula continued, "If I can spot which bears are volkolaks, then I can misdirect the hunters. Maybe I can set up fake accounts and tell them where I've seen targets but actually give the wrong information."

"You could just do that seeing us as bears too and not knowing the difference." Peter had a good point.

"But you, Peter, they're specifically after you. Travis would love nothing more than to make Walker a trophy. Stuffed and mounted in a place of honor. I don't want anything to happen to the other bears. You know that. And after seeing Rona in action, I think she'll be able to take care of herself. But Walker has a target on him."

"And you think I can't handle myself because of my hands? You saw me in action too. You could have been mauled by those Musky bears for being in their den, but we're the ones who saved your ass."

Nothing Ursula said ever came out right. She continuously made herself look like a jerk. In the case of conversations with volkolaks, intentions were not coming through with clarity.

"No. I'm not saying that!"

"Then what are you saying?" Peter stepped closer to Ursula.

She didn't back away. She wasn't scared of his anger. She wanted to show him comfort.

"I'm saying I care about you and if I can't change your stubborn ass and convince you to stay hidden or to stay human for a couple weeks, I will do whatever you think is best to help all of you stay safe. Especially if that means Travis doesn't get any kills this year. How does that sound?"

Getting revenge on Travis would definitely be the icing on the cake. Sweet, sweet buttercream icing on the cake loaded with revenge against him and his club. She imagined its perfection. After what he did to her shop, he was going to pay. Somehow. Even if the police never bothered to look into him for the crime. Ursula knew it was Travis.

"What are you going to do about Adriana?" Rona wasn't ready yet to let down her guard.

"I've thought about that too. I was wondering if you wanted her to also go through the ritual. It would be one more human, yes, but she's also been fair about helping get the media coverage for SOAR."

The twins looked at each other without saying anything. They had that twin ability of telepathy that scientists still refute. It was real though. Peter spoke first.

"We're not sure if we can trust her. We let you in and that didn't work out so well."

"But she already knows."

Rona picked up the thread. "But you said she doesn't believe you."

Peter dropped another heavy topic to digest. "At least give us time to talk about it with Devora. She's thinking of going to elders in a few days to let them know the whole situation."

"Elders? What do you mean?"

"We told you we weren't the only volkolaks. We have ways of keep track of other families and they can reach out to ones they know. Like a network. And part of that network is made of the oldest volkolaks," Peter said.

"They make the most important decisions for our kind. Aunt Devora is one of them." Rona showed her pride. Shoulders back. Stature tall. Chin up. Arms crossed though. She was still pissed off.

Ursula let them know she would abide by whatever was decided. She would tell Adriana that she was probably right and that it was probably exhaustion making her say she had seen shapeshifting bears.

Rona wouldn't admit it, but she took a little bit of pleasure in knowing Ursula's actions had personal consequences.

"All right. I guess you can drink the tea since we're here." Rona softened just a smidgen.

"And you think it's fine that the lunar phase isn't right?"

"We'll never know unless you try it." Peter nodded to the mug in her hand. "Drink up."

"Do I have to say anything or do anything? Is there like some kind of chanting part?"

"No idea. The last time Aunt Devora tried, whatever she did failed." Rona watched with scientific interest and curiosity. It was an experiment after all. If something went wrong, none of them had any way of knowing what to do short of calling poison control or nine-one-one.

Ursula looked into the liquid one more time. It looked like a bottomless wishing well. "Up to my lips and over my gums; Look out stomach, here it comes."

***

Adriana spent Wednesday researching and getting lost in thought. She spent hours on any message boards she could find that mentioned shapeshifters. She came across the only credible link to people believing in the ability. It was about Navajo skinwalkers. It was a lead but probably a dead end. None of Ursula's friends were from any Native American nation or tribe.

That led Adriana's curiosity to look into Inuits and then any possible connection to the people who would be considered indigenous of Russia. It was getting her nowhere. Land bridge theories. Colonization. Wars.

It wouldn't be exactly out of the realms of her job as a journalist to contact Devora Zhukov and request a full feature about her family's history from Russia, living through Communism, and then making a new life here.

The news was saturated with international tragedies: attacks in Syrian and Pakistan; typhoons and floods; the Zika virus which sounded like a plague to end all humankind. Maybe readers would want something filled with dignity and hope about a family that found freedoms in the U.S. that they couldn't find in their home country. Maybe it wouldn't look too much like prying into private lives since Devora Zhukov was a candidate. She surely would have been prepared for her life and family members to be under the microscope of journalists looking for scandals, mishaps, or treason. But, Adriana Garcia would be the only journalist looking to for a groundbreaking historic record of shapeshifters living among humans. She'd win more than a Pulitzer if it was true. She'd have her pick of job offers, book deals, a lecture circuit. All her dreams would come true.

There were other questions with vague, untidy answers to the Devora Zhukov biography. What really happened to her sister and brother-in-law leaving Rona and Peter adult orphans? Was there something more to how Peter's hands were injured? What other family do they have? Do they ever go back to Russia?

Adriana's call was answered by Devora Zhukov personally. She was still trying to make it through a campaign without a full-time assistant.

"A feature about my family? I don't know, Ms. Garcia. I think I'd have to ask them how they would feel about that."

"Of course, but I'm particularly interested in the people who aren't still alive. Your parents, grandparents, ancestors."

Adriana laid out more of her pitch regarding her interest in a Russia family turned loyal American family which produced someone devoted to legislation and public service.

"I always welcome opportunities to get publicity for the non-profit I founded."

"Yes. The Root to Blossom Foundation? Is that correct?"

"That's right. It's a small operation, but we aim to help children from less privileged areas by providing school supplies, tutoring, and low cost after school care."

"I would love to discuss that more and also your interest in saving wildlife. Do you have any time in your schedule today? I'm in the Newark office now, but I can be over to you in about forty minutes."

Devora invited Adriana to her house for the interview. She did most of her work from home and it was far away from prying eyes that would snap their picture and blog wild speculations about what they were discussing.

The home office reflected more personal style than the rest of Devora's house which had been kept up for mass appeal. One wall was taken up mostly by the glass doors leading to a patio. The rest of the walls were a basket weave texture of birch squares, rough with beautiful grains showing. The squares alternated vertical and horizontal grain direction. The Mission furniture with an espresso stain contrasted the walls. There were two Tiffany lamps. One was next to a cozy chair and then there was a desktop one on the immaculate surface of her workspace. The lamps were genuine and precious with the enchanting glow of light through the amber glass. The dragonflies looked real as if they could take flight at any moment and decide to land on Devora's shoulder if she so wished.

Adriana studied the room and took the seat offered to her in front of Devora's desk. The questions were professional, but Adriana sensed there were things being held back in Devora's answers. They discussed what she knew of her heritage from Russia, but the most information she shared was about the more recent generations.

"It's not like we were famous and had biographers. I'm sorry I don't have much to say about the family pre-1900."

"That's not that unusual. I thought I'd do the most thorough job possible though to get a full view of the Zhukov and Medvedovich history."

"Yes, Peter and Rona are my sister's children as you know. Unfortunately I have very little to say about the Medved lineage." Devora interlaced her fingers. They were freshly manicured, but the skin was rough like someone who worked with their hands all day in physical labor rather than at a keyboard.

"Was saving the wildlife something that you learned from your family or did that become your own personal crusade which then influenced your niece and nephew?"

"It was Peter's accident that compelled all of us to do something about stricter hunting regulations."

"Can you tell me about that?"

"I suppose he's already a public figure after his arrest, but it's really his story to tell. I'll give you the basics, but if you want more, you'll have to go directly to him. He's not the one running for office."

"Fair enough." Adriana picked up her recorder to make sure it was operating and that the batteries had enough juice.

Peter Medvedovich was always drawn to the outdoors. He spent a lot of nights directly under the stars. In 1999, Peter was on one of his photography adventures. It was a hobby he took up at a young age. That year, for their twelfth birthday, Rona wanted a computer and Peter wanted a new camera and lens. He had such strong legs and lungs that he could walk farther than most people or kids his age.

He followed a creek to a marshy area and began taking pictures of the birds. As he headed back towards home, he tripped over a root and fell. His left hand landed on a hidden snare trap intended for fur animals.

"Between 1998 and 2000, snare trappers killed approximately two thousand foxes, over seventy river otters, almost nine hundred minks, and fourteen coyotes in New Jersey."

"I can't believe you have those statistics memorized." Adriana paused the pen over her steno pad which she used to make note of when the conversations had particular interest or to scribble out follow up questions she didn't want to forget.

"It was a significant moment for my family and the cause of Peter's disabilities. I studied why it happened."

Adriana asked her to continue the story. Peter's strength with his right hand and feet were enough for him to rip his left hand out of the trap, but not without causing permanent damage. Doctors were fortunately able to save the blood supply to both hands, but the nerves of the left were far too damaged; and the ulnar nerve on the right couldn't be repaired which is why he had partial use of his right hand. Now that science has had time to advance, Peter is totally comfortable with who he is. He's not interested in more surgeries.

"He's a wonderful photographer. In fact, my editor would like to use some of his photos from the bear hunt protests and the ones he's managed to capture of the bears in the wild."

"You'll have to talk to him about that. I'm sure he'd be happy to help. For his professional rate, of course." Good ol' Aunt Devora letting the press know that they couldn't take advantage of Peter's talent and expect the use of his photos for free.

Adriana let it slide. Any compensation negotiations would be between the freelancer and the publisher. She didn't care. They never paid her extra when she provided photos for her own stories.

"Speaking of the bear hunt protests, what was it about them that got you interested? They aren't hunted with snare traps. Only bows and firearms."

"Regardless of how they're killed, our black bear population is not out of control as the gun lobby would like people to believe. The heart of the issue is habitat loss. There are cities all over New Jersey, all over the whole country, where land is deforested, developed with buildings, and then never used. You can go through any corporate park and find half or more of the buildings empty. Same thing with strip malls and shopping plazas. We, as living beings sharing this planet, can't expect the wildlife to magically move on. All of this affects them in ways humans rarely consider. Migratory patterns shift because of climate change. Territories are forced to intersect. Reproduction goes down while mortality rates go up from starvation. There's a lot that humans should be answering for, Ms. Garcia."

"Are you more attached to the bears for any particular reason? I noticed outside by your front door you have a sign with the Ursa Major constellation and bear etched on it." Adriana had a feeling it was a pointless question, but she needed to try anyway. She leaned forward in her chair and made eye contact to let her subject know she was listening attentively.

"All of nature is important to our family. As I said, Peter spends the most time outside out of the three of us. He can commune with them in a special way."

"Them, meaning the bears? Like Grizzly Adams?"

"I guess you could say so, but Peter is smart enough to let wild animals be wild. They're not pets."

Adriana felt that was the perfect segue into discussing the local community bear, Walker. The bear that plenty of folks in northern New Jersey regarded as a pet.

"How about Walker, the black bear that walks on its hind legs. He's made national news because everyone thought it was a hoax at first."

"Walker is special to a lot of people. He's a perfect example of what's wrong with the regulations. Not just hunting regs, but the land development as I said. He comes around and doesn't bother anyone. If you see the videos, he looks so scared. All he wants is food and water and to be left alone to be a bear."

"Do you know what's wrong with Walker's front arms that makes him walk on his back legs like that?"

"The most accepted theory is that he was hit by a car when he was smaller and learned to adapt."

"Do you think he's in pain? Suffering?"

"I have no idea. I'm not a veterinarian. And to my knowledge, no vet has ever examined him."

There was something in how Devora's brows tensed inward when she answered the questions about bears. Adriana's instincts told her she was on the right track of a good story, but that didn't mean something as ludicrous as volkolaks being real. What Devora had said made sense. Peter was injured by hunters and the family has become anti-hunting or pro-conservation whichever way one wanted to look at it.

"Do you feel especially merciful towards Walker because he's disabled like your nephew?" Adriana saw Devora's brows lift in surprise. Nailed it, she thought to herself.

"You know, Ms. Garcia, I guess I never realized that, but you might be right. And like a human who needs compassion, so does Walker. I want the bear hunt canceled."

"For the five year hiatus that current senators have proposed?"

"No. For at least twenty years, but I'd be willing to get to a negotiating table as soon as I'm elected and if that means starting with five years, I'd take it."

Adriana checked her recorder again. She had to make sure she didn't miss this next part.

"Ms. Zhukov, did you or anyone in your family break Walker out of Musky Park?"

"Why would we, Ms. Garcia? We want him to be safe."

"Well, I interviewed your niece Rona and she believes Walker should be free, not caged."

"That's true. I've heard her say so as well."

Adriana asked for clarification whether Devora disagreed with her niece on the Walker situation. Devora collected her thoughts before answering.

"Ultimately, Rona, Peter, and I want the same thing. We want the bear hunt canceled and none of us want to see Walker harmed in any way. When Walker was tranquilized and taken to Musky Park, he was further injured. You were there. You know it's true. So as much as I'd like Walker to be some place safe in case the hunt goes on, I don't think permanent captivity at Musky Park is the answer."

Adriana felt like she was on to something, but struggled to make two plus two equal four.

"You know something — I found an interesting bit of information in my research of Russian culture."

"What's that?" Devora's mounting tension showed in her stiffer shoulders and clenched teeth which she tried to force a smile through.

"Have you heard of volkolaks? I'm sure you must have. It's quite fascinating."

Devora amused Adriana, but not for too long.

"Yes. I can remember hearing them mentioned. It's like werewolves, right?"

"Except instead of humans turning into monstrous wolves, they turn into bears. It's not something you see much in American folklore."

"I guess not. You probably know the younger generation better than I do. They're all into vampires these days. I guess bears aren't as appealing or romanticized since they don't look like humans or glitter in moonlight. It's just fairy tales. That's all."

"Fairy tales. Sure."

Devora politely brought the interview to an end. Adriana pretended to look at the time on the clock on the shelf behind Devora's desk and gave one of those pretentious "I must be going anyway" excuses. She thanked the candidate for her time and said she looked forward to speaking again soon.

"I think there's even more to your family's story and I hope you'll go on the record for the rest of it."

"I assure you, that's all there is to know." Devora walked around the desk and gestured for Adriana to find the way to the door. "I'll show you out."

***

There was a proper coffeehouse on Kirkland Boulevard. Adriana found parking in front and a few shops down from Drip & Sip. In all honesty, she preferred it to Applegate's Country Store. There was a selection of coffees and teas and the quality of them was superior. At Applegate's, the coffee was good — for a breakfast diner. It was also cheap despite Ursula's attempt to modernize the selection. Adriana couldn't wait to place her order for an enormous flat white and pay over five dollars. She carried her leather computer bag to a small table against the front windows. She placed the table placard with the number "6" on it at the edge so the server could see it clearly.

The guest login for the Wi-Fi was typed on a small tented sign with a list of dessert specials. Adriana held it to read, then put it out of her way so she could boot up her laptop. Her fingers typed out "b-e-s-t-i-n-t-o-w-n" in the password field.

Sure, the cafe made far more in profits than Applegate's even though they only served small pre-packaged desserts or cups of yogurt with granola and no hot meals; but they had what a lot of people wanted. Better coffee and more tables, almost all of them wired up the center with outlets for charging. Customers could stay as long as they wanted even on one cup of coffee. Plus, they were opened later in the evenings than Applegate's. Drip & Sip even started a slam poetry night and acoustic music nights over the summer. Their walls featured paintings for sale by local artists and changed the gallery every two months. The young woman who lettered their chalk signs was an artist in her own right. If a Hollywood director needed a charming cafe bustling with people under forty, Drip & Sip would be the ideal set.

Adriana's flat white was set down while her fingers blazed across the keyboard. She told the server she didn't need anything else and kept her head down as the black letters appeared on her screen one click at a time.

After an hour, Adriana looked back over what she had so far. She prided herself on being objective. She had received praise for fairly reporting more than one side of a story. This was her first chance at a feature. It had to show flourish and enough intrigue to make people continue reading passed the first two paragraphs and skipping to the end.

"This is crap." She was quiet, but didn't care if anyone heard. Unfortunately, someone did.

"Is the coffee that bad?"

"Travis. What are you doing here?"

"Getting coffee now that I don't feel so welcome at my usual place."

"You haven't been welcome at Applegate's for a long time. Ursula was just too polite to kick you out sooner."

Without an invitation, Travis pulled out the chair opposite of Adriana and sat down.

"She's probably just about done with her lezbo phase and then she'll be kicking you out too, Garcia."

"Unless you're giving me a story, Travis, go away."

"My story will be front page once I take down the biggest black bear in the state. Probably break a new record."

"I thought you were after Walker? He's not the biggest bear by far."

Travis stood up and placed a foot on his chair to rest his upper body on his thigh like some kind of country-boy-pirate.

"Maybe you didn't do all your research, Garcia. We're allowed two tags in different zones. I can shoot Walker over here in zone one then bag another in zone three. I hear they got some big bastards over there by Hewitt."

Adriana heard the barista call out Travis' name. She firmly suggested he get his coffee before it got cold. When he walked away, she looked at her empty mug. She closed up her laptop, put on her blazer, and got out the door before he had a chance to catch up to her.

Her car was practically invisible parked behind Travis' monster truck. She turned back to see if he was behind her. He wasn't. Probably took the opportunity to try and flirt with one of the girls behind the counter.

He kept the truck in decent shape, but ran it hard. He would leave mud on it for a few days to drive around and show off to the world that dirt meant he was some kind of manly-man. On that day, Adriana noticed it was reasonably clean. She had a twisted curiosity about Travis because he was Ursula's ex-boyfriend. She looked through the passenger side window; fortunately, she was tall enough. Empty soda cans and sports drink bottles littered the interior. She looked back to the cafe again. He still wasn't coming. She peeked into the truck's bed. It had a plastic liner, a foot locker bolted in place, and miscellaneous crap. His camouflage jacket was in a heap, stuffed between the foot locker and boxes for his hunting gear.

He's got everything all ready to go, Adriana thought. Then she noticed something that didn't look like it was used for hunting or fishing. There were two cans of spray paint. One red, one black. She was about to reach over the truck bed to try and reach one, when she heard his voice.

"You stalking me, Garcia? If you want to leave me a love note, you should put it under the windshield wiper."

His smile made her sick to her stomach. Even if he hadn't dated her girlfriend, he was a vile creep.

"Heh, no. Just admiring this massive beast you have here." Adriana patted the truck pretending to appreciate it.

He leaned in close to her, making her wince. "Truck's not the only thing massive, sweetheart."

She couldn't muster the words to tell him to back off. She turned away as quickly as possible and clicked the key fob for her own car. She slid inside and locked herself in before he had any ideas of chasing her. He laughed, took a sip of his coffee, and watched her pull away.

Adriana turned off Kirkland and mindlessly made other turns until she realized she was by the police station. She didn't know how things were between herself and Ursula so she wasn't ready to find sanctuary at Applegate's or at Ursula's apartment.

"Why did I come here?" She asked herself aloud in private. The spray paint. Could it actually prove Travis was the one who vandalized Applegate's? Adriana sat behind the wheel deciding if it would be better to go to Ursula with the information or the police. Ursula would believe her and say, "I told you so," but that wouldn't do any good. The police would tell her spray paint is common and there's no way to link one particular can of it to the damage done on the shop. Would it make her look like a decent, good-hearted citizen or a nosy busybody? Cops already had strained relationships with journalists. They used each other mutually, but there was no real love between them.

Adriana's thoughts whirled around as she tried to connect the dots. She decided to drive all the way home to Harrison before she gave herself a headache. No one would be able to do a damn thing about spray paint cans in the back of a truck.

It was the right thing to do. In her own apartment, Adriana mixed herself a cosmo with hardly any cranberry juice and breathed a sigh of relief for the first time all day. She sat at her kitchen table. Laptop on. Cursor blinking.

"State Senate candidate Devora Zhukov prides herself in being an advocate for the less privileged class and a wildlife conservationist. Her journey to this point in time goes all the way back to Russia and her great-great-grandparents. She's the first of her family to pursue a political career. Even though she's been in Frankhurst her entire life, no one seems to know much about her and her family. Peter Medvedovich, Zhukov's nephew, was arrested recently and charges were reduced to trespassing at the Musconetcong Animal Park. His arrest and the related animal rights protests have gotten more attention than any of Zhukov's political aspirations. One would expect her to seek out the spotlight and welcome public interest. It's almost as if she's trying to hide something."

Adriana knew it was garbage and no editor would ever publish it. She stared at the open document and downed her cocktail. For kicks, she typed what she really wanted to say.

"State Senate candidate Devora Zhukov is the current matriarch of the Frankhurst volkolak species. What's a volkolak? They're people who can become bears. And yes, that makes her niece Rona Medvedovich and her nephew Peter Medvedovich volkolaks too. So if you see bears wondering around, there is the possibility that it's someone you know."

"It's so outrageous. It's probably true and I can't tell anyone," she said to her screen.

Adriana fished out her steno pad and reviewed her notes. Snare traps. Foxes. Minks. "Where is it? There's something here. I know there's..." she found what she was looking for scribbled and underlined twice. Why did she underline it? WALKER. In the middle of the page glaring as if it was it was written in neon. She circled it and banged her pen on the pad. "Walker! That's it!"

CHAPTER SEVENTEEN

It took some convincing, but Adriana got approval for a feature to run on Friday. Only it wasn't the story about the life of a state senate candidate.

October was approaching. People's houses were being decorated for Halloween already. Kids were banged up and bruised from soccer games. It felt like every other person needed donations for a fundraiser. The fall definitely exhibited unique attributes other than going back to school and looking at the leaves change color. It was the perfect time to talk about urban legends of New Jersey.

Adriana's boss wanted to hold the story to run it with other Halloween pieces, but she said Friday's news was light and it was a full moon. It would give people something to read on their website instead of OctopusSmiles.com or BuzzFirst. Old media had to keep up with the frivolity of new media somehow. They still had some luck with syndicated comic strips and horoscopes, but even those dwindled to nearly no traffic hits. People used apps on their phones for all that stuff.

A post worth reading could get attention if the right Boffo users shared it. Adriana made sure to bring her article to the attention of everyone in the weird and paranormal circles. They had decent fanbases and appreciated that she gave them mentions in the section on who to follow. When Adriana first typed the names of ghost hunters and paranormal investigators into her article, she did it out of jest. Then she caught her own duplicity in the making. She couldn't mock the weirdos chasing spooky sounds in old houses if she was about to imply that the northern part of the state had monsters just as intriguing as the Pine Barrens' Jersey devils.

Volkolaks could be the new cryptid people thought of when horror stories were told. Adriana built it up positing whether a volkolak could beat a Jersey devil. That alone would stir up controversy in the state where people were either from the north or the south; either New York sports fans or Philly fans (most of the time they forgot about their own). Back in the days when there were two area codes, that's what defined what type of Jersey person you were, a 201 or a 609. Adriana wanted to build on that rivalry in a brand new way.

Before her article ended, she hinted a bit too much about what it would mean if volkolaks were real:

"Imagine looking into a bear's eyes and seeing something familiar, but you can't place it. Maybe it's how it cocks its head to one side like that girl you know in math class. Maybe it's a limp or a disability you recognize in the man who frequents your favorite sandwich shop. After all, Jersey devils don't disguise themselves as human and do things like infiltrate the highest echelons of our government. If cryptids are real, it's monsters like volkolaks we should watch out for more than Jersey devils."

Ursula was busy helping Kylie and Manny clean up from the breakfast crowd. She hadn't had a chance to look at her phone each time it vibrated in her back pocket. When she finally did, her blood boiled. Rona's text contained a link to Adriana's story. It was the first time having a search alert for the word "volkolak" paid off.

"I haven't seen you or Peter since the ritual. Can you come over to talk?" Ursula's hands shook texting back to Rona. The bear root spell didn't work immediately in a poof of magic like an illusionist making an elephant disappear.

It was difficult for Rona to accept the invitation. She was furious at Ursula all over again. They wouldn't be in this mess with Adriana if Ursula hadn't opened her big mouth, especially to a reporter.

They had to continue speaking in code and low voices with people around. Ursula didn't want to leave Kylie high and dry to manage everything again. There were only so many times in one month she was willing to put her personal life before her business.

"Can I get you a decaf?"

"A decaf?" Rona looked insulted.

"Herbal tea?"

"What?"

"I don't think you need any caffeine right now, but I'm trying to be cordial. On the house." Ursula had been serving Rona regular coffee as long as she had known her. It was Peter who preferred herbal tea. Ursula had already decided their personalities matched their choice of beverage.

"Boss, I could really use more hands on deck," Kylie said as she whizzed by with arms full of hot plates with eggs and toast.

"I'll see if Tayleigh can come in early." Must be the full moon, Ursula said to herself. She excused herself from Rona's table, texted Tayleigh, and rang up a couple of tables waiting to pay their bills. Tayleigh agreed to come in after she had time to shower and get ready. That meant it could be another hour. Some day that girl was going to have more important responsibilities and a boss who isn't willing to cut her so much slack.

Ursula made her way back to Rona and hadn't noticed that Peter arrived when she was running dirty dishes back to the kitchen. She offered to get him whatever he wanted and was soon on her way back behind the counter for his orange spice tea. She hoped he appreciated the gesture of her stocking more tea even though it was way too small of a gesture to repay him for all he had done in defending her from Travis and sacrificing himself at Musky Park. She put the hot cup and saucer with a lemon slice in front of him.

At the neighboring table, one of the chairs was empty. Ursula checked with the person there to make sure she was dining alone before absconding with the chair.

That's when time slowed down. Ursula felt like she was in water, moving against the force of resistance. Her sight wasn't the same. It was blurry in waves, yet when she looked directly at something it was the best vision of her life. She looked around and wondered what other people saw looking at her.

She slid her butt onto the chair at the third side of Rona and Peter's table. Her head swiveled back and forth between them, looking from one to the other. She continued to feel the waves of energy pushing into her like the edge of the tide on a beach. She asked what was happening but had no idea if the words came out.

Peter reached his right hand over and placed it on Ursula's. She looked down at it because she knew in her mind-trip that he was still Peter and that his hand was on hers. What she saw though was his furry black bear paw with its healed injury, but still deformed.

"I guess it finally worked."

"Seems so." The twins said to each other. Ursula understood them, but wasn't a hundred percent sure they spoke in English.

There was a swell of new and confusing feelings inside Ursula. She couldn't figure out how much time was passing. She saw customers coming and going. Kylie was busting her ass taking care of all of them, but Ursula didn't feel like she could get up and help. Her legs didn't feel like her legs. Her hands, her whole body — everything had sensations surging through muscles, nerves, blood, organs and her bones.

"We did this. I guess we have to see it through."

Which twin said that? Ursula thought it was Peter. It was only a guess though. Their voices no longer had the human distinctions she knew. Her eyes followed the beefy paw on her hand. She scanned up his arm and saw the shift. She looked at Peter's face and it felt like she was looking at those old foil hologram stickers she used to collect when she was a little girl. She saw Peter, the Peter she knew. If she moved her head half an inch, she saw Walker looking back at her. She turned out of wonderment to Rona. It was the same experience. She had been with both of them in their bear forms up close at Musky Park, but this was different. She could see their forms overlapping.

"Whoa! Did you guys slip an edible to my boss?" It was Tayleigh chuckling at the sight of Ursula spacing out with each of her hands fondling the cheeks of Rona and Peter.

"She's having a bad reaction to some cold medicine. That's why she called you in early." Peter made up the lie quicker than Rona expected.

"Yep. We're going to take her upstairs to lie down. If her girlfriend happens to come by would you send her up?"

Rona was ready for the confrontation with Adriana despite not having heard back from Devora yet. Devora had only left that morning to meet with the elders of the other volkolak families.

They helped Ursula to her feet and guided her to the back hallway where they took the stairs to the apartment. She held onto the railing as she slightly swayed. Inside, they steered her to the couch and she plopped.

"Wushappng?"

"We think it's the ritual kicking in. You'll be fine in a little while. Rona is calling Aunt Devora to let her know everything is going according to plan."

Rona finally reached her aunt on the phone. The conversation was brief. Since no one had performed the ritual in ages, there was no way of knowing if this was to be expected. Devora was still in her car but promised to ask as many questions as possible of the other volkolaks. Between all of them in the northeastern states, there had to be a way to piece together enough clues about the ritual's effects on humans.

Ursula continued to feel the funkiness for a couple hours. In time the sensations mellowed to a humming vibration through her whole body. It was more subtle than when circulation is cut off and a foot falls asleep. Her body felt the colors in the room around her. She tasted the sounds of the twins' voices. She saw the aura of the only plant in the house. The synesthesia slowly diminished.

"Did you poison me?" Her first coherent words could have been more respectful, but considering Ursula had never been through an experience like that before, she lost grasp of etiquette.

"If anything, you poisoned you," Rona pointed out.

Peter asked Ursula how she was feeling and she admitted that she felt better than fine. She had a hard time describing it and didn't care if she sounded like a lunatic.

"I felt like I tapped into part of the universe that I never knew was there. It was beautiful. Frightening, but still beautiful."

"We need to figure out what to do about Adriana. I don't mean to rush your recovery, but..." Peter wanted to get to the heart of the troubles instead of leaving it up to his sister who might have taken a drastically different direction.

"No. No. You're absolutely right. You're not rushing me. It's my fault you're — we're — in this mess. Honestly, I think the story would most likely be perceived as a fun bit of spooky history. How many people could possibly take Adriana seriously?"

"Let's see." Rona helped herself to Ursula's desk and computer. She navigated to the comments of Adriana's article. "Most of them, like you said, are people finding this cool. It's something they didn't know. There's a fair share of them that took the bait about south Jersey having a weaker monster."

Peter sat on the end of the coffee table. Ursula shimmied down to the other end of the couch. Both leaning forward waiting for any bad news.

"And here we have three people talking back and forth in a thread about volkolaks being real. The original poster said he saw someone running naked through the woods right after he saw a bear."

"So? Isn't it possible a person was just naked in the woods?" Ursula wasn't a prude. She knew there were naturist clubs around. New Jersey supposedly had some kind of secret beach at the shore.

"I think what Rona is getting at is that once the idea is out there, humans have a way of building and adding on to stories with each iteration. This person might say that they saw a naked person running. The next person might say that they saw a half man half beast running. And the next might say they noticed their neighbor transform into a bear and eat from their garbage cans. It's the way legends are made."

"Ursula, it's not only being discovered that's a danger. It's how humans react. You can see by how Adriana compared us to devils and demons, things to be feared. It's a stigma about black bears being man-eaters and going into people's yards to eat their toddlers. It's that shit we have to deal with on top of worrying that the government and scientists might actually find us."

It was the first time Rona presented her case without Ursula thinking it would all blow over after Halloween's ghost stories were told.

"I'll fix this, guys. I promise. I'll make sure Adriana's story is discredited."

"You're going to set up your own girlfriend?" Rona squinted at Ursula, only half disbelieving since she knew Ursula was capable of betrayal.

"If it means making things right and protecting all of you? Yes. Yes, I have to do this. It's not like things are working out between us anyway."

"Well don't use us as the excuse to dump her just because you're unhappy." Rona had a point.

Ursula hated herself for what she had done to the volkolaks. Deep inside though, she also had resentment for Adriana and their relationship for other reasons. Adriana's ambition was part of it. Two people being inconsiderate doesn't make anything right. Adriana wanted commitment and cohabitation and a happy ending. Ursula never had that dream with Adriana the same way, and it was time to put on her big girl pants and own that. She had to come clean with Adriana and break up.

CHAPTER EIGHTEEN

The autumn darkness was broken by the full moon gleaming through Ursula's living room window. Rona and Peter left her alone to deal with her mess. Despite their disappointment in her, they assumed their presence would continue to stimulate the new sensory experience of the bear root ritual until Ursula was fully acclimated.

She stared at the computer monitor. Browser tabs were opened to several social media sites and the *Jersey Express* local site. Ursula tried to focus and do her volunteer work for SOAR. She had photos from Peter to share with updated facts on hunting and advice about how to live with bears in the area.

As urban sprawl of real estate development escalated every year, there were more people moving into the rural areas who lacked the common sense about keeping garbage cans locked up or making loud noises to scare away a bear rather than call for their extinction. It was important information to share, but humans were ultimately lazy creatures. Ursula had seen how they'd rather be reactive to the bear situation. They'd rather wait until the habitats were lost and then call for the killing under the guise of it being merciful so the animals don't starve to death or get killed by traffic.

Devora's moonstone was on Ursula's desk. She found herself carrying it around with her and looking at it no matter what she was doing.

The full moon lit up her living room like a soft flashlight beam. Ursula held the crystal in her fingers in front of the moon and created a make-shift moon-over-moon eclipse. The radiance of the real moon gave the stone a halo. It was more magical to her eyes in that moment than when she saw it brewing and charging the bear vision ingredients. The surface was so smooth that no matter how she turned it around, the opalescence remained brilliant.

The crystal made more sense to Ursula now. She could understand how it harnessed Devora's energies. Devora had a welcoming softness to her personality, but no matter what cropped up, her family's wellness was her focus. She had clearly defined directions for her energies to penetrate. Yet, underneath it all was mystery and magic. It was a core that so few were allowed to witness that it could be considered rumor.

Ursula put herself in Devora's shoes. If she had the sort of mindset to run for public office, she would be inclined to make the world a safer place too. There wasn't room to consider safety a selfish campaign platform or a non-political desire. Everyone wanted it. The difference was when humans divided living beings up into *Others*. Other color of humans. Rich humans. Poor humans. Beautiful humans. Cute animals. Working animals. Food animals. Ugly animals. Trophy animals. Humans needed to put everything an appropriately labeled checkbox.

Volkolaks wanted the freedom to exist. They weren't rising up and demanding any other rights of the nations. They weren't asking for special considerations or voting amendments or medical care. All they wanted was to exist in secret without constant fear. Not being known or in the spotlight was their goal.

With her thoughts finally giving her some clarity, Ursula's fingers tapped across the keyboard. She left anonymous comments on Adriana's article about cryptids. It was time consuming as someone who didn't have hacking skills to create a hundred sock puppet accounts. She had to painstakingly do it manually and she had no knowledge how to falsify the IP address; it wouldn't take long for an IT professional at the newspaper to see it was all from one person. Ursula's fake users ended up in conversations with each other as they belittled Adriana's writing and mocked her. She felt the pain crush her heart as each of these accounts tore through Adriana to discredit her. She wavered each time as she felt the emotional challenges. Coming up with what to say was that boggled her intellectually. As long as Ursula's fake users didn't post threats, there wouldn't be much likelihood anyone would try and track her down. At worst, they would block her IP address from ever commenting again.

Random people around the state had already posted their speculations that Walker the bear was a volkolak. It made sense to them. They used his bipedal stature as a determining factor rather than admit it was an adaptive use of his legs once his hands were damaged.

Ursula didn't expect so many people to give credence to Adriana's piece. She thought they would see it for a fun story about fictional creatures. There were enough true believers or those with open minds that Ursula figured anything she could write wouldn't make a difference.

She finished up in the comments and returned to sharing heartbreaking photos of murdered bears, particularly the little cubs. It made her cry to look at them, but it had to be done. Humans had to see the results of the legislation they allowed to pass. They couldn't sweep every unpleasant thing they did under the rug. At SOAR meetings, they had many discussions about what the federal government should be doing to protect the ecosystem; Election Day was close and if it didn't go the way they expected, the whole planet would pay for it.

The way that Boffo and LifeLook worked, anything someone posted publicly could be shared. The original poster could click an icon and see all the user accounts who shared an individual post. Ursula didn't usually bother to deeply analyze those users. She was grateful for anyone willing to spread the message about SOAR's objectives and the controversies on legislation pertaining to the environment. She paid extra for a third-party software that enabled her to extract information about the users in easier to read formats. She could create reports on demographics, for example, that showed most people who shared SOAR photos had things in common: animal rights, vegetarians/vegans, spirituality, liberal politics, and on and on. As long as a user allowed their information to be publicly displayed and not set to private accounts, Ursula could also see their names and whatever they filled in for their small biography sections. That's how she noticed Travis Iver's name and birthday in one particular user.

She hadn't thought to keep an eye on SOAR's enemies on social media. She should have been doing that all along. When Ursula clicked over to Travis' Boffo feed, she saw he and he friends sharing the photos all right, but not way she intended.

"Damn you, Travis."

Ursula's screen sat there and mocked her. She knew it was exactly how Adriana would feel if and when she read the comments on the newspaper article.

Travis and his ilk posted the photos claiming credit for the kills and taunting the activists. They openly posted their plans to target Walker. They even picked on each other about who was the better marksman or how bows were superior to the sport than guns. It was an online pissing contest. Ursula's blood boiled through her as she thought about what hunting was really like. There was no sport in luring an animal with bait while it could be shot from a hunter a few feet away up in a tree. Something about the land animals felt so much different in process than fishing, not that she endorsed fishing either.

Photos of Walker and other bears had been altered to show them already bludgeoned and bleeding or with sight markings over them. It resembled the vandalism of Applegate's windows enough for Ursula to know for certain Travis had done it. It still wouldn't be enough for the police to do a damn thing though. Even if she wasn't considered one of the local liberals, she was the only black merchant in the small historic downtown district.

The horrific visuals compelled Ursula to pick up her phone and text Peter to see if he was all right. He didn't reply until morning. He had transformed and spent the night as Walker as he often did. She had to let it go until he was available to talk. She hoped he would respond to her then.

Travis' posts were narcissistic, filled with his typical bravado. Everything was shallow. He occasionally tried to make a point about the Second Amendment and gun owners' rights, but Travis was not gifted with eloquence for debating.

"What the hell is this?"

Ursula had to enlarge the photo of a post a few days prior. It was the scene of the protest outside the local police station when Peter was arrested. She saw Adriana there so that wasn't the surprising part of the photo. It was the presentation. Adriana wasn't an on-camera reporter. She didn't have to fake smiles regardless of who she interviewed. Yet there she was with Travis. Standing close together, shoulders touching. There was no way to tell where his hands actually were. The shot was captioned: "The press loves me! Adriana Garcia knows the Frankhurst gun club is right!"

"I can't believe he spelled her name correctly," Ursula said audibly to no one. She silently questioned why the heck Adriana allowed the photo to be taken and why she looked more than happy to pose with him. She had always taken Ursula's side that Travis was an enormous creep to be avoided. If she had to do her job and interview him, she didn't need to stand so close to him to do it.

Ursula took screen captures of Travis' feed and included them in an email to SOAR's executive board along with the comprehensive social media reports. It was clear that they would have make decisions about how to handle the press, namely Adriana, and the gun club.

As for her personal relationship, Ursula needed the courage to do what was right. She had to dive in to the deep end without swimmies on her arms and get the hard part over with.

Adriana sounded wide awake when she answered her phone. She refused to drive out to Applegate's just because Ursula wanted to see her in person.

"You know what? You can come over here for a change. If you have something to say to me that can't wait until tomorrow, you can make the effort. Unless of course you need to be in Frankhurst for Peter and Rona."

"I am worried about Peter, but that's not why I'm unwilling to drive to Harrison. I don't know what your problem is with either of them anyway."

"My problem is that you'll drop what you're doing for them, but when you need something from me, I have to come to you. You've been treating me like crap since you started hanging out with them and their kind."

"What's that supposed to mean?" Ursula didn't want to know the answer, but she knew what was coming. Her mind quickly calculated that Adriana could have meant white people when she referred to their kind. She hoped that's where Adriana was taking the conversation, but was disappointed.

"You claim they're supernatural creatures and I'm going to be the one to break that story. I'm going to prove that they've been brainwashing you or poisoning you or I'll prove that they really are monsters. And if they are, they need to be in cages." Adriana hung up before Ursula had a chance to say anything else.

It wasn't the ideal way to handle it, but since Adriana refused to talk civilly Ursula took the chickenshit way out and texted her break up speech. It contained the basics of what she wanted to say in person. They were on different paths; Ursula wanted to stay in Frankhurst while Adriana he big dreams of working in a city; and the accurate admission that she didn't feel comfortable taking their relationship to the next step. The reply wasn't pretty though it was brief.

CHAPTER NINETEEN

It was October and the day before bear hunting season officially began. The SOAR members had been in contact with each other daily through emails and weekly meetings held at Applegate's. Mick Hoffman had a schedule of protests printed for everyone and the designated checkpoints where the murdered bears would be taken for weighing, cataloging the date and time, the location of the kill, the sex of the bear, and confirmation of the hunters' Conservation ID number.

The previous Wednesday meeting at Applegate's was publicized as "activism and environmental protection 101" workshop. It became a gathering of emotional people assembling their protest signs using the large photos and graphics Peter printed for them. New members signed up. More members of the community were talking about the hunt online. Ursula reported that people who weren't card-carrying SOAR members responded to her LifeLook posts that they would also show up to the protests.

What was obviously missing was coverage from the *Jersey Express*. Adriana hadn't given up on the story. She continued to sleuth for any dirt she could get on Devora Zhukov's family. Besides the hunt, the election was on people's minds too. The jealousy didn't end because Ursula dumped her. If anything, it grew inside Adriana. It made her obsessed with the alleged volkolaks. She spent every chance she could following one of them, taking notes, talking to anyone she saw them talk to. For the first time, she felt like a real investigative reporter.

Ursula continued to beg Peter and Rona to stay in their human forms for the next week. Rona had plenty of grad school work that would force her to be human; she spent a lot of time at her home studying or helping Devora with her campaign. Peter, however, refused to bow to the real predators. He visited Applegate's on that Sunday morning alone.

"Can I get you some tea while you wait for a table to open up?" Ursula was happy to see him. She sensed that he had at least partially forgiven her over the last few weeks.

When he accepted the tea, his eyes locked with Ursula's as they had done in the past. This was different now with her new vision ability. She adjusted quite well considering that none of them knew what they were doing when she decided to go through with the bear root ritual. She saw Peter, all human and as handsome as ever. The sensation she felt is what changed. It was even more intense which Ursula hadn't thought possible. It wasn't lustful like vampires of lore. She felt consumed, comfortable, and at ease. The dinging bell telling her Manny had an order up to be served jolted her from the trance.

A few more people showed up in line behind Peter to wait for tables. Ursula couldn't wait to have some time after the hunting weeks to buckle down and interview people for part-time help.

"If it would make it easier for you, I can take mine to go. You can seat these people instead." Peter's offer was sweet, but Ursula rejected it.

"If I could chain you to one of my tables so that I'd know you're safe, I would. As long as you're here, I'll do whatever I have to in order to make room." Ursula pointed for Peter to head over to the table that she would bus as soon as she could.

She simultaneously handed back one person's change while ringing up another. The few people still in line looked around to see what everyone else was eating. Ursula finally made her way back to bus and clean two of the tables including the one for Peter.

"Ursula?"

She didn't realize that she had her ample behind directly pointed at Peter while she was bent over a table to scrub it. He didn't mind the view, but that's not why he called her name.

"One sec." She placed the sugar, salt, pepper, and ketchup back up on the table and turned around. "Do you know what you want already?"

He smiled with his eyes and couldn't help let out a tiny laugh to a joke only he must've heard. She didn't know what was humorous.

"What am I missing? Is there ketchup all over my butt? Wouldn't be the first time."

"No. Not that. I just want to talk to you when you get more than one second."

"Tayleigh is scheduled to come in at noon. Do you want to eat your breakfast now and then come upstairs where it's less crowded?"

Peter agreed and ordered a bowl of oatmeal with dried cranberries, almonds, and maple syrup with an additional cup of mixed fruit on the side. When he was finished, he left more than enough to cover his bill which she put in Kylie's tip jar under the counter instead of keeping for herself. As Peter headed for the front door, he told Ursula that he'd meet her upstairs at noon. In the meantime, he took the opportunity to get his camera from his car and go to the riverbank to see if any of the water fowl were in the mood to model.

As soon as Ursula had the chance to stand still, she closed her eyes and saturated herself in the three seconds of silence she was allowed.

Her phone alert went off as it had been all morning. She knew the SOAR members would be busy corresponding all day. Most of them didn't have a business to manage on a Sunday. She swiped her screen open and saw that Jon McHugh sent a link to a *Jersey Express* letter to the editor. What shocked her was that it was from Hank Iver, Travis' father and recent retired supervisor of the public works department.

It had always been discouraged for employees of the municipal government to voice their political opinions — or any opinion at all, truth be told. Hank Iver is the one who set Travis and his brother Junior on the path of hunting. He had a superior way with words compared to Travis who spelled almost every word phonetically and often, maybe intentionally, screwed up people's names. Hank, though had some wisdom that came with age and paying attention to things other than girls and trucks.

The letter to the editor called for the arrest of any protesters who refused to allow hunters their legal right to hunt. Ursula was familiar with all of the debated bullet points. They saw it an opportunity not only for sport, but for food and to cull herds that would otherwise starve to death. The part that did take Ursula by surprise by the mention of specific candidates. Hank Iver said that Devora Zhukov would be no good for the district because of her views which seemed to redefine the Second Amendment.

This is typically where Ursula noticed arguments going off onto tangents. Firearms were only part of the hunting practices. There were days for archers and trappers too. It wasn't a pro- or anti-firearm argument. The only time SOAR ever brought up gun technology was to point out that some of it is ridiculous to consider for non-military uses; and certain technology removed all the alleged sport from the hunt anyway. If you couldn't find your target without night vision lenses and laser sights, maybe you shouldn't be hunting three hundred pound animals.

The real kicker was at the end of Hank's letter. "If Devora Zhukov takes the state senate seat for District 24, I will run against her in four years."

No wonder Travis' ego was more inflated than usual. He probably had visions of his father starting a political career late in life. It would bring them more attention and awareness for their pet projects like the Frankhurst hunters. It would make Travis more unbearable than ever if he thought he couldn't be touched by the law.

Ursula felt guilty wishing she had been able to do more for Devora's campaign. She was already stretched too thin doing so much for SOAR and working. Maybe she could use the little time she afforded a relationship with Adriana and reallocate her free time to help Devora in the final few weeks before the election. Something good had to come from a break-up. Helping someone who was fighting to protect the less fortunate (human and otherwise) wasn't such a terrible option.

She couldn't wait to get up those stairs and change her clothes before Peter arrived. She smelled like fryer grease. Plus she wanted to let her hair down as soon as she didn't have to serve customers. She didn't care if it was a mess. Pulling it up looked nice and neat, but when she had a tension headache setting in, massaging her scalp right at the roots and let the curls drop or stand on end naturally was a requirement of daily life.

***

Ursula hurried to get out of the clothes she wore for the morning shift. She pulled on a pair of comfortable yoga pants and a Black Lives Matter long-sleeved shirt. It was the best thing she could think of to wear when watching the debate between Hillary Clinton and Donald Trump. She honestly wanted to watch it alone since she didn't have Adriana to be with her. She had plenty of hours before it began and in that time, there were things to do.

Peter's knock was a welcome way to be startled out of her thoughts. Ursula had a paring knife in her hand and jabbed herself while trying to cut lemon slices for glasses of water to serve. She yelled out that the door was open giving herself time to hold her finger wrapped in a paper towel.

"Hello?" Peter's footsteps barely registered.

"In the kitchen."

"What did you do? Do you need stitches?" His face showed genuine alarm. He looked around and saw the lemon on the counter with two glasses of ice water.

"I'm fine. I run a diner. I have mishaps in the kitchen all the time." Ursula dug through a junk drawer and found a box of bandages and antiseptic ointment. "See, no hospital needed. What's that?"

A small gift wrapped box was in Peter's right hand. Ursula didn't expect them to be gift exchanging friends yet especially considering it wasn't close to Christmas. It wasn't her birthday or any other reason she could think of that would warrant Peter getting her a present.

"Oh, this? Um, it's for you. You can have it when we sit down. If you're inviting me to sit down that is. I don't mean to imply that I can barge in and do whatever I want."

"You're being ridiculous. Of course you may sit down. I'll get the drinks. Do you eat chips? That's about all I have to offer."

Peter took off his jacket in the living room and saw an empty hook on the wall in the hallway he could use. He took a seat on the couch, contented that Ursula decided to sit next to him.

"Okay, tell me what's going on? You look nervous to see me." Ursula curled her legs underneath her and rested an arm across the back of the couch.

"Me? No. Nope. I'm not nervous. Why would I be nervous?" He put the gift box on the coffee table and ran his right palm over his thigh as if it had gotten clammy with sweat.

"I don't know, Peter. I'm the one who's nervous though. Anxious, maybe is a better word. I haven't heard from Devora since she got back from upstate. Do I have to face some kind of punishment or go swear to them personally that I'm sorry and I can be trusted to know about volkolaks?"

"Devora was going to call you and come deliver this," he pointed to the box, "but I volunteered. She's swamped with campaign stuff and Rona is helping her as much as she can. They're both kind of operating like tornadoes right now."

Ursula looked at the box. She raised her eyebrows wide in exaggeration and looked at him then the box then him again.

"Okay, yes, you can open it!"

She leaned over and grabbed it. It was about the size of her palm. The paper was brown craft paper like it was a reused shopping bag. The bow was soft and velvety the color of black cherry soda.

"Before I open this, I just want to say again how sorry I am about breaking your trust and telling Adriana about your secret. I'm hoping she'll forget the whole thing now that we're not together. I haven't heard from her. She said I was having one of those cases of exhaustion like they say about Hollywood starlets who accidentally overdose. I'm fine if she thinks that and leaves all of you alone."

"Even if Adriana or anyone out there tries to reveal the volkolaks, they'll have a pretty hard time being believed. Look at how many times the Loch Ness monster and Bigfoot have been investigated. It might make some people hitch a ride on those waves, but I'm not worried about Adriana."

"I'm worried about you though. I read the comments of all her articles about the bear hunt. I read Travis' social media feeds. There are plenty of reasons for you to be scared right now."

Peter said he appreciated her concern, but he's been through the bear hunt before and managed to stay safe living life by his terms. He wasn't going to let a man like Travis Iver or members of the media create another diaspora.

"I'm serious, Peter. I'm a black woman in a white town full of rednecks with pick-up trucks. I am plugged into the news. I know the realities of what can happen when a pissed off white man from the suburbs has a weapon and an obsession."

"I'm a white man too."

"Only half the time. And don't get coy with me. You might not know what racism feels like, but you know what it's like to be a target."

"Will you open the box now?"

Ursula pursed her lips and shook her head. It was awkward opening a present while lecturing him about staying alive. She took the lid off and saw a gorgeous jewel inside resting on a circular nest of grass. It was a moonstone. It was smaller than the one Rona carried, but in a similar filigree setting like an antique amulet.

"Peter." She didn't know what else to say. There were so many words trying to come out of her mouth, but she sat there staring at its beauty with her jaw hanging open.

"It's for you. From us. The whole family. Devora said the rest of the volkolak elders were more understanding than she expected. They had strong suspicions that in this modern age with surveillance everywhere, we'd be outed soon. So, hopefully, we aren't quite outed yet, but since you've shown great courage at the animal park and you've dedicated yourself to protecting the environment, we wanted you to know that you're part of the inner circle now."

"This is amazing. I don't know what to say. Thank you. I guess, thank you is all I can get out right now!"

"Thank you is enough. And you're welcome."

Ursula remembered that she still had Devora's moonstone in her possession. She put the gift down and hurried to the bedroom. She returned with the stone and handed it to Peter.

"Tell her thanks for letting me hang on to it. I've been meaning to return it. I thought she was avoiding me."

Peter assured Ursula that the only reasons she hasn't seen their family members is because of the campaign. There were non-stop phone calls, emails, interviews, and appearances which they had to set up. It wasn't like anyone was knocking down Devora's door for her opinions on the issues. She had to hustle.

"You've been helping too? Stuffing envelopes and telemarketing?"

"Not as much as Rona. I've been kind of selfish these past few weeks. It's not that I don't like the people in SOAR, I do, but all the loud voices can be overwhelming. I've been spending most of my time outside being away from it all."

Peter's face revealed how deep his melancholy was. His family had spent their lives trying to get things accomplished through human channels and they were still losing their habitat and resources.

Ursula's heart broke for him, for all of the volkolaks. She knew she had a part in their situation as all humans do. Her mistake in believing Adriana could be trusted was simply one more stupid human thing that could lead to the volkolaks' demise.

"If there is anything I can do for Devora's campaign, let me know. My offer still stands for her to hold an event at Applegate's."

"I'll mention it to her. I think we're all a bit stressed about the hunt starting tomorrow. You going to one of the protests?"

"I can get there later. Probably three or four. Over at the Whittingham area checkpoint station. I'm not looking forward to it to be honest."

Ursula had seen enough dead bears hanging from cranes and hoisted into trucks. She and Peter had the unfortunate and gruesome task of choosing which of those photos to use on their promotional materials and protest signs. They had seen the corpses in person and it never made them numb. Gut-wrenching. Heartbreaking. Rage-inducing. Of all the possible emotional sensations in the body, neither of them ever went numb from the public displays of the slaughter.

"I just remembered that this must be especially hard on you, not just because of the bear connection, but because of your father too." Ursula didn't balk at bringing up the family history now that she was welcomed into their circle of trust.

"Yeah. It is. My father was killed in a hunt like this. Up in New York though. It's a bit different there. In some ways, it's a lot safer for us there even though they have more kills. But there were others besides my father. Regular bears that I got to know." His wistful eyes broke from looking at Ursula.

Ursula was astounded by the information that Peter shared. Since joining SOAR, she had learned a fair amount about the bear hunting regulations in New Jersey not New York. Some of her biggest grievances with her state were how they allowed bears to be killed. Targets could be any age including baby cubs or new mothers. And then there was baiting; Ursula couldn't understand how that attributed to the challenges of a "sport". To her, when a target stood right in front of an armed archer to eat berries it didn't take much skill to find the center of their chest to murder them. In New York, it was even illegal to kill a bear if it was in water; or to target one bear out of a group standing together. The standing in water caveat was probably more for the safety of the human than having anything to do with hunting skills.

If people truly needed bear meat for food, Ursula was likely to compromise her ethics. Those compromises were harder to step towards now that she had a deeper connection to the volkolaks.

The story of how Peter's father was murdered broke her heart. His name was Pavlo, but he Anglicized it and used "Paul" instead. The twins called him Pop or Papa. People often made comparisons of children to their parents and the Medvedovich volkolaks were no exception. Everyone said Rona had the adventure and wild side of their father; while Peter had the quieter, artistic nature of their mother, Irena.

It was November of 2000 when Paul traveled across the border to New York State's Orange County. He was supposed to go through Harriman State Park to get to Bear Mountain. On the way, he was shot with a three-oh-eight. The volkolaks have an insider who has access to the more detailed environmental reports than the cumulated statistics found in the public digests online. When Paul didn't return home, Irena called and gave a description. It was their insider who saw the matching information in the harvesting database.

They lived their lives knowing the risks, but ninety percent of the volkolaks chose to spend part of their time in their natural bear form. The ones who remained human were generally folks that had content lives in urban areas. They may be the types to vacation in the mountains and occasionally spend a week letting their bear selves loose.

For the twins it was a different mindset to know that there were certain days that might be their last. Peter described it to Ursula as being a whole family in the military. There were months or years when their parents left, the children went separate ways, and the families were worried while still trying to have their own lives.

"I guess there's nothing I can say to convince you to stay human for the next six days, huh?"

"Sorry. I hope you understand. If you're going to be my friend, you have to accept me for who I really am." He shook his head from side to side, his eyes lowered. His lips rolled in like he wanted to say more but wouldn't allow himself.

"I understand, but I also care a lot about you."

"I appreciate that, Ursula. I think Rona and Devora will be fine. You can always go to them and talk about things."

"I will."

Ursula reached out and put her hand on his arm. Her vision kicked in and she saw her hand move through the shape of where his bear form would be. She needed more time to practice controlling the power so it would feel natural when she looked at the volkolaks.

"And plus, I have some friends out there in the woods that I want to check on."

"More volkolaks?"

"No, I mean regular bears and a couple herds of deer. I love to spend time with them. So the way you are worried about me, I'm worried about them."

Peter agreed to check in with Ursula and his family at regular intervals. They hadn't invented cell phones for bear paws yet so they had to expect long hours with no word from each other. He agreed to meet up with Ursula at the Whittingham Wildlife Management Area for the Monday protest at four o'clock.

Her hand was still on his arm when they stood. She didn't want to let him go out. The hunt was scheduled to begin a half an hour before sunrise. He wrapped his arms around her the best way he could with the mobility limitations in his left forearm and hands. He didn't say a word. He let his energies flow around them. It was that soothing warmth Ursula felt when she looked into Rona's eyes or felt Peter nearby. It was the same feeling that Peter exuded every time he knew Ursula or his sister needed to calm down during the SOAR meetings or while fighting with each other. It was nothing short of a magical drug willingly piping through her nervous system that felt like nothing she had ever known before.

***

It was a different kind of Sunday for Travis Iver and his friends who were getting their bows and arrows ready for the first week of bear hunting. They had three days for archery followed by three days with muzzle loading rifles.

"I cannot wait to take down a beast with this!" Travis showed off the new Remington he bought with his tax refund money. The weapon was considered a feat of firearm engineering. It could fire accurately at three hundred yards with a special type of bullet moving at a velocity of two thousand four hundred feet per second.

Dante, Brandon, Mike, and Bruce eyed the rifle with as much jealousy as little kids seeing a new video game console. They had been hunting together for a few years. Dante and Travis were the only ones who grew up surrounded by it though. They started out when they were thirteen. Their fathers were friends from the local volunteer fire department. The four of them plus Travis' brother, Marlon, used to get decked out from head to toe in camouflage, spray themselves in animal pheromones, and paint their faces like they thought they were Seal Team Six. But they had to abide by the laws and still cover their heads and torsos in safety orange which made their camo efforts even more ridiculous.

"Brah, we got bows for three days and I'm the better shot." Dante's rivalry was tougher for Travis to handle than with his own brother. Dante usually was the best at things. He was a starring running back in high school who dated a cheerleader. He left home for college in West Virginia and returned with a job lined up as a salesman for his father's auto dealership. He was so attractive they put him in the local commercials and on the billboards.

They sat around in Travis' garage drinking beers and sitting on furniture that was as old as they were. The garage bay had been made over into a man cave with essentials like a refrigerator, battered pool table, dart board, widescreen TV, and the crappy stained, ripped furniture. It was heated with a kerosene unit that Travis hoped to replace with a small wood stove at some point when he had the money. His house wasn't much. It was a cottage behind his parents' house on their property, what used to be called a "mother-daughter" set.

The rancid stench of the kerosene mixed with cigarettes, marijuana, gun oil, and years of sweaty dudes permeated the small space. Individually, someone might not mind those smells, but together it was pungent.

"Trav, what's the weird shit going on between you and that hot Hispanic reporter? You banging that 'spic?" Bruce always found the time to run his mouth about the women his friends were seen with, yet he never had any luck in the dating scene. Probably because he was still a closeted gay man filled with self-hatred and denial. He had had sex with only three women and didn't even seem to like them enough to give them the time of day. They were hook-ups he felt he had to perform to try and cure himself and to get other men off his case about never getting laid.

"Dude, she's a lez." When it came to Travis, his bros, and other men like them, meeting a bonafide lesbian was complicated. They wanted to think they were born of a magical bloodline that could suddenly make a woman's sexuality into their own porn-fueled desires. They also loved to mess with women regardless of their sexuality. They thought it was just teasing. Boys being boys. They said they didn't really mean anything by it. Travis and guys like him didn't care that their antics sent otherwise strong, determined women like Adriana Garcia to her car crying, locking all the doors and obsessively checking the mirrors.

"Isn't she dating your ex? The black one?" Mike was the least horrible of the lot. He was the only one in a long term relationship. He even bought an engagement ring and hadn't told any of the guys. He needed more self assurance to know it was the right thing to do. Lacy had started to put the pressure on him after five years of dating. Mike didn't have the confidence Dante had. A part of him worried about being the first one to get hitched. Things would change. Babies would come soon after. He didn't know when to take a step forward or if what he wanted was to stay still and hang out in Travis' garage drinking beer.

"I bet you turned her gay, man," Bruce egged.

Travis took an extra-long chug from his beer while he thought of what to say. "I guess they're dating. Don't know. Don't care. Ursula is batshit crazy if you know what I mean."

"You had it bad for her, man. Admit it," Bruce said.

"You know what they say about girls crazy in the head." Travis grabbed his crotch and shook his head.

Dante was normally polite to Ursula's face when she and Travis were together. He learned the art of schmoozing from his salesman father. "I never understood how you ended up dating Ursula if she hates guns so much."

"She's hot. Ya know, in her way. A great ass. And it's not just guns. She hates all hunting. She's a complete whackjob. She'd rather talk about saving some frog from extinction if it lives where there's oil under the ground that could heat people's homes."

"I'm outta here. Meet you losers at oh-six-thirty." Brandon had to take vacation days and rearrange his schedule for the two part-time jobs he had working in retail and as a bartender for a chain family restaurant. He didn't have much of a personal life because he had originally moved to New Jersey for a great IT job for a coal engineering corporation but was laid off. His family was in Pennsylvania, three hours away.

Brandon always got at least one deer a year. The meat lasted a long time cooking for one. Last year, he even donated half of it to a food bank program set up by hunters. He had never eaten bear before and this was the first time he would hunt for one. He didn't feel the same way about it as Travis and the others. He wasn't after the trophies.

While Brandon gathered his coat and fished for his keys, Travis thought about Ursula. He made sure she caught sight of him at the protest for Peter Medvedovich. That was when Adriana interviewed him. Ursula was always there for the protests — on the other side, with her liberal bleeding heart trying to save the animals who would otherwise starve because their resources had been depleted.

Travis remembered how he used to tease her about becoming vegetarian. She didn't know what she was missing. But she made them enemies, as far as he was concerned. And that friend of hers, the crippled guy, Peter, with the hipster beard — he was on Travis' list for sure. There was no way Travis would let self-righteous activists stop him from getting what he wanted. He wanted victory. He wanted the adrenaline rush. He wanted to fire off arrows and bullets and feel the cold air on his face. He wanted a trophy — the biggest one of their club, a state record would be even better. He was all set to do anything to get what he wanted and then throw it in their faces. Show them that there's a reason man is at the top of the food chain.

The boys broke up their little party at a reasonable time in order to try to get some sleep. They planned to spend a few long days in tree stands and walking through thick brush.

CHAPTER TWENTY

It was dark outside when Ursula gave up trying to sleep until her alarm. She looked out the window and felt the anxiety swell in the pit of her stomach. The hunt would begin in about ninety minutes. SOAR failed in stopping it. The best they could do was continue their plan to protest and spread awareness about wildlife safety and conservation. Once the first six days were over, SOAR could go back to pushing the state legislature to cancel the second segment which was on the books to take place in December. It was the second year since reinstating the bear hunt that the season was expanded to two six-day segments and SOAR blamed it on the gun lobby which had more sway over politicians than experts in wildlife population did.

Ursula told herself to keep going along with the plans. Keep chugging through the motions. One foot in front of the other. Adriana might be out there at the protests looking for evidence whether volkolaks were real. The rest of SOAR couldn't know — no one could. Ursula had to fake everything about why she was really so overly anxious.

Her shift at the diner went by in a blur of pancakes and eggs. She couldn't wait to get out of there. At least Rona had the good heart to text her at eleven o'clock that everyone was fine.

"Boss, your head is not in the game today. You really that upset about hunting season?" Manny knew Ursula better than most people, probably even better than Adriana. The thing about Manny was that he could know you with few words spoken. Day after day, he saw Ursula and absorbed all the information she sent out through her movements. She had her confident gait, her welcoming smiles for the customers, and her furrowed brow when Travis Iver was around.

"To be honest, I'm not okay. This year is different. It feels personal."

"I've never heard you say that you're not okay before. It's good. You're human. It's okay to have those feelings once in a while, ya know?"

"You're right. I'll be better once I see my friends later. I hope I see them anyway."

Manny couldn't possibly know what she meant in proper context. He assumed reasons for her not seeing people she cared about would be mundane reasons: working late, stuck in traffic, flaked out. Manny knew about violence, but the thoughts of accidentally being killed by a hunter with a bow and arrow was not the sort of thing he'd imagine. He did however know the fear of the government and immigration raids. If the election didn't end well, and a candidate who promised to deport hundreds of thousands of people won, then he and his family could be in serious jeopardy. He was so grateful to Ursula that he didn't talk about those fears. He never wanted to upset her.

Ursula sent another text to Rona who was practically glued to her desk at home. There were phone calls for her aunt's campaign to make every single day. She had her own share of social media activism that was important to her. Meanwhile, the chapters she was supposed to be reading sat untouched.

"Still home. I don't want to be here!"

"Helping your aunt is critical." Ursula knew something like a singular hunting regulation was not the sort of platform that would get a person elected to state senate. Devora's campaign was diverse and that meant Rona and all of the volunteers had to be well-versed in the proper way to share Devora's opinions on healthcare, casino developments, education reform, and a hundred other hot topics that bombarded the state.

Devora's campaign strategy was to make appearances at each different checkpoint station throughout the week when she wasn't speaking elsewhere. Rona wanted to be there with her. The number of bears killed had nearly doubled from 2014 to 2015 when the additional week was allotted. Devora wasn't running for office back then and their grassroots efforts couldn't stop that additional wave of slaughter. The changes had to come from the top. It may have been the primary reason she threw her name into the hat, but all of the issues had significance.

Devora was one of the few candidates who started out with wanting to make the world better and safer. She knew that real estate development was linked to environmental upsets which were also directly linked to tax breaks and lenient regulations of Big Pharma and Big Oil (two of New Jersey's major industries). As the rural areas were lost, that meant social-economic turmoil for the lower class. Even moderate families had more expenses than they had fifty years ago. All of it was connected. Standing up against the bear hunt was a subtle visual aid for constituents who didn't know the real risks for Devora's family and friends.

There was enough money in the SOAR war chest to offset some of the bail that would inevitably be needed when members got arrested for civil disobedience. They were used to it. Those funds were specifically raised for that purpose so there was no confusion that donations for other costs like the website hosting, mailings, and other administrative expenses were being used for legal trouble. The legal fund also paid a non-profit lawyer who was willing to help them out for a fraction of his usual fee.

Big game hunting is considered a rich white person's domain normally because the permits for exotic animals are expensive, not to mention the travel costs. However, local big game hunting is dirt cheap and written off as population control. The black bear permit only costs two dollars and the firearm and archery licenses are around thirty bucks. Of all the permits regulated, black bears were the cheapest ones. The expensive part was the weaponry and none of that went into conservation efforts. That was flat out retail sales.

The state police had a designated zone cordoned off for the protesters. Juan Rivera and Gabriella Goldberg were the first to break the rule. Each of them tried blocking different pick-up trucks and were promptly arrested and it wasn't even noon. Adriana wasn't the only reporter there. Since it was hunting week, the other regional papers would be willing to buy some of the coverage from stringers.

Hunters couldn't have asked for a better day. The weather was sunny with a few puffy clouds. The temperatures were mild. Travis, Dante, and the rest of their boys had their bows ready. Bruce and Mike were tree stand hunters. The rest were stand and stalk types. Brandon was still more interested in getting a medium-sized whitetail buck, but hadn't spoken up much around the guys.

Autumn's arrival was pushed back by more heatwaves and reports about the ice caps melting. There was no frost that October morning. The ground was wet under Travis' boots. His weight caused sinking footprints. He felt the adrenaline and the stress in his muscles as he tried to walk quickly but silently at the same time. A twig snapped under him. He stopped and held his breath. He used his eyes to look around for other movement before breathing and turning his head from side to side.

The squirrels were startled. They ran from an oak to a black walnut tree. Between their noisy rustling of the branches and their screeching chatter to warn every critter around, it sounded like monsters overhead. Travis remembered when he was kid learning the ropes. Every single noise made him tense up. What he had to learn was that it was the tiny critters that made the most noise while big game like the deer and bears were so graceful that you had to listen for the silence and watch for movement instead. Two hundred pounds of animal could have stepped on that twig and it wouldn't have broken, but his lumbering human body wasn't so lithe.

Most years, Travis was able to get a respectable kill on the first day. It was the most popular day and with so many hunters out there, the animals were spooked and on the go.

There was another advantage to focusing on the bears instead of the doe. None of the guys had to cover themselves in synthetic deer urine as a lure. It always took a while to get used to the smell. The bonafide urine lure wasn't illegal, but was discouraged because the prions in it stayed viable for years. Whether the urine got into the soil or on foliage, it could continue spreading Chronic Wasting Disease which was one of the worst conditions an animal could get. It was the "mad cow disease" of the deer family. However, no one knew if Chronic Wasting Disease could be transmitted to humans the same way as mad cow disease. The earth stayed infected and if a deer or elk caught it, they were in for a long, suffering, decaying death. The guys decided not to take that risk and switched to synthetic urine when they were after deer.

All of them had deer permits anyway in case a prime opportunity presented itself. The rivalry between Dante and Travis pressured them into focusing on the black bears. As for Travis, he had his sights set on a particular one.

"You know people are going to hate you if you kill Walker?" Dante tried to warn him before they split up.

"You think I have to worry about some vegan coming after me? Bro, get real. They're all talk. And there's nothing illegal about killing that bear."

"I still don't think you should've trashed your ex's place. That was low, man."

"I think it was gentlemanly of me to give her a warning before I kill one of her pet projects." Travis checked his archery gear and let his eyes linger on the carbon steel broad head tip the way other people admire art.

Mike didn't agree with Travis' reasons for targeting Walker, but he didn't disagree with the action. "The bear has broken hands. It's got to be a lot harder for it to survive anyway. You'd be doing the humane thing."

Travis appreciated the validation of his fantasy kill. Not to mention, Walker was a big ass bear estimated around three hundred pounds if not more. Taking him down would be the same kind of accolade as his largest kills any other year.

"Why aren't any of you interested in taking him down?"

Dante sported a shitass grin. "Because killing a disabled beast isn't a big enough challenge for me, bro. It's like going after an old lady with a cane."

Alone in the woods, Travis continued to hear the heckling from Dante in his head. None of them had problems killing the cubs and yearlings, but they had the nerve to mock him for wanting to target a disabled bear? Who the hell did they think they were?

Travis lost focus arguing with the voices in his head. Had to keep his mind clear. He felt himself come back to the present and to the environment. A chickadee landed in a bush. The leaves rustled. A crow cawed from somewhere up high in the canopy. Squirrels were all around like their world was ending, but that's how they always seemed to act when Travis was in the woods.

The smell of dirt and moss were strong, almost like they were trying to mask other scents around. Mother Nature was at work as she tried to protect herself. Travis preferred those familiar scents of the northern hunting grounds. Down in south Jersey, the Pine Barrens were close enough to the shore that he could detect the salt water on the breeze. And each time he put a foot down, he wanted to feel solid ground or a rock not sand. Travis liked a challenge, not as much as Dante though he would never admit it. He preferred to feel sure of himself with confidence in his surroundings.

The glorious serenity of the forest enraptured him for hours. The sun's movement told him how long it had been. His cell phone was on silent in the cargo pocket on his thigh. The club members always sent out messages when they got something. Some folks even paired up, but Travis and his boys liked to embrace the solitude.

He needed a break. His shoulders were starting to hurt from the constant tension. He felt for the phone and saw there were already a slew of messages. It was eleven-twenty and a lot of people already took their shots and were rewarded with kills. The photos sent around showed guys posing with deer carcasses and bears of different sizes. Carl Kowalski, a guy Travis knew well enough but not part of his inner circle, smiled for the camera while he cradled the head of a cub not more than seven months old. A kill is kill. Carl might have saved the little thing from being squashed on the highway.

While Travis was trying to read the messages, more kept popping into the conversation. It was a good day for the club. Brandon got a doe that looked larger than average, probably one-twenty if Travis to guess by the photo.

Bruce and Mike shot down black bears. The one Mike showed off was a photo taken at the weigh-in. Eyes opened. Blood smeared over its nostrils. Paws wrapped with chains to hoist it. Bruce's photo was a selfie of him holding up the head of young adult bear the way someone might have an arm around a drunk friend at a party.

The guys with kills could go back out for whichever animal in the combo deer-bear hunt they didn't get. But there was a fair amount to do once something was killed. It had to be registered, weighed, and dressed before butchering and taxidermy. There were five more days. The only reason to rush was if they had only taken the first day off of work.

***

The aromas of the dirt and moss enthralled Peter too. It was his home. He loved that he knew every tree by its features watching them grow taller and sprout new branches. He raises his nose in the air and soaked in all the information. He knew humans were all around within miles. Humans armed with bows and arrows and muzzleloaders were traipsing through the acres that were his sanctuary.

Before he left the cottage at Devora's property, he sent a message to Rona, Devora, and Ursula that he was about to go out. They knew what that meant. Peter took off his clothes, left his phone on the table, and walked out the door. His body cracked, tore, and popped into his bear form. He promised them he'd be back by three to return to being Peter and then meet Ursula at the protest at four.

A few miles away from where his human self lived, he walked upright on his back legs through the wildlife preserve. Funny how it was considered a preserve yet allowed the wildlife to be slaughtered.

Peter rubbed his cheek against an elm tree leaving his scent there, but also for the love of it. He knew that tree the way he knew all of them. He wanted them protected too. The elms were some of his favorite trees. They were capable of growing into uniquely magical shapes with enormous branches in all directions. The oldest ones radiated centuries of stories. Every bird that landed on them. Every person that hiked by. Every squirrel that ran from the tip of one branch to the tip of another. Peter stood there looking up this old friend to admire the way it managed to survive humans invading its home.

All the whitetails knew what was happening. They were trying their best to run to safer land. It was daytime. They were normally ambling slowly while grazing or resting. The birds and rabbits were scared too even if they weren't the targets that day. Muzzleloaders boomed through the serene oasis. At least the noise helped to know where some of the humans were unlike the silence of archery.

A doe was nearby. Peter could smell her of course, but she also let herself be known. She made a huffing sort of half-bark to scare anyone away from her babies. There were fawns two with her. Their spots barely noticeable anymore. Their eyes dark and filled with innocence. This expansive world was still new to them. The mother and Peter exchanged glances as he walked by them with an understanding that he wasn't something to fear.

One thing humans did make better was giving Peter an easier place to walk. It was dangerous, but he could move on the trails more quickly than navigating over piles of boulders glaciers had dumped. He was so used to being around humans and being spotted by them, but the weeks of the hunt he felt inadequately able to protect the place and creatures he loved. These weren't people gawking and stumbling to get their cameras out. There were two thousand bear permits issued throughout the state. The odds were not in any bear's favor of surviving.

Beauty was near. Peter sensed it. Not that the entire wilderness wasn't beautiful, this was specifically a scent he loved to consume. It was Darla, a female bear he cared for deeply.

Peter lost his opportunities to mate with her each time because of healthier, stronger males. He had to remember he was a volkolak and their mating was different. They had a reasonably strict code to only mate with other volkolaks, but it wasn't always followed. If he had ever mated with a bear like Darla, they wouldn't be volkolaks. They would be genuine bears. Volkolaks could mate with humans and birth new volkolaks, but that wasn't a guarantee.

She wasn't actually named Darla. That's just what Peter called her. Bears had unique identities but it was all explained somatically. In his human form, he called her Darla to tell Rona about her.

Darla was gentle towards him and didn't want anything from him. She shared her food with him. He saw her litters of cubs growing up. He remembered how fond he was of those two little girls. They used to get so excited to see him visit. They'd roll around playing just like human kids that loved to expend their energy. They didn't make it. They were killed in the 2014 hunt.

Darla was blessed with three more in 2015. Two boys and a girl. Peter was as protective of them as he was allowed to be.

Human women hadn't impressed him; that is, until Ursula came along. All the others that showed him romantic interest were more into the idea of him. They wanted to take care of him because of his hands. He could tell he was a prop to those women. "Hey, look at what a good person I am for dating a disabled guy." Of course, they wouldn't admit that. They wanted to be needed by someone and thought he'd slide into that role. It's not what Peter wanted.

Something inside his soul told him that he wasn't going to have the cute fairy tale relationship with anyone. Still, when he saw Darla and her kids coming, he couldn't think of anything else. He had no idea how any commitment could work unless it was with another volkolak who had the same needs for duality that he had. He wanted life in both worlds. With

Ursula's acceptance by the volkolak elders, she had gotten closer to his worlds than any other woman.

Little did Peter know that as Ursula said goodbye to her failing relationship with Adriana, that she was opening herself up to him. Ursula knew the reality of the situation. She didn't want to move too fast after a break up. Peter and Rona already felt like family of choice to her. Secretly, she felt a fear so deep that it pained her heart. The fear of them only being in her life for a short while and then leaving. She loved their companionship, even Rona's willingness to break the law and take every risk when life called for it.

"My brother asked me to keep an eye on you during these protests. To look after you and keep you out of trouble. I guess he expects me to get you arrested or hurt." Rona told Ursula when they finally met up at the Whittingham Wildlife Management Area.

"Funny, he asked me to keep an eye on you." Ursula gave Rona a playfully bop on the arm.

"So who's gonna look out for him?" Rona said more to her subconscious than to Ursula. "My aunt is over there talking to a reporter."

Ursula turned to see where Rona was looking. Devora was being interviewed but not by Adriana. There was no sign of Adriana in Whittingham's designated protest area. Ursula took out her phone to scroll through the Boffo feeds. She saw that Adriana was posting from there. She went to look around, but a cop told her if she walked out of the designated spot for protesters, she'd be arrested for civil disobedience. She tried arguing and explained that she had a friend who wasn't a protester that she wanted to say hello to, but the cop didn't buy it. He warned her again to stay put.

"I think Adriana is over where they weigh the corpses," Ursula told Rona.

"You mad at her about this whole break up? I thought it was your idea?"

"No. I mean, yes, it was my idea, but no, I'm not mad at her. Not exactly. I just want to know if she's seen Travis and his stupid friends."

Rona suggested texting Adriana, but Ursula felt that was even more awkward. Plus, if they were talking in person in front of people, there wouldn't be any fighting while Adriana was there for professional reasons.

Instead Ursula looked up Travis' Boffo feed. He hadn't made any posts since six in the morning. It was a group selfie of his band of hunting brothers. They looked like a militia. Ursula was disgusted and the feeling of defeat crept through her.

"Rona? How would you feel about not listening to Peter and perhaps taking off with me to one of the hiking entrances?"

Rona's eyes widened. It was a wild idea. A dangerous one. An exciting one. She was all in.

They left the way that protesters were allowed and drove in Ursula's car. They headed south on Wolf's Corner Road then circled around to the other side of the two thousand acre preserve.

They parked in a shady spot and Rona got out first. She looked all around with a specific purpose: to see if there were cameras. If anything were to happen which would draw police interest, she didn't want Ursula's car to be identified. She waved for Ursula to get out of the car and told her the coast was clear.

"Will you transform? Do you think it's too dangerous?" Ursula saw the familiar look in Rona's eyes that matched how she looked in Musky Park when Peter had been captured.

"I'll do whatever I have to. My brother is stubborn. He knows it's dangerous and he still went out there."

"He told me he had to check on some friends. Do you know them too?"

"I think I know who he's talking about, but he spends way more time out here than I do. That's not necessarily my choice, mind you. I'm just so damn busy with school and everything."

It was the first time Ursula was going to put her ursine vision to the test. She knew she'd be able to spot Peter in an instant because of his unique bipedal walking. Rona would be seen differently too. And it was the first opportunity to see other volkolaks in the wild.

"So is there like — some kind of signal I can do to show bears or volkolaks that I'm not going to hurt them?"

"We're testing out your abilities here, so maybe you'll get lucky and just talking to them will be understood. I wish I knew, but that ritual wasn't exactly well documented." At least Rona was honest. She didn't get Ursula's hopes up.

There were only a few other cars in the parking lot. Most people used the main entrance where the protests were taking place. The women headed through the entryway to the northwest trail where there was a bulletin board showing maps and fliers with important safety information.

Rona carried her backpack as she usually did for venturing out. It was mostly empty except for her phone, wallet, a health food snack bar, a roll of duct tape, and her multi-purpose tool that folded up. She mostly needed it as a place to stash her clothes if she went into bear form.

Ursula didn't want to be weighed down by a lot. She wore a flannel shirt over her Save New Jersey Bears t-shirt. A small purse fit diagonally across her body to hold her phone and essentials. She would have to take the backpack so it wouldn't be left behind in a park full of people. She kept her dense curls off her face with a bright pink headband. She never invested in hiking boots before. She was out there with sneakers on her feet and realized that with her new volkolak friends in her life, she should get around to upgrading her footwear.

There weren't many other hikers which didn't surprise them since it was a Monday, but it was a perfect day for being out in nature. The sun was going down and sparkled through the tops of the trees. The air was around sixty degrees, comfortable for Rona, but Ursula preferred the heat. Unfortunately, they weren't there to enjoy it. They had to check on Peter since he hadn't shown up to the protest at four like he promised.

"Would Peter ever miss an appointment to meet you?" Ursula tried to think back on Peter's exact words the night before. He never specifically promised to be there, but he did agree to it.

"Yeah, it wouldn't be all that unusual for him to disappear and lose track of time. When he gets out in the wild, he's different. Ya know what I mean? You should probably accept that part of him if you're going to stick around with us."

The hunting hours were set to end a half an hour after sunset. Ursula made sure to check all the regulations again to post facts on the SOAR feeds. Sunset would be around six-twenty. Peter was an hour late checking in with them at four which left ninety minutes to go in the first day's hunt.

CHAPTER TWENTY-ONE

Feelings of failure inched through Travis' bloodstream making his heart pick up pace. He had days to get the perfect kill shot, but there was something even more celebratory bagging one on the first day. He didn't want to be left out either knowing his friends took home trophies. By the end of the hunt, a target would be harder to come by. He had the deer license too. He could have taken a shot at a doe to end his day. It wasn't what he truly wanted. He wanted to see the dark eyes of Walker and put him down. He wanted Ursula to feel the pain. It wasn't out of anguished love and heartbreak. It was all about revenge. Power. A way to hurt her without hurting her directly. To show her who was boss.

Travis had walked miles throughout the day. He didn't want to get cozy in a tree stand and feel limited. His hunting wasn't about good luck as the right species of the right size happened to cross his path. He went in search of it. He believed in making opportunities happen for himself.

He took a step out of the brush and planted his feet onto a trail. The dirt was smooth from all the hiking traffic that made it worn and easily visible. Travis knelt down and saw the hoof tracks heading northwest. If the deer headed that way, the bears probably did too. He took out the compass his father gave to him when he was a kid. It was an old Army-issued one in an olive green metal housing. He stuck it back in his pocket and followed the tracks. They led him back off the ease of the trail and into the thicket of prickly bushes covered in razor hairs and thorns. His clothes got caught, but he tore his way through without any of the grace the animals had. So much for silence.

The sun changed from its bright golden yellow to a darker orange. Travis was losing time. His thoughts took him back to 2003 when he shot a doe with twenty-gauge shotgun. It wasn't a good shot. Hunters were supposed to only go for it if they had a clear sight to the target's center mass chest cavity. The doe took off and led him on a chase until she couldn't stand anymore, some three-quarters of a mile away. He had to deliver a better shot once he found her. That wasn't the only time, but he had an outstanding record since taking up the compound bow. He grew more selective with which shots were worth taking.

Voices jarred him out of his memory and back to the real world. Had to be hikers. Hunters knew to shut their mouths. The voices were coming from deep into the woods though, off trail where they shouldn't have been.

Rona and Ursula continued to head east into the park. Ursula stuck her hand inside her jeans pocket to feel for the moonstone Peter had given her from his family. She was so afraid of losing it, she checked for it every five minutes. When this was all over, she promised herself she would take it to a jeweler to be fitted as a necklace charm.

"I can tell he's not too far away, but I don't want to call out to him in case a hunter is looking for movement. Someone else is nearby too. Stay alert." Rona read the scents on the air and pointed in the direction they should continue.

First, she needed an isolated spot to morph out of her human body. There was a small red maple tree surrounded by blackberry bushes and covered in an unkempt nest of grapevines. She told Ursula she'd be right back and crawled under the branches into the botanical cave. As soon as she filled her backpack with her clothes and shoes, she threw it out of the hiding spot. Ursula picked it up. She could hear the transformation Rona put herself through. That snapping of bones. The tearing of skin. Rona couldn't help but let out some moaning noises going through the process.

Ursula heard a footstep nearby. She wasn't sure though. The squirrels made a lot of noises. The birds made their share too as they flitted through small bushes looking for insects. But if it was a footstep, a human one, and Rona's sounds were heard, they could be in trouble.

Rona's bear body exited the shrubbery. She saw that Ursula had her backpack and led the way following Peter's scent. They didn't have far to go. They kept to a side of the hill where the landscape was in shadows. They had to stay safe another hour. Then they could breathe easier.

Ursula's foot slipped and she fell to her hands and knees. She yelled out of reflex when one of her knees landed on a rock and cut open her jeans. The abrasion bled a little, but not enough to stop her.

"Just a scrape. Keep going. I'm right behind you," she said to her bear hiking guide.

Something behind her caught Ursula's periphery vision. She held onto a thin tree trunk and tried to test out her powers. No radiant auras or holographic bodies were in sight. She couldn't shake the feeling of being watched though.

On the other side of the hill, they saw one of the ponds that offered the park wildlife a place to bathe and drink. It provided the right habitat for some of the state's threatened and endangered bird species like the long-eared owl and pied-billed grebe. The deep rich aroma of the eastern red cedar trees normally would have brought a sense of soothing comfort. Not then. Not when so many lives were in danger.

Ursula watched as Rona picked up her pace. She found Peter, Darla, and the cubs. He walked on his two back legs to Rona and they rubbed their cheeks on each other. Ursula had never seen a more perfect sight. Rona and Peter's forms had multi-colored waves around them. Not too bright, not glowing. It was more like the heat waves coming off hot asphalt on a summer day. But the colors were transcendent and she didn't want to take her eyes off them.

The little ones and Darla greeted Rona like it was a family reunion. Peter stood back up to his more comfortable posture and looked at Ursula a good distance away. He could smell her presence and knew exactly where she was. She swore his head nodded to say hello, but she wasn't too sure of anything except how she felt about him. It was surreal seeing them like that again particularly because it was a moment of happiness. She walked closer and felt assured that she was safe. Darla backed away from her and tried to wrangle her cubs, but they were having too much fun.

"I'm Ursula. You must be Darla?"

It was worth a shot to see if the ritual made her everyday English understood by the authentic bears. There seemed to be some recognition from them, but Darla was not ready to be friends yet. She raised her chin and circled it around. The babies were too curious though. They got closer to Ursula against their mother's wishes. Peter had told Ursula that he called them Big Guy, Queenie, and Jester. She could see why. The smallest was more reserved and stayed closer to mom, probably the female he called Queenie. Another seemed to be coaxed into wrestling by the third. That fuzzy goofball had to be Jester which meant Big Guy was the tolerant brother willing to roughhouse.

They were still wild animals, but Ursula wanted to go over and hug them and join the wrestling match. It looked like so much fun. That freedom. That spirit. That pure innocent joy.

Rona's attention was pulled towards something in the woods. They had to get out of the open area near the pond and take cover. Darla was already in action trying to command the cubs to safety. Jester ran over to Peter instead. Ursula spun in circles looking for whoever was out there.

Hidden by the foliage, Travis Iver slowed his breath. He couldn't believe what he was seeing. Ursula Applegate frolicking in the woods with Walker and a whole family of bears. How was she able to do it? He couldn't think about that now. She was the best bait he ever had and that was all the mattered. It made the revenge that much sweeter.

Peter roared trying to get Jester to follow his mother. Rona went over to them and picked up the cub in her jaws. She wasn't a mother, but the instinct was there. He was heavier than she expected, but got him off the ground and his struggling stopped. Peter leaned down to nudge the cub with his snout letting him know it would be okay. Queenie and Big Guy cried for their mother realizing she wasn't in sight.

"They're over there." Ursula pointed for Peter to get the other two passed the treeline.

Ursula was too close to Walker. If Travis took the shot, he'd maim or hill a human, not that the fine was that bothersome anyway. First offense was only up five hundred to two thousand dollars. He didn't want to answer for it publicly even if the monetary payout was minimal. Ursula was clearly attached to all of them and in his way.

A cub wasn't sure whether to run towards the woods for its mother or to go to the bipedal bear for protection. The other female had a cub in her mouth and she just made it back to the woods.

"Take the best shot. Don't miss." Travis whispered to himself as he stood tall out of the foliage. His bow drawn back and ready. He watched as Walker ran as fast as he could on those hind legs towards the little cub.

"No!" Ursula screamed so loud she shocked herself. She saw the arrow pierce through Peter's torso as he blocked Big Guy from the shot.

Rona heard the scream and turned around. She dropped Jester who thankfully ran to his mother. Big Guy was confused but at least ran away from the shrieking human.

Travis came out from his hiding place to claim his kill. Rubbing it in Ursula's face in person was beyond his wildest dreams. He was covered in his camo except for the required safety orange turning him into a bizarre tropical land fish. He didn't relax his bow and had another arrow ready in case Walker wasn't dead. By the time Travis was a few feet from the body being cradled in Ursula's arms, he was smacked with tunnel vision.

The impact of Rona's behemoth body knocked the air out of Travis' lungs when his back hit the ground. The bow dislodged from his grip. The arrow fell next to him. Two enormous paws crushed down on his chest. The fur pulled back from the teeth of the beast about to take his life. Travis heard Ursula scream out, "No!" If she could command these animals somehow, he was praying it worked. The snarls and low growls came through the mouth only an inch from his face.

What Ursula actually said was, "Ro!" She looked down at Peter as his final breath escaped. His heart stopped. Uncontrollable tears gushed from her eyes. She gently put Peter's head down on the ground before walking over to Travis trapped underneath the weight of a bear. Ursula made it there in time as Rona was swinging a paw back and ready to clobber Travis' brains to mush.

"Stop! Don't do it!" The bear waited to hear what else Ursula had to say. "If you hurt him you'll only give them what they want. They want to keep these laws allowing them to turn you into trophies because they can paint this exact picture. How wild you are. How dangerous you are to people. Don't play into their hands."

The bear lowered its face back down. Travis could feel its mouth on his neck. Its snout and fur touched his skin. It roared right in his face while pushing down harder on his chest. He was dizzy. Close to fainting. Multiple ribs on the verge of snapping. But then the beast backed off. Travis didn't get up right away. He tried to get some oxygen into his body and coughed. He curled his legs in and rolled to one side trying to sputter out words.

"How?"

Ursula knelt down, saw that he was able to breathe, and walked back to Peter. Rona was there at his side lying next to him. Animals can cry. The agony Ursula felt was nothing compared to what Rona was going through at the loss of her twin brother. Ursula whispered to her that she could go into the woods and transform into her human body.

"I'll call out your name like I'm looking for you. It should be a decent cover to fool Travis."

The bear didn't want to leave her kin though. Not yet. She laid her head down on top of him.

Travis rolled over and got to his knees. He supported himself on one and planted the front foot on the ground. He had his arrow focused on Rona.

"Ursula! You better move!"

"Travis! Don't you dare! You already killed one! Stop it!"

"No! I'm sure when I show the rangers all this bruising, self defense will be justified. Now move!"

"No!"

Ursula covered as much of Rona as she could with her own body, spreading her arms out wide.

"Look at what you've done, Travis. Just look at him! You murdered a gentle animal that never bothered a single human being. And why? Just because this is fun for you?"

He lowered his aim a little so he wouldn't accidentally shoot Ursula. His mind was already plotting out a story in case he did: the bear that attacked him went after his ex-girlfriend next and he tried to save her life but she got caught in the line of fire.

"I'd be doing the world a favor if you'd just move. That bear is clearly willing to kill people."

"That's not for you to decide! Put the arrow down. Now!"

Rona and Devora wouldn't get to give a proper memorial for Peter now. He died in bear form that meant he would be treated as Travis' trophy. He would get the body. He had to clear Ursula and the vicious bear out of the way so he could properly dress it. But first, he wanted pictures.

"Do you have any idea what's going to happen to you when people find out that you killed the bear they loved?"

"What? A bunch of vegans are doing to threaten me? Thought y'all cared about 'all' life? Now move." Travis was closer. He could kill Rona at point-blank range which wasn't optimal for archery.

"Travis, if you do one decent thing in your life let it be this. Let her go and I'll get out of your way. You got your damn trophy. Just let her go. That's more than fair." Ursula reached her arm around and petted Rona's head still on top of Peter's body.

"How are you doing this anyway? How are you getting them to listen to you?"

She should have expected this was a possibility. Time to think fast. "These were trained bears. Rescued from a circus and set free. I heard about it and I've been trying to find them ever since I heard the rumor." Ridiculous, but Travis wasn't exactly a rocket scientist.

"A'ight. Doesn't mean she's not dangerous. The DEP loves to have nuisance animals put down."

Ursula watched his body language. His arrow was pointed to the ground. He was about to disengage it completely and then they'd be safe. She kept trying to reason with him. He was smart about certain things, like the local political sphere; but still, he wasn't as tuned into the bears as Ursula was. Not after she gained her abilities.

"Look at this way. You have the rest of the week to try to prove that this one bear is a nuisance and a danger. You and I both know it's illegal for you to shoot a second bear this week. You'd lose your hunting license. You'd have to pay a huge fine. You might even lose all your weapons. Let me see if I can guide her away from here. Okay? Is that a deal? Can I try?" She exaggerated on purpose.

He didn't like it, but the thought of never hunting again or even owning his guns and bows was out of the question.

"Fine! Get her out of here."

Ursula could not believe she convinced him to let her and Rona go. She bent down and whispered into Rona's ear, pleading for her to walk away from her twin brother.

Rona got on all fours and stared at Travis. He started to raise his arrow again, but Ursula yelled out a reminder that he promised to let them leave. He took steps forward which forced them to back up. Rona wouldn't do what Ursula wanted. She wouldn't flee into the woods. She couldn't look away. She stood there at the treeline and watched as Travis nervously took pictures of the body and then of her. He would plaster her photo all over the internet with a call out for fellow hunters to target her, another black bear with a small pale patch on the chest. Rona knew he would do it and it didn't matter anymore. Peter was gone. Her father was killed. Her mother was stolen from them. Devora lived most of her life as a human. The rage and sadness turned to despair as Rona's mind wondered how she could go on living. She was tempted to charge Travis and force him to kill her too.

Ursula couldn't watch Travis gut her friend. He had texted his location to Dante and the guys so one of them could come out with an ATV and pick up the body and give him a ride back. The sun was down. Day one of the hunt would be officially over in thirty minutes. Ursula quietly begged Rona to move into the woods.

"I have your clothes. You can go change and we'll say I texted you to meet me if he questions it." Ursula waited for Rona to show any sign of listening.

***

As soon as Rona heard the motor of the ATV, she turned and shuffled into the trees. Ursula followed and finally heard the noises a few minutes later. The bear root ritual hadn't given Ursula volkolak-level hearing, but it was enhanced compared to before. The ATV crunched along the nearest trail which opened to the pond at the far end. The driver parked it there and walked to Travis and the carcass.

Ursula stopped to watch through the trees, her back to Rona. She saw that the driver was Dante. He patted Travis on the back for a good job with the kill. They bent down to finish cleaning the guts out of the carcass that used to be Peter Medvedovich or Walker depending on how well someone knew him. Ursula lifted the front of her shirt and wiped off her face. She kept watching as they took pictures of her fallen friend.

"Can I have my clothes?" Rona stood naked behind Ursula. She didn't care if she was out of a hiding place where anyone could see her body. That didn't matter before and certainly didn't matter now.

"Sorry." Ursula took the backpack off and handed it to Rona. She wanted to say a lot more than sorry, but she wasn't ready. Ursula had lost a lot of family, but couldn't imagine how losing a twin must feel. Her inner voice reprimanded herself for not doing better. For not saving Peter. For not letting Rona tear Travis to shredded meat. For not finding the right words.

"Look at them. And they call us savage animals." Rona slid her shoes on and finished buttoning her pants.

"Do you want me to call Devora for you?"

"No. Let's just go back. I'd rather tell her in person."

The walk back to the parking lot was in silence. They didn't stick around to watch Travis and Dante drag Peter's body along the pond's edge to the ATV. The women had seen enough to sicken them for a lifetime.

They weren't even sure how to break the news about Walker's death to the animal activists. Ursula considered not saying anything at all since it would be discovered when Travis brought the bear in for weighing.

Then there was Peter's absence. That would be noticed. His family needed to come up with a believable lie. Ursula thought back on what they had told her. If someone died they came up with explanations for the missing person: moved far away, died but the body was never found, and a few have used the humorous "gone into witness protection" excuse. Peter was in his prime, enjoying his life and his work. He stayed in the town where he was raised so moving out of the country wouldn't necessarily sound like a plausible reason. To say a body was never found in a death when the person was connected to a public figure like Devora Zhukov would draw even more suspicion.

One more turn and Ursula would have the car back on the road to the main entrance. She held herself together. She surprised herself how she managed to do that. She had to hold space for Rona and allow her to emotionally release whatever she needed to in the car. Ursula reached over and rubbed her friend's shoulder and back as best as she could while driving.

"Hey. Let me text Devora to meet us in the parking lot. You shouldn't be seen like this yet. No one except Travis knows that we know about what happened. We have to wait for Travis and Dante to get back to the checkpoint."

Rona nodded her head. Her crying girl speak came out more like a gurgling growl than words, but Ursula understood her. Rona had known the pain of bereavement before, but there was something worse about it being for Peter. She spent her life watching out for him even before the snare trap incident. She was suspicious of everyone who tried to date him. She encouraged him to come out of his shell. She wanted his work to be known. This wasn't a hole in her heart. It felt like her entire heart was ripped out.

Ursula checked her face in the reflection of her window when she closed her car door. Devora was already there waiting. Rona barely let the car come to a complete stop by the time she bolted out into her aunt's arms.

Ursula gave them privacy and walked back through the gate to the mass of protesters and park rangers.

The weighing and identification verification was done far enough away from the protest barrier that none of them could tell what was being said. Adriana was over on that side though along with the other reporters and photographers. Everyone could see Dante's ATV coming through the woods with Travis on the back of the seat and a huge bear corpse being pulled by a trailer attached to the back.

The crowd screamed louder. Their anger elevated even more each time another carcass came into the checkpoint. The activists were not going to let each bear's death go unrecognized.

"Monsters! You bastards! Murderers!" And more colorful words were shouted across the expanse between the crowds.

The police jumped into action when two protesters crossed the line and ran towards the ATV. They were tackled, handcuffed, and led to a patrol car. Adriana's article later identified them as Donovan Mercer, 22, of Hackettstown; and Bambi Sullivan, 21, of Mendham. Both were students at the county college.

People had their phones out live streaming the arrests. Others were trying to get shots of the bear being attached to a crane and weighed. He was too far away for anyone to notice Walker's primary distinguishing feature, his front paws. Word traveled over from a member of the press that had been up close.

Mick called the guy over and asked to see his photos. The man normally wouldn't have obliged since it's his shots that get him paid, but this circumstance was different. People were heated.

"All right. I'll show you. On one condition." The photographer wore old jeans, dirty sneakers, a plaid button-down shirt that wasn't flannel, and a trilby on his head emphasizing he was middle-aged and trying to appear younger. He looked like he lived on a steady diet of Chinese takeout and pizza.

"What's that?" Mick reached his hand into his pocket to feel for a couple twenties. He sized the guy up. He was about Mick's age, early forties, but not nearly as in shape as Mick.

"Can you get me the number of the girl that was arrested?"

Mick tilted his head. He would've rolled his eyes, but there was something he wanted from this douchebag.

"Sure."

The photographer held up the camera so Mick could see the large viewing screen. He showed Mick how to go forward and back and zoom in.

"If I'm not mistaken, I think that bear is the one who walks upright, but I can't tell." The news was not delivered gently. Emotionless was more like it.

Mick's blood was about boil. He kept studying the pictures instead. "These recent ones are that bear here now?"

"Yep. Now about that phone number?"

"Sorry, man. She's not part of my group. Don't know who she is." Mick shoved the camera back at the guy.

The photographer huffed on his way back to the parking lot. It was the end of the day. Nothing left to see after the last bear was brought in.

***

Ursula caught up to the pack of activists. She saw the two kids in the back of the squad car. They didn't seem too upset at being arrested. Her cried-out, bleary eyes continued to survey the scene. Reality slapped her again when she saw her ex-girlfriend was interviewing her ex-boyfriend about his bear harvest, the final bear of day one.

She watched from the distance as Peter's furry body was hoisted by the crane and weighed. His insides removed. His tongue hanging out to the side. Blood around his snout, mouth, and chest. The only day more gut-wrenching was when she got the news about her parents' deaths. Fortunately, she didn't have visuals of their massacred bodies.

Adriana turned around, recorder in her hand, and she caught the eyes watching her. Ursula was relieved to see that Adriana was neither smiling nor smirking. She was just doing her job which unfortunately included interviewing Travis Iver.

People on the hunting side dispersed. A few lingered back to brag and take pictures for the internet. That's when Mick noticed the absences.

"Ursula, you left with Rona before." It was a statement more than a question. She confirmed. No sense denying it. "I don't see Devora either. Did both of them head out?"

"I'm not sure. I last saw them in the parking lot. Why? What's up?" She had to play stupid.

"I was just hoping someone knew where Peter was. Maybe he's been at a different checkpoint all afternoon. Sometimes he does that. Makes the rounds so to speak."

Ursula tried to swallow, but her throat was too tight and her mouth lined with cotton.

Mick called the group to order so he could speak without having to using the megaphone. He first thanked everyone for showing up to support the conservation efforts. Then asked for a moment of silence for all the bears who lost their lives that day. He broke the silence with the announcement Ursula knew was coming.

"I have some information. Now, it's not confirmed. I don't know if those authorities over there will validate anything. But, I was told that the last bear brought in was most likely Walker."

The crowd gasped with heavy sighs and denials. A woman shouted, "Murderers!" at the top of her lungs. The official tally of harvests for the day wouldn't be ready until later that evening. The reporters would get their first bits of coverage out there and then have morning updates with statistics and what people could expect on day two based on weather forecasts, anticipated drop-off numbers for a Tuesday, and a lot more pictures and quotes.

Adriana walked up to Ursula. Her face still showed signs of the emotional hurt; yet her posture showed off her confident demeanor.

Ursula didn't want to be there. She wanted to be with Rona and Devora mourning or all alone in her apartment to cry. She didn't want to be there pretending that she didn't witness Peter's or Walker's horrifying death. She most certainly didn't have the stamina to get into a fight with Adriana.

They greeted each other with, "Hey," and a nod as a check to see if they could talk civilly. It played out like watching wildlife interact with each other.

"I have to tell you something." Adriana slipped her recorder into her bag. She crossed her arms defensively over her chest.

Ursula waited for both barrels to be fired at her, not that she didn't feel like she deserved it. She hurt Adriana and that pain does take a while to heal.

"I'm listening."

Adriana looked over at the crowd and the cops. They started to collect all their protest gear and walk back to the parking lot.

"Let's walk."

Ursula continued to wait for the barrage of emotions to come, but they didn't. She nervously looked down at herself and it was the first time she realized she had blood all over the front of her shirt.

"Why do you have blood on you?" It obviously wasn't why Adriana wanted to speak to her.

"Oh. It's fake. For the protest."

"Oh." Adriana bought the excuse. "So there's something I think you should know."

"Look, it's been a really difficult day. If you want to scream at me and tell me how much I hurt you, believe me that I already understand. I already know I was a total bitch for not ending things as soon as I felt it wouldn't work out. Can it wait until tomorrow? I promise, I'll set aside all the time you need to get it off your chest."

"No, that's not it."

People loaded up their cars and trucks. Mick and Jon filled the back of their vehicles with signs, posters, and the supplies to make new ones. It was after sundown so the park was officially closed. The rangers moved the wooden horses into place along the trail entrance.

"Oh. Sorry. What then?"

They got to Ursula's car and stood at the back of it. Adriana's eyes scanned the back end of the body to look at all the bumper stickers: Obama/Biden 2008; World Wildlife Fund; Save NJ Bears; I Stand with Planned Parenthood. There were enough to make a type of paper skin over a quarter of the back.

"The other day I had a little run-in with Travis and I noticed something."

"That he's a complete racist ass who exoticizes women of color?"

Adriana cracked the slightest hint of a smile. "Besides that which I already knew. No, it was about his truck."

"Pfft. He loves that damn thing. More than he could love a person, I think."

"Ya know how high up it is. He has trunks in the back for all his crap."

"Yeah, I know. So what?"

For the briefest moment, Adriana reconsidered whether to tell Ursula what she saw.

"Maybe it was nothing. And it's not like it actually confirms anything."

"But...? Just spit it out."

"There was a milk crate type of box in the back and I could see spray paint cans in it. Red and black. Like what was used to vandalize your place."

Ursula knew in her gut that Travis and probably one or two of his goons were responsible for the vandalism, but she didn't have proof. Possessing paint wasn't the proof she needed to go to the police, but it was all she needed to remove her own doubt.

"Thanks. I knew he was the one."

"You gonna go to the cops with it?" Adriana didn't want to get in the middle of anything. She preferred if the cops did their own investigation.

"Nah. It's not enough for them. It is enough for me though." Ursula fantasized about reaching into the back of the pick-up, removing the spray paint, and covering his precious truck in her own graffiti. She would never actually do it though. Still, the revenge fantasy felt pretty good to her.

"I gotta go. Need to get this written up."

"Thanks for the information." Ursula waved when Adriana began to turn away from her and walk towards her own car.

The drive home gave Ursula a feeling of being in a mental fog. She was on auto-pilot. Gas. Break. Blinker. Keep moving forward towards home even if nothing was there to welcome her. One small bamboo plant wasn't going to give her the hug she desperately craved. She felt her phone vibrate with each new text notification. She didn't look at them until she entered her apartment.

No news from Rona. All the messages were from SOAR members. There was a more clearly stated email from Jon McHugh with a press release attached. She would have to take it and save it as an image in order to post to the social media feeds she managed for the club. Jon and Mick updated their own feeds. Before Ursula even got out of the shower, Jon had a Walker the Bear Memorial Page set up. He smartly set up a button for donations to SOAR on it.

The hot shower got the blood and dirt off her skin. She wrapped the towel around herself and sat on the closed toilet. Her filthy clothes laid on the floor. It looked like the scene of a murder, but a lot less blood than TV shows had. She stared at the pile and thought of Peter. Peter, the human, the disabled photographer who showed courtesy and gallantry. Peter the bear, who died by her side. Peter the volkolak, who was so much more than most people would ever be allowed to know. Peter, her friend.

She shifted her butt off the toilet lid and knelt by the clothes. She picked up the blood-stained shirt and stared at it. She kept her fingers on the cleanest parts not wanting to touch the blood again because it was too real. It was too much a part of this mundane, physical world.

Real blood.

Peter's blood.

She moved the shirt around in her hands. There was still fur on it like a cat had shed on it, but that belonged to Peter too. Black and tan thick hairs, some caught in the stains. She didn't know what to do with the clothes. Irrationality told her not to wash them. On the other hand, no one should see them and question her again about whether it was real or special effects. She folded everything she had worn and carried the stack to her kitchen. Her towel fell to the floor as she stood. She didn't care. She was alone.

The plastic grocery bags were in a low cabinet behind paper towels and garbage bags. She pulled one out that was yellow with black ink branded by the local supermarket chain. She put the clothes in and tied the handles. She couldn't explain to herself why, but she put the bundle back into the cabinet out of sight, preserving them.

She wanted water to drink, but her hands shook too much to hold a glass so she left it there on the counter. She walked her naked self into her bedroom and climbed under the covers of her cold bed waiting for it to give her any sense of warmth and comfort. Her obligations to SOAR would have to wait.

CHAPTER TWENTY-TWO

The sunrise didn't provide any sense of potential happiness when Ursula got out of bed. For a half of a second, she forgot that the day before was real. It came back to her in flashes of blood, tears, and memories of begging. She thought about Travis' eyes and that for a short moment in time, she saw something resembling compassion in them. He probably could've killed Rona and gotten away with it as a case of defending himself and another human nearby. He could've looked like a hero to the people who believed it. Instead, he relented and gave Ursula the gift of only murdering one of her friends.

Work beckoned. Ursula knew there would be at least a few hunters among her customers going out for the second day of black bear and deer hunting. She spent her life at that diner and had the muscle memory to smile on her worst days. That morning was definitely one of them. She didn't remember a single thing people said to her when the breakfast rush was over.

Tayleigh was fifteen minutes late for her shift. She thought she would be able to pretend she had been in the kitchen talking to Manny for a bit, but he hung her out to dry.

"Tayleigh! Nice of you to show up."

Manny may have been just giving her the business playfully, but it was enough to steer Ursula back to the kitchen at lightning speed. By then,

Ursula was fuming and a lot of her anger about Travis got misdirected. During the quieter minutes, Ursula read timelines and texts about Walker being presumed dead.

"You're late."

"So I guess it's a bad time to ask for tomorrow off, huh?" Tayleigh had youthful attitude, but did not have the maturity nor experience of her irate boss.

"No. You may not have tomorrow off unless you can miraculously pull a trained replacement out of your ass. I need all hands on deck this week."

When asked why, Ursula tried to explain without giving too much away. She said the shop would be busy with hunters and reporters flocking to Frankhurst. Afternoons in town were busy whenever the weather the nice and October was turning out to be mild.

"And I have things to do. I have hardly ever taken time off for myself, but it's a difficult time right now. And I'm the boss!"

"Well, can you come in and close for me so I can leave a few minutes early at least?"

"Why? What is so important that you need off at the last minute?"

Tayleigh shrugged one shoulder and her eyes looked down and away from Ursula's brutal stare.

"I have a date?"

"A date? Is that a question? Is that your real question? You want to shirk your obligations because of a date? I need you here for your entire shift. If you can't do that, then don't come in at all."

Tayleigh was smart enough to wait to roll her eyes until after she turned away from Ursula.

"Did you just say something?" Ursula heard a mutter and considered letting it go, but she was in no mood for bullshit.

"I said you're being a bitch. You're usually real cool, but whatever is up with you lately, you're taking it out on all of us. We covered for you and that wasn't good enough!"

"That's it. Get out. I'll have your last paycheck ready for you by tomorrow."

Tayleigh petulantly attempted to claim that her comment was a compliment about what a great boss Ursula normally is. It didn't fly. Ursula followed Tayleigh out of the kitchen into the main part of the diner. There were still customers waiting for their orders to be taken.

An apron flew by Ursula's face as Tayleigh threw it.

"Oh by the way," the girl didn't know when to shut her mouth, "my date is with your ex, Travis. And he's the one who killed that stupid bear you're always talking about!"

Ursula refrained from shouting all the things she wanted to get off her chest. It was nothing short of a miracle. People watched and pretended they weren't. Noses went down into their phones except for a couple still more interested in the drama than their lunches.

"Anyone want a job?" She said it with the coolness of a powerful woman who was so absolutely done with the universe taking a shit on her.

Fortunately, Kylie was able to come back and help out as soon as her kids were home from school. She made arrangements for them to stay at a friend's house and then drove back to Applegate's. Good help was too scarce considering how many people wanted extra work. The problem was doing something like waiting tables didn't bring in much at place like Applegate's. It wasn't a fine dining restaurant with a full bar. Ursula wished she could pay them more than minimum wage. Even that was more than the state required of wait staff who were expected to live off tips. Gratuity on ten dollar tabs couldn't even fill a gas tank. Kylie worked at Applegate's because she liked the job and she liked her boss. She had gotten to know a lot of regulars and anticipated their orders like a pro.

Now with Tayleigh out of the picture, Ursula really had to find extra help. She printed out a help wanted sign and taped it in the front window. Leaving the place in capable hands, she went up to her apartment to see if she could get a hold of Rona.

There was no good news from the Medvedovich family. Rona and Devora tried to step up their campaigns to bring an end to the bear hunt. They were on the phones and sending emails filled with their passionate pleas about the importance of maintaining the ecosystem. They tried to play on any heartstrings about how much Walker would be missed. Pretending to be fully human while in mourning was the hardest thing either of them had ever done.

Ursula offered to go over and help them make calls or do whatever they needed. The despair coursed through their words to accept her company. Ursula checked her wallet wanting to stop at the store to bring ingredients to cook them something, but she didn't have much cash to her name. Manny answered when she called his cell. She requested three garden salads and three deluxe veggie burgers with baked potatoes. No sense in spending her last dime when she could write it off as a business lunch even if it technically was for free home delivery to a politician.

In Devora's kitchen, Rona helped Ursula unpack and plate the food for her aunt. Ursula stepped up her initiative by cleaning the coffee pot and starting a new brew for all three of them.

"How's it going over here?"

Rona kept her face in the refrigerator pretending to take longer than needed to fetch the ketchup. "Not good."

"I figured as much. I meant it when I said I'm at your disposal. Let me know what you need. I don't care if it's bringing over breakfast, lunch, and dinner; or taking Devora's dry cleaning to Schubert's; or just being here to give you a hug when you need it. I want to be here for both of you."

"Thanks. It's not only losing Peter. She doesn't have time to grieve. The campaign is so demanding. It's taking all her energy and money. And she's a longshot. She's not well known. She's trying to win on ethics and that doesn't fly when it comes to New Jersey politics."

Three plates were made up with the burgers and potatoes. The salads were in small wooden bowls. Rona dug out the flatware while Ursula found paper towels to use as napkins.

"What are you guys drinking?"

"Just water. The coffee will be fine when we're finished."

"Do you think you can convince her to eat somewhere besides her desk?"

"I can't, but maybe you can."

Rona pulled out a small wooden folding table from a closet in the kitchen. It would be cramped, but it would have to do for all three of them if they could convince Devora to leave her desk.

"You can step away for twenty or thirty minutes to nourish yourself." Ursula spoke from experience. She usually ate on a different cycle than anyone else because she was too busy serving and helping prepare their meals.

Devora dropped her hands to the arms of her chair and pushed herself up. The aroma more than anything they said convinced her to move over to the little dining station they made. Even the smell of out of season tomatoes made her stomach gurgle.

Cell phones kept bleeping and chiming with notifications. Ursula knew hers were from SOAR members because of group conversations and social media notifications.

"How about we turn off our phones for a half an hour while we eat?" Ursula was anxious about the disconnection considering how much turmoil SOAR had during hunting weeks. If she expected Devora to relax for one meal, she had to be willing to do the same.

"This is why I rarely have notifications on." The only people that would text Rona were with her at the table. Emails might come in from her professors, but nothing that couldn't wait.

"You two are more demanding than I expected." Devora pressed the button on the side of her phone until even the vibrate setting was turned off.

Before Ursula changed her setting, she caught a glimpse of the conversation in her message thread.

"Is something else wrong?" Rona decoded the expression on her friend's face.

"I don't know." Ursula punched down the setting and stuffed the phone into her back pocket. "It seems Travis' name is out there now. He's getting a lot of publicity for what he did."

"I hope it's bad publicity." Rona still wanted to kill him.

"Some of it. Of course, there are people congratulating him, but now he's also got death threats. Karma's a bitch, son."

"He deserves worse than threats. I don't know how you managed to refrain from turning him over to the police when he vandalized your storefront. Rona told me all about it. Plus, there was that big article in the paper."

"Couldn't prove it was him. I don't have cameras anywhere. I was thinking of getting those fake ones to see if they would help. But honestly, I think now that Travis got what he wanted, he'll probably leave me alone."

"That's not how violent abusers work, you know." Devora hit a nerve that no one else ever did.

"Abuser? Travis is an ass, but he never touched me."

Rona chimed in, knowing exactly what her aunt meant. "Seriously? He calls you racial slurs. He trashed your business. And he murdered my brother. He's an abuser."

"Did he call you any names like that when you were together?" Devora wiped her hands on her paper towel and waited patiently for an answer from Ursula.

"Once. During a fight. I laid him into hard. Not physically and trust me, that was hard for me not to pound the crap out of him for it. I guess I never put harassment in the same category as abuse."

Rona and Devora had no problems agreeing that people knowing his name was a public right since the bear known as Walker was a local celebrity of sorts.

"I suppose death threats are wrong, even against people like Travis Iver." Part of Devora relished the thoughts of him bombarded by hate messages and threats for what he did. The politician inside her though had taken a stance against harassment especially from internet commentators who felt safe spewing whatever they wanted.

Ursula almost choked when she remembered something she wanted to share with them. She told them that Tayleigh was officially fired and that she's apparently dating Travis now.

"I can't wait until she threatens me with wrongful termination over who she chooses to date when that girl has a history of being disrespectful and late all the time."

"Well if any lawyer sends you a letter just bring it to me and I'll take care of it." Devora wasn't a lawyer but she had some clout. Plus she had her own various lawyers who specialized in services she needed from real estate to non-profit to campaign funds.

CHAPTER TWENTY-THREE

The subject was bound to arise. Ursula asked if there would be a memorial for Peter or if his death would be kept a secret.

"I just want you to know that SOAR will have a vigil on Saturday for all the bears killed this week. They do it at the end of every hunting week, but I'm sure this one will get more attention."

"Thank you. Rona and I discussed it and we'll have a service telling people that Peter died unexpectedly from an aneurysm and that we had him cremated per his wishes." Devora left half of her veggie burger uneaten. Her normally larger than average human appetite was affected by her grief.

"I don't think I could handle it if people kept asking where my brother was and when he'd be back. I keep forcing myself to stay alive. Be what he wanted me to be. Finish school which I don't care about at the moment. A memorial would hopefully help all of us who miss him so much."

"But you should know, Ursula, that the volkolaks will also have a gathering to mourn him and you are invited as long as you don't tell anyone." Devora explained that it would be up to the individual whether they appear in human or bear form.

On Wednesday night at eleven, the volkolaks gathered in order to avoid humans as much as possible. They met in secret at the side of the pond in Whittingham Wildlife Management Area where Peter was murdered. Six volkolaks were in human form including Devora. They held lanterns for ambient light. Rona and the remaining twenty chose to be in bear form.

Ursula turned off her flashlight and stood close to Devora who introduced her everyone. For those in bear form, Ursula followed the instruction on how to greet them by placing her hand at their snout and if they felt comfortable, the bear would sometimes rub their nose against the human hand. When they came to bears who didn't give Ursula special auras, Ursula pulled her hand back instinctively. Then she realized who they were. It was Darla and her cubs Big Guy, Queenie, and Jester.

Devora turned to Ursula when she noticed the situation. "I understand you met."

"Yes. I wish it had been under happier circumstances. Can you tell her that for me?"

Devora translated and replied back to Ursula that Darla was not interested in making the acquaintance of a human at that moment. She couldn't however, stop her children from their curious inspection of Ursula's feet, legs, and butt.

A woman held a small wood box covered in symbols. She opened the lid and revealed rows of identical blue bottles. Devora introduced her as Anya and said the bottles contained a healing drink that was optional for participants.

Ursula plucked a bottle out of the box when Anya stood before her. The label had a broken heart wrapped in vines on it. She guessed it was around two ounces of liquid inside; and even though it was from friends, she was skeptical about drinking something before knowing what it was. She whispered to Anya and asked for the ingredients.

Anya's lips and eyes showed the slightest hint of smiling merged with her intense sorrow. She seemed to understand the concern of the stranger among them.

"It's only an infusion of herbs. Elder berries, rose hips, hawthorn berries, valerian root, cinnamon, and skullcap. We take it for healing despair, broken hearts, or in some cases, extreme night terrors. It's prepared in a ritual with sacred words and a moonstone like the one you're wearing." Anya nodded her chin toward Ursula's pendant hanging on a necklace then took a step to her right to continue around the circle.

Ursula decided it was safe enough to consume. They were ingredients she had heard of from natural supplements and teas. While she contemplated drinking it, one hand unconsciously went to the new necklace on her chest. It wasn't so much new as it was repurposed. She found an old chain and soldered a loop to the filigree around the moonstone so she could wear it and stop worrying about it falling out of her pocket or ending up on the laundry by accident.

For the volkolaks and Darla's family, wooden bowls like the ones Devora had in her kitchen for salad, were placed in front of them. Anya walked the circle again, this time carrying a larger glass bottle. She poured the same infusion into the bowls. Her ankle length brown dress billowed as she made her way around and returned to Devora's side when she was done.

Anya led the service instead of Devora or Rona to Ursula's surprise. It made her think back to her parents' funeral. She realized it made sense. In that situation, a priest led the mass. She wondered if Anya was a religious leader among the volkolaks or why she was chosen.

The air was still over seventy degrees in mid-October. The sky was perfectly clear showing off every star. Anya and Devora chanted together in their dialect of volkolak language. Ursula understand their words this time now that she had been through the bear root ritual. When she first heard their language, Rona chanted it over Peter at Musky Park.

"We're here under the waning moon to remember and honor our kinsman, Peter Medvedovich. As our requiem says, he has gone home to the sky and will become a new star until he's ready to return."

Anya's words did provide some soothing comfort to Ursula and others present. Ursula didn't notice how much her heart was broken. Right after the murder, so much energy poured out of her. Multiple times in the last forty-eight hours she had found herself scrolling through Peter's incredible wildlife photos. He was so generous with his gifts and loved to share it with the world.

"Volkolaks have always been able to support each other through difficult times. Death is no different. We are a community. Devora, Rona, you will mourn in your own ways, but it is our bond as volkolaks to be of assistance to you if you need it." Anya held Devora's hand and spoke from her heart. She introduced the part of the service where family then friends could speak about Peter if they wanted.

Rona was content in her stoicism. She bowed her head in gratitude, but chose to remain silent. Rona would save her remembrances and stories for reaching the human population about their misunderstanding of how to coexist on the planet with natural life. In that outlet, she would be loud and roaring through her human voice and spreading her displeasure through her written words.

"My nephew Peter was a remarkable individual." Devora let go of Anya's hand and clasped her fingers together at her chest. "All of you knew him and had different relationships with him. But I think we can agree that Peter showed courage, strength, and compassion in ways so many people can't find in themselves. He overcame odds. He chose a life of non-violence. He kept believing in the goodness of others even though he was harmed multiple times by humans. The human friends in Peter's life will have their own service to remember him and I'd like you to consider being there as one of them for support. I'd like to put an end to that bear hunt and his human friends do too. If we work together, there's a chance we can make this happen in Peter's honor."

Devora looked at every face around the circle. She smiled at the little ones who had now survived their first brush with death.

"I just want to say thank you for being here, for being his friend."

Anya checked again with Rona to see if she wanted to speak. Again, she replied with a bow to say no. It was time for the medicinal philtre for broken hearts.

"Our Maker of Spirits granted volkolaks the wisdom to learn the ways of the forests, meadows, and towns. With this knowledge, we have understanding for the laws of nature and come to grips with the laws of man as we try to make our world better. If you feel that you need this libation of healing, it's time to hold your serving of elixir in a joined salutation to help mend your heart. *Moye serdtse*."

They toasted to their own heartbreak in the Medvedovich's native Russian language and drank from the bottles or the bowls. Rona nudged a bowl with her nose to Darla and the cubs to see if they were interested. It wasn't bear food and they were content with spring water. Instead of drinking it, Darla dunked her paw and applied it to her head and did the same to the kids. It ended up being a little like a baptism for them anyway since they had to learn this phase of life — the death of someone they loved.

Anya walked around the circle to collect the bottles and bowls. She had one more part of her liturgy before concluding. She offered Devora a small honey cookie then went around to everyone with the offering. She returned to her spot in the circle and took Devora's hand once again. They raised their arms up and gazed at the stars while singing a departing chant.

The circle of mourners broke apart. It was before midnight, but for those who lived in the human world, they still had to get back into cars, drive home, and get up for jobs in the morning. Ursula kind of wished she had their stamina. She wasn't going to leave without saying goodbye to Rona for the night, but when she turned to look for her, all she saw was Rona's bear hind end at the edge of the woods and then she was gone. Ursula wanted to hold her and tell her it would be all right in time, but Rona took her pride with her into the woods alone.

"Ursula?"

She looked around to find the source of the voice. It was Anya still next to Devora. She waved her hand to signal.

"Thank you for coming and participating tonight. I don't know if a human has ever been allowed to do this before, but we all agreed your compassion for Peter and your love for his sister and aunt have earned forgiveness."

"So you know that I told Adriana about you? I'm genuinely sorry, but I thought it would be..."

"Shhh." Anya had a more delicate delivery in her voice than Devora, but her command was equally tangible. "You thought it would be good for you and now that you've learned from your mistake, we formally forgive you."

"I don't know what to say. I'm so honored and so overwhelmed to be invited here. I promise you, all of you, that you can trust me. I want Devora to succeed so you can be safer. I want to help you keep your natural resources." Ursula nervously gripped the strap of her messenger bag at her chest. She knew she was babbling, but couldn't seem to stop. She was grateful when Devora interrupted her.

"It's okay now. I'm done being angry about it. You've shown that you do want to help me and Rona and the campaign. I'm sorry if I was too harsh on you."

"No. No! You weren't. I deserved it. And I know bringing over burgers isn't the biggest gesture in the world, so if there's anything else I can do, please let me know."

"There is."

"Name it."

"Can we use Applegate's on Saturday for the reception after the vigil at the checkpoint station? I'm sure your fellow activists would appreciate a good veggie burger after a week of protests and arrests."

"Yes! Absolutely! I'll see if I can find some extra help before then."

It wasn't easy, but Ursula did manage to post an ad online that night when she got home. She had several messages in her inbox by the end of the morning shift on Thursday. She was so desperate for help, anyone who could carry a plate would be better than Tayleigh.

CHAPTER TWENTY-FOUR

Applegate's had never seen such a turnout for anything like Peter Medvedovich's memorial and the reception for the bears. It made sense to have one big merged event. The public didn't know about Peter and the other volkolaks, but they knew he loved those bears and all the wildlife. His photos showed them the way he saw them. Majestic. Peaceful. Sometimes fighting. Often in families. Applegate's walls became a gallery of Peter's vision completely organized and hung by Rona and Ursula.

"I don't think you should quit school. You've missed a few days. You can make it up. I'm sure they understand." Ursula was surprised to hear that Rona would quit anything, but she did understand how hard it had to be to focus after such a tragedy.

"I'm still thinking about it. It might just be a year off or maybe only a semester. I don't know. What good is a Master's degree these days anyway?" Rona pulled out a flask from her bag and poured some whiskey into her coffee.

"I have more of that upstairs if you run out, but you're sleeping over then."

"You got it, boss."

Rona had agreed to work part-time at Applegate's for only a few hours a week and be the on-call substitute if needed. Fortunately, Ursula was able to hire two young people to replace Tayleigh. She hoped James and Tasha would be quick to learn everything they needed to know. She also hoped that it wouldn't be so devastating if she needed a few hours or even a day off each week. Plus, she promised Manny that she's get him an assistant for thirty hours a week. Paying bills just got a whole lot harder.

"You guys did a great job making this exhibition of Peter's photos." Devora smiled for the first time in weeks or so it seemed. She glowed in the revelry of her nephew's friends and admirers. "I'm glad to see we were able to invite more than the SOAR members. No offense."

"None taken." Ursula knew what Devora meant. She had a tray filled with soft drinks and empty glasses waiting to get back into circulation.

"It's just that Peter's work had a way of touching lives silently. I think it's important that everyone who loved his work get this chance to say goodbye." Devora had something in her hands — large, thin, and rectangular. The item was wrapped like a present and she did a terrible job of hiding something so big behind her back.

"What's that?" Ursula tilted her head to see if she could get a better glimpse.

"You'll see. And thanks to Rona's hard work, I'm happy to say that the party has finally taken notice of me and the support has been pouring in for the campaign. I mean look around. There are more assembly representatives, senators, and freeholders here than my largest fundraiser."

"That's all you, Aunt Devora. I answer the phone and sort the mail."

Ursula said she was intrigued by the mystery item, but had to excuse herself and get back to serving. It was all hands on deck in Applegate's. Kylie trained James and Tasha whenever there was a different kind of request. Rona pitched in once in a while when she was inundated by handshaking and condolences. She was also in charge of any gallery sales as noted by red dot stickers that she placed on the tags of photos as soon as someone's credit card charge processed through her phone.

The cacophony was indecipherable until Ursula heard two words clear as day: Travis Iver. She looked around and saw a small cluster of people leaning into each other like they had the juiciest gossip to spread. Travis' name had gotten out, but some people not plugged into the hunting news had only just started hearing about it.

"Yes, the newspaper said that they can't one hundred percent confirm that it was Walker, but the bear Travis brought in matched his description."

"So that's proof, isn't it?"

"They mean DNA proof. Who knew they took DNA from bears? I didn't."

"Maybe it's for science. Like tracking them or something."

As long as Travis and his band of murderers stayed out of Applegate's, she couldn't ask people not to discuss him. She knew they would want to know why and she couldn't say Travis killed Peter when they were told Travis killed Walker the upright bear.

Ursula broke her concentration on that conversation and got back to her tasks of taking empties to the kitchen and setting up a new tray of sodas and water. She checked on Manny's creativity in the kitchen. Catering wasn't their norm and he managed to come up with a variety of hors d'oeuvres and tapas for the mostly standing crowd. Almost all the tables were stashed upstairs crammed into Ursula's apartment.

"Senator, another Coke?" Ursula found Senator Lester Maxwell as he broke away from a constituent wanting a selfie with him.

"I think I'm good for now. I hate to have clammy hands from the glass when I'm meeting people, you know?"

"I do. Good thinking. I don't believe I've seen you here before, but you do look familiar."

"Devora Zhukov and I have become good friends over the last couple months. I love her dedication to wildlife conservation. I've gotten to know her and fully support her."

"Were you at the protests? In Whittingham?"

"Yes, I was there for one of them. I think my picture got in the newspaper when they were arresting protesters."

Ursula bit her tongue when he reached out and patted her on the upper arm. She normally would pull back, but if the senator wanted to support Devora, Ursula did not want to compromise his backing. She knew there was a harmless, probably friendly meaning behind it, but Ursula had gone through life with people expecting her to be open their unsolicited touching. Whether it was her upper arm, her ass, or her hair, she wanted none of it from strangers. She told herself to keep smiling and make nice for Devora's sake.

People came and went. Soon the place was overflowing. Jon McHugh from SOAR stood at the door outside allowing people to go in only if the same number of people exited. The Applegate's maximum capacity was sixty-five according to the fire marshal's sign discreetly hanging on the wall behind the cash register.

Ursula stood in the kitchen and thought about how they were running out of food. "Oh well. We said we'd host a reception cocktail hour and did it with one day to prepare."

"Then what do we do?" Manny gestured at the empty shelves of the glass-front double-wide refrigerator.

"I can't worry about it. Neither can you. You've busted your ass, Manny. If the food runs out, it's a sign that it's time for them to wrap up what they're doing and go home."

"Are you paying for all this, boss?"

"Thank God, no. I thought it was going to be an even smaller affair for Devora Zhukov. Fortunately, some of the SOAR members have deeper pockets than I'll ever understand. They're covering this cost which is even better for Devora. She can keep her money for the campaign expenses."

As if on cue, Devora opened the kitchen door and poked her head in looking for Ursula.

"It's time to unveil the mystery. Can I pull you away for a few more minutes?"

"Sure thing." Ursula held up a fist towards Manny for their fist bump explosion. Manny was the kind of person whom Ursula would hug or welcome a friendly "atta-girl" pat, unlike strangers. Manny was family.

Devora began her speech while Ursula found her way from the kitchen. Rona stood next to Devora on one side. Assemblyman Walter DeGroff stood on the other with the mysterious wrapped present held up between them.

"My family has been through a tragic loss and Rona and I have been so blessed by all the support we've received from people like Assemblyman DeGroff and Senator Maxwell. Walter sacrificed a lot of his time to help draft a bill that simply could not wait until after the election to discuss."

Devora unwrapped the object to reveal a framed document, enlarged to almost poster size. It was filled with legal paragraphs no one could read from their place in the audience. Next to the document was one of Peter's photographs. It was one that Ursula had never seen before. It was Peter in his bear form. A self portrait of him loving his life walking through the woods.

"Did you take that shot?" Ursula leaned in Rona's ear.

"Not me. He set the timer and did it himself to sell to the image service. The ones citizens had taken were blurry snapshots taken from videos." Rona's smile curved up more on one side. She knew about her twin's trick on the press and public.

"How very Peter Parker of him." Ursula didn't know if Rona understood the Spider-Man reference, but it wasn't important.

"Assemblyman DeGroff, and hopefully myself should I win the election in a couple of weeks, are honored to have written legislation putting an end to the New Jersey bear hunt. We present you with the draft of Walker's Law. I have confidence this will pass the Assembly and once I am elected, I will proudly sponsor it in the Senate in honor of Walker, a bear that my nephew Peter Medvedovich dearly loved."

Everyone applauded the presentation and congratulated Devora on her compassionate gesture to memorialize her nephew. People came closer to glance at the framed document and get a better look at the uniquely stunning photo of Walker the bipedal bear on top of a mountain at sunrise. He stood majestically overlooking the ridge and the Delaware River below.

"Devora, when did Peter take this picture?"

Everyone wanted to know how he did it. How had Peter been lucky enough to be in the right place at the most perfect time to capture Walker in a way no one else could ever have done?

"Oh well, that's what made Peter so special. He had a way with the subjects of all his photos." When Devora turned to wink at Rona and Ursula, it was easily assumed by anyone who noticed that it was only meant to convey her pride in her family.

The bustle and celebration continued, but with the highlight over, more people took the opportunity to leave. Someone tapped Ursula on the shoulder while she collected more empty glasses from people.

"Adriana! I didn't know you were here."

"I'm sorry if I'm not welcome. I came here for the story."

"Oh. No, of course you're welcome. I only hope that our issues aren't interfering with your job."

"Not exactly."

"What do you mean?"

"Can we talk? In the kitchen maybe?"

Ursula led the way and dropped off the dirty glasses in a bin on the other side of the wall from the main room. Manny was just about finished cleaning up, but Ursula told him it was okay if he took off and she would finish loading the dishwasher once everyone was gone.

"What's wrong?"

"It's about that crazy story you told me. About the were-bears?"

"The volkolaks?"

"Yeah. Do you really believe all that stuff you said or were you freaking out from stress or something?" Adriana had let the unbelievable story pass for a while. It seemed more logical that Ursula was making it all up. Then she saw the photo in that frame. The glory of the scene gave her reason to pause and reconsider.

Ursula drew the corners of her mouth down and shook her head. "I think you were right. I think I had a kind of mini breakdown. A lapse in judgment about reality. I got emotionally invested in Walker's capture and then Peter's arrest. Tayleigh was a pain in my ass and I fired her. And I'm real sorry you got hit with the brunt of that."

"Yeah. I guess that makes sense."

Neither of them felt the confidence in their relationship to question the other about reconciliation. Silence hung in the air. James, one of the new part-timers, burst through the swinging door unaware of the tension in the kitchen. He gave an expedient greeting before dumping off more dirty glasses and bolted right back out the door within seconds.

"I guess I have all I need for now. I'll get the text of the legislation from DeGroff's office."

172

"Thanks for coming. I mean, I know you had to, but thanks anyway."

"Peter was a good guy from what I could tell. I'm gonna head out."

"See ya."

Ursula stood alone in the immaculately clean kitchen. All she had to do was finish loading the dishwasher and say goodbye to stragglers before locking up. Her reflection in a hanging ladle caught her attention. Her face was warped in it like a funhouse mirror. She couldn't hold back her stress any longer and let the tears of anguish flow.

CHAPTER TWENTY-FIVE

The 2016 election left the United States in a state of perpetual shock. It was a devastating presidential upset. Almost everyone was focused on how the Electoral College sealed the fate of Hillary Clinton, former Secretary of State and Senator of New York. Millions of people lost hope. Despair encompassed them and their allies.

Local races didn't garner much attention because of the impact of the national disaster. There were plenty of other celebrations for Congressional seats at least. As far as predominately white small towns like Frankhurst were concerned, people's lives would miraculously be transformed into idyllic existences of yesteryear. That wasn't Devora Zhukov's vision. She embraced her win and credited her left-leaning platform on land preservation, education funding, and accessible healthcare for the less privileged areas in the district.

Ursula opted to wait for the results with Rona at Devora's house. Devora was with the rest of the party's officials in a diner since they didn't have the resources for a permanent headquarters office.

As soon as the text from Devora came in, Rona popped open the bottle of champagne. She wasn't smiling though. Neither was Ursula. Their sadness smothered how genuinely happy they were for Devora.

"Drink up. Cheers." Rona's toast was flat.

"I think we need something harder hitting than bubbly."

Both of them cried on and off. The stress of the presidential disappointment compounded with all the efforts they put into Devora's little campaign. Exhaustion. Relief. Fear.

"I'm glad we're here. I don't want Aunt Devora to think I'm not happy for her. She'll be great in the state senate and who knows? Maybe, she'll go on to even bigger things."

"I hope so. We're gonna need people like her."

Ursula's mind went to the worst case scenarios. She had already experienced hatred and racism from Travis Iver, a local hero as far as other people were concerned. She could never prove he vandalized her shop. With elected officials winning seats quite literally on the platform of the 1950's before the Civil Rights Act, Ursula wondered if her business or her life would be in greater danger.

"Now that it's over, sort of, I have something to tell you."

Rona didn't mean to sound alarming, but Ursula immediately felt the hairs on her arms stand on end.

"What's going on?" Ursula sat up straighter on her kitchen stool unconsciously altering her posture to appear taller.

"It's nothing bad. Take it easy." Rona flicked her hand in the air. She took a sip of the champagne, sneered at how much she didn't like it and continued to twist the glass on the counter.

"Okay. You have my attention."

"I'm leaving. For a while anyway."

"What? What about school? Your aunt? Where are you going?"

"Easy now. My aunt knows and she's on board. She's paying for this sabbatical actually."

"Well? Spill it!"

"I'm going to California to try and find my mother. After losing Peter, I finally convinced Devora that it couldn't possibly be more painful to find my mother in a zoo than anything I've already experienced. If she is in fact, still there in California, she's probably being taken care of pretty well unlike some other places in this world."

"Wow. I can't believe it. I mean, I'm here for you. I support your decision. I just can't believe everything that's going on." Ursula gave Rona a hug to try and prove that she was supportive of her quest. "So, all this time, since she was captured, your mom has been living as a bear? She never transformed into her human form to try and get out of there?"

"I honestly don't know anything. I don't know if there have been any external reasons why she couldn't transform. Maybe there are cameras on her all the time. Maybe they keep her on some of sedative or medication that would prevent her from thinking clearly. I have no idea, but I'd like to find out. I'd like to reach her."

"And if she's happy? Then what?"

"Obviously I don't want to find her in the condition I found Peter at Musky Park. I hope she's at least comfortable. And, well, if not, I'll do whatever I have to. If she wants to come home, I'll will not stop until I get her home."

"I know that's true." Ursula clinked her crystal flute on Rona's and held it up to toast her friend's tenacious spirit. "When?"

"I was going to wait until after Aunt Devora took her oath of office, but we talked about it, and there's no time like the present. I'm leaving on Monday."

"Monday! Short notice!"

***

Ursula was able finally take a day off without worry since hiring additional responsible employees. She took Monday off so she could drive Rona to Newark airport. She got to say goodbye and wish Rona well on her new journey.

The 2017 legislative calendar included the State Assembly and State Senate versions of Walker's Law sponsored by Assemblyman DeGroff and Senator Zhukov. They were assured that even if the governor vetoed, the party had gubernatorial candidates who were willing to end the bear hunt should any of them win the seat in the next November's race.

Travis Iver got to experience the other end of the stick for a change. Once it went viral around the world that Walker, a disabled bear loved by locals, was murdered without remorse, Travis was driven off social media for months. He was compared to the dentist who murdered Cecil the lion. Extreme activists harassed his employer too. His precious pickup truck was vandalized — not by Ursula nor did she know who the culprit was.

As for the other guys, Dante started dating a woman who wasn't fond of him being friends with the hunter who killed Walker. Dante occasionally connected with the Frankhurst hunting boys online, but none of them really wanted to be associated with Travis anymore. Mike finally proposed to Lacy and promised they'd get married within the year. Brandon decided it was smarter to move back in with his parents in Pennsylvania since the job market all over was horrible. That left Bruce. Bruce discovered an online app for hooking up with other men and continued to keep his secret.

Applegate's featured the work of Peter Medvedovich for three months. The photographs sold quickly. Ursula resolved to make local art a part of Applegate's from then on. She featured other photographers who could find the beauty of New Jersey like Peter did. She opened up the exhibitions to oil and watercolor painters, pastel artists, and illustrators. The newspaper even did another story on the shop. This time a feature about the art gallery was something worth hanging up in a frame unlike the crime blotter coverage from the vandalism.

Ursula's prized piece of artwork was her own enlarged framed copy of Peter's "self portrait" of Walker overlooking the Delaware River and mountains.

ACKNOWLEDGEMENTS

This whole story is because I grew an attachment to wildlife around me. When I first saw the news reports on TV of this alleged bear walking through New Jersey neighborhoods on hind legs, like many others seeing grainy footage, I thought it was a "Bigfoot" type hoax – a person in a bear suit. Once local papers gave better coverage and confirmed that it was indeed a real black bear, I wanted to make sure it was safe from the dreaded bear hunt instituted by then governor, Chris Christie.

I discovered there was an activist group called *Save NJ Bears*, or more formally, the *Bear Education and Resource* program of the Animal Protection League of New Jersey. APLNJ is a 501(c)(3) nonprofit organization. You can learn more at savenjbears.com. They've done an incredible job protesting the bear hunts at checkpoints and urging legislators to pass a five-year ban on the bear hunt. I wore my Pedals the Bear necklace charm every single day until I finished this book.

Unfortunately, Pedals was murdered during the 2017 bear hunt. Though it's considered "unconfirmed" by the DEP because Pedals was never microchipped, all the identifying characteristics were present on one of the bear corpses.

Thomas Boatwright was kind enough to fit another cover into his schedule. He's one of my favorite people for collaborations. You can support his work at *patreon.com/boatwrightartwork*.

Thanks to Joe, the cats, and my family for allowing me time to write when I know they'd probably wish I was doing something else.

Peace,

Amber

ABOUT THE AUTHOR

Elizabeth, "Amber Love" to her friends, is an author and model who openly discusses her life at AmberUnmasked.com and on her podcast Vodka O'Clock. She's the author of the *Farrah Wethers Mysteries* series and the short horror novel *Misty Murder*. She's written comics, short stories, and a memoir. She's been published in the Anthony-nominated charity anthology *Protectors 2: Heroes* and the adventure anthology *Athena Voltaire Pulp Tales*.

If you appreciate a lot of cat pictures and selfies, you're welcome to follow Amber Love on Twitter @elizabethamber and Instagram @amberunmasked.

2014 Bear family in our backyard

www.ingramcontent.com/pod-product-compliance
Lightning Source LLC
Chambersburg PA
CBHW011437170626
46808CB00009B/3075